Also by Sarah Jamila Stevenson

The Latte Rebellion

underneath

underneath

sarah jamila stevenson

Woodbury, Minnesota

First Edition
First Printing, 2013

Book design by Bob Gaul
Cover design by Ellen Lawson
Cover photo compilation by John Blumen
Cover photo © Titled "Drop" by Alex Stoddard
Cover images: Woman © Glow Images/SuperStock
                        Space/cosmos image © DigitalStock

Flux, an imprint of Llewellyn Worldwide Ltd.

This is a work of fiction. Names, characters, places, and incidents are either the product of the author's imagination or are used fictitiously, and any resemblance to actual persons living or dead, business establishments, events, or locales is entirely coincidental. Cover models used for illustrative purposes only and may not endorse or represent the book's subject.

Library of Congress Cataloging-in-Publication Data
Stevenson, Sarah Jamila.
   Underneath/Sarah Jamila Stevenson.—First edition.
       pages cm
   Summary: "When her cousin Shiri dies, sixteen-year-old Sunny Pryce-Shah is suddenly able to 'underhear' people's thoughts, which raises questions about what is truly going on with her friends and family"—Provided by publisher.
   ISBN 978-0-7387-3596-2
[1. Psychic ability—Fiction. 2. Friendship—Fiction. 3. Death—Fiction. 4. Family life—California—Fiction. 5. Diaries—Fiction. 6. California—Fiction.] I. Title.
   PZ7.S84826Und 2013
   [Fic]—dc23

                                                                                2013001175

Flux
Llewellyn Worldwide Ltd.
2143 Wooddale Drive
Woodbury, MN 55125-2989
www.fluxnow.com

Printed in the United States of America

For my family

one

The whistle blasts three times and Coach Rydell yells, "Take your marks!" Fifteen seconds more. I step up onto the starting block. My feet are poised on the dark, sandpapery surface, toes hanging slightly over the edge, my body tense and ready to dive into the lane.

I take a deep, slow breath and expel it in a quick puff of air.

Looming in my peripheral vision are all of the other swimmers lined up on either side of me. I try not to look at them; instead I focus on the abstract pattern formed by everyone's legs on the blocks, the different colors of swimsuits, the faint reflection of the cloudy sky in the surface of the water. I look at people's toes. Cassie, as always, has a perfect, glossy pedicure. Not me. The light-purple nail polish I painted my toes with is starting to scrape off.

Glancing back up, I see my mother sitting on the lowest bench of the small bleachers on the south side of the pool. For some unknown reason she's on her cell phone. Why now, when my race is starting? I frown.

Five seconds. Almost time. I push everything out of my mind—Mom, cell phones, even Cassie, who's in the lane to my left, adjusting her goggles.

The whistle shrieks, and we're off. It's my best event, the 100-meter freestyle. My arms and legs cut into the cool water with hardly a splash, and then I surface, sucking in air. It's only an off-season invitational, but I push my muscles that extra little bit because I know I've got this one covered. I barely notice that I'm gradually edging ahead of a girl from Lakewood in the lane to my right. I'm focused on my rhythmic breathing, my legs churning up the water, the exhilaration surging through me.

This time, I'm leaving Cassie behind, and for once that makes me glad. She can go ahead and look perfect all the time. But guess who's going to win today's race? Not Miss Fancy Feet. I file that one away for post-race teasing at Spike's house.

After a perfect flip-turn, I try to add an extra burst of energy for the last length, even though it doesn't matter because I know I'm going to be the first one in by a long shot. Soon the familiar calm comes over me. I'm in the zone, quiet, just me and the other end of the pool beckoning me, coming inexorably closer with every stroke. My happy place. One of the reasons I swim. Really, the only reason I—

ohgod, ohgod—
NO! no. no. no. no—
dead.

I pop my head up, my legs floundering in the pool. My heart pounds. Who's dead? I hear screaming, and my hands go reflexively to my ears as I try to block out the sound threatening to drown me.

The wake of the person in the next lane washes over me, pushing chlorinated water into my nose and mouth. I cough and sputter, my sinuses burning, and take a quick glance around. But I've realized by now that nobody was screaming. It was all in my head. I'm in a race, at the school pool.

Was in a race. A race I am now losing as Cassie swims past me and tags the end of the pool, me belatedly pulling up a few seconds behind her, my head spinning.

Elisa is already there, her long dark hair tucked tightly into a swim cap, ready for the relay in a few minutes. She high-fives Cassie and shoots me a sympathetic smile.

I shake my head. This is not good. I heave myself out of the water and head over to the junior varsity bench, not wanting to meet my mother's eyes. I can see her out of the corner of my eye, sitting like a statue with her cell phone in her lap. She looks shocked. I am, too. Everyone else is looking at me as if I'm mentally unstable. Did *I* scream?

Cassie squeezes my shoulder before sitting down on the bench next to me. "Wow," she says, and pauses for a moment to catch her breath. "That should've been you, not that Lakewood chick." I nod, then shake my head, still in a daze.

Coach Rydell is not happy. Not happy at all. She stalks right up to me, brandishing her whistle, as I'm drying off by the benches.

"Pryce-Shah," she says, with a measuring glare. The dreaded last name. "What happened back there? That was your race. You had it."

"I know," I say hoarsely. I clutch my towel around me, dripping, and shiver a little in the breezy October air. "I ... I don't know what happened." It's a pathetic answer, but it's true.

"Well, I don't want to see it happen again. We're lucky this is the off-season." She sighs, straightening the Citrus Valley Vikings baseball hat that's mashed down over her sun-bleached hair. "And your form was looking so *good* before you just ... freaked out and bailed. I hope this doesn't become a habit, Sunny. I'd hate to see you drop in the team rankings before the season even starts." Coach peers at me over the top of her sunglasses. I swallow hard.

"I'm just—maybe I'm getting sick," I say. Coach makes a frustrated noise and moves down the bench to where Cassie is celebrating with James, who won earlier for backstroke. I should be there, too, but I can't even manage to be happy for my friends.

Maybe it's true. Maybe I *am* sick.

Sick in the head.

Because nobody just spaces out mid-race and dreams they hear voices.

But it's not real, either. Nobody's screaming. Nobody's dead.

As I'm heading to the locker room to change, I catch sight of Mom hurrying to her car to pick up Dad from work. I'm kind of glad I don't have to talk to her about how I messed up my race. She'd say something well-meaning, but she's never been part of a school sport and she wouldn't understand how it really feels, how I didn't simply disappoint myself. I drive home in silence, still trying to figure out what happened, but all I can think is maybe I didn't get enough sleep last night.

I pull our old green Volvo into the driveway next to Mom's hybrid. As I drive up, I notice the mailbox door is open and a big puffy envelope is sticking out. I walk to the curb and grab it. It's addressed to me, from my cousin Shiri. She hardly ever sends me snail mail from college, so I rip it open eagerly.

A small notebook falls out. The hard cover is dark blue, plain. I open the front; turn a few pages. I flip to the middle. All the pages are covered in Shiri's neat, rounded handwriting. I frown, perplexed, and rummage in the envelope for a note or a card or something. As I do, a folded slip of paper falls out of the back of the notebook. I bend down to pick it up.

"Sunny!" My mom is standing in the doorway. There's a strange note in her voice.

"Yeah, Mom." I straighten up, juggling the slip of paper, the notebook, and my backpack.

"I'm so glad you're home. Come in right now—we need to talk."

"Is this about my race? Because—"

"No," she cuts in, and this time her voice wavers. "No, honey, it isn't." She goes back inside, and I'm left standing on the front lawn, suddenly shaking for no reason I can name.

From Shiri Langford's journal, January 18th

My grades again. Dad was livid. Not that I care what he thinks. Why should I?

It's not like I was planning to get a C in Math 75, but everything just seemed like too much last semester. At least this semester I have Existentialist Lit. I don't care if he says it's useless.

But while I was home, THAT happened. Again. I thought it stopped about a month ago, but it happened every night, while I was trying to go to sleep. One night I must have screamed or made some noise, because Mom came in to check on me and stroked my hair like she used to when I was small.

I miss it. I miss my family, the way it used to be when I was little. Before THAT started happening.

two

The air in here smells like sour dirty laundry. The heavy yellow curtains are closed and it's too dim to see much, but I can feel the lump of bedspread bunched up under my right shoulder; I feel my dry, cracked lips and swollen eyes but I don't move. I should probably go downstairs to get cucumber slices to put over my eyelids, but it doesn't seem important.

I haven't gone downstairs in two days.

I haven't changed out of my pajamas. I haven't showered. I haven't talked to Cassie, or Coach Rydell. I haven't called Auntie Mina or Uncle Randall to say ... what? What would I say?

My mom brings in tomato soup, my favorite creamy kind that comes in a box from the organic section of the grocery store. She's even grated cheddar cheese over the top and brought a small plate with a slice of buttered toast. I only make it halfway through. It doesn't taste like anything to me, and when I swallow my throat is sore. I put the plate on my nightstand and pull the covers up to my chin.

"Sunshine," my mom says gently. "Please try to eat something before we leave."

We're leaving in an hour. It's my first funeral.

We're here, and it's awful.

I stare at the dry skin on my knees, at the white specks of lint on my navy blue skirt. In my peripheral vision, everything I see is black—black dresses, black suits, Mom's black crocheted handbag on the floor next to my chair. Dark wood-paneled walls.

All I want to do is go home and crawl back into bed. Mom squeezes my hand and doesn't let go, as if she's afraid I might bolt. Her hand is freezing, and her elaborate silver wedding ring dents my skin.

Of course, it isn't technically her wedding ring, since my parents didn't "technically" have a wedding. Instead, they eloped on the beach during a yoga retreat in Santa Cruz. And since both sets of grandparents are holding grudges about that, now I only "technically" have grandparents. You know; on holidays and birthdays.

And funerals.

"We are here to console one another during this time of grief and to remind ourselves of our love and respect for Shirin Alia Langford." I jump as the chaplain's voice blares out of the speakers that sit on either end of the dais.

"This young woman was just twenty years old, but she was universally loved by family and friends alike... blah blah blah dee blah." The chaplain is obviously using a pre-fab introduction, something he downloaded off the Internet or pulled out of a file folder. His reedy voice rises and falls, punctuated by frequent sighs. I can't help but wonder if that's rehearsed, too. It makes me angry. It seems so insincere, so flat and empty and forced.

When Shiri first decided to go back east to Blackwell Cliffs College, it felt like part of me was getting ripped away. I knew she wanted to get as far away from her family as possible, but she was pushing me aside, too.

I was furious. I imagined the East Coast turning all her familiar Southern California habits into something I couldn't recognize, some uptight, work-obsessed go-getter with a New York accent and no more interest in me.

Little did I know how much she really would change. Little did I know that my anger then would be nothing compared to now. When she choked down all that pain medication and drove off into the mountains, did she even think about what would happen to the rest of us? Is she somewhere out there looking down at us, regretting what she did, or worse, *relieved* she's not here? My teeth ache, I'm clenching them so hard.

Auntie Mina, tiny and forlorn, goes to the front of the room. She starts talking in a small voice about how much Shiri was their little girl, how proud they were of her, and then she breaks down and I can't make out the words through the crying. Uncle Randall and Randall Jr. go up and lead Auntie Mina back to her seat.

Randall Number Two, as Shiri and I used to call him when we were little, is dressed in a dark three-piece suit, his brown hair slicked down and a somber expression on his face. Uncle Randall's son from his first marriage, his golden boy. The one he always indulges, while Shiri has—*had*—to excel at everything just to get acknowledged.

When Number Two gets up to speak, he manages to stop being an asshole for five minutes and sound like an actual human being. He even squeezes out a few authentic-looking tears for his poor departed half-sister. But I'm not convinced.

I look at Uncle Randall. He sits there rigidly, his face not showing any emotion at all. Auntie Mina can't or won't stop crying.

I don't feel like I'm about to cry. I'm not even sure what I feel.

I guess I just don't understand—not any of it.

I think about the journal Shiri left me, the one that arrived the day we found out about—everything. The note, scrawled on a half-sheet of paper, that fell out of the journal. *Dear Sunny: I don't expect you to understand any of this yet, but we'll always have yesterday . . . and today, and tomorrow. Maybe one day you'll figure it out. I never could.*

I squeeze my hands into fists in my lap, digging my fingernails into my palms. I don't know why she thought I'd be equipped to figure anything out. She was always the brilliant one. And me—I wanted to be just like her. My whole *life*, practically, I wanted to be like her; to have all the boyfriends, the tennis awards, the scholarships. By the time I started high school a little over two years ago, I was able to bask in her reflected glory, even though she was a senior while I was only a freshman.

Insipid as it sounds, the chaplain was right—everyone did love Shiri.

I didn't just love her, though. I idolized her.

An imam from the local mosque gets up and says a few words at the request of my Pakistani grandparents, Dadi and Dada. On my right, my dad shifts awkwardly in his seat. He's not religious at all; Auntie Mina isn't either, and Shiri certainly wasn't, so the imam's words seem just as false as the chaplain's address.

"No vanity or dark rumors will they hear," the imam quotes, describing some heaven that I can hardly imagine exists; "only the call, 'Peace! Peace!'"

He rationalizes Shiri's death for my more traditional relatives, reassuring them that she will still make it to Paradise, since she was obviously suffering some mental afflic-tion that made her not responsible for her actions. I glance around. On the other side of Auntie Mina, Dadi is rocking back and forth in her seat, her gauzy shawl wrapped around her head and tears trickling down her wrinkled, nut-brown face. Dada just sits there looking miserable.

After the lanky, skullcapped imam concludes his part of the ceremony with a brief *sura* from the Qur'an, there's a viewing of the deceased so people can go up and pay their respects. My dad puts a hand on my shoulder as we stand, so I know I can't avoid this.

Even though all my shaking legs want to do is run out of here.

The wooden casket lies on the carpeted dais at the front of the room. The top half of it is open. It's surrounded by arrangements of white and yellow flowers, and black plastic stands holding blown-up photographs of Shiri: her senior portrait with the fuzzy filter that makes her look like a movie star; an action shot of her whacking a tennis ball that appeared in the local paper her junior year. In the tennis picture her long brown hair is tied back in a ponytail, flying behind her as she hits the ball; her tiny features are scrunched in a grimace of concentration.

I stop, reach one hand up, and lightly touch the edge of her senior portrait, my other hand knotted into a fist at my side. In that photo, she's the epitome of calm, her makeup perfect and her mouth curved slightly as if she's smiling at someone off camera. But she's got that little line between her eyebrows that she only gets when she's upset. I wonder what made her so unhappy that day.

I wonder what made her so unhappy, period. She seemed embarrassed about taking antidepressants; she only told me reluctantly, after I found the bottle in her purse while rummaging for hand lotion. I can't help feeling like I should have known, should have been able to figure it out somehow. But how could I? How could anyone?

Earlier today, my mom told me something else I hadn't known. Shiri had been put on academic probation after last spring and would be in danger of losing her scholarship if she didn't get a good enough GPA this fall. Even worse, she'd gotten a stress fracture during a tennis match that left her on the bench for the duration of the season.

"None of us knew that was going on," my mom said this morning, looking at me with red-rimmed eyes across the kitchen table. "She must have been feeling so much pressure. We never want you to feel like you're under that kind of pressure, Sunshine."

I let out a shaky sigh. There was no chance of that happening. Sure, they're always telling me I have to "live my ideals," but I don't think the words "parental pressure" are in their vocabulary. Not the way Uncle Randall put pressure on Shiri. They're probably just glad I'm not like they were at my age, ditching school to smoke pot at the nude beach or whatever. They have nothing to worry about. I'm a swim jock, not a hippie. I have popular friends. I fit in at school. I'm happy there. I am *nothing* like them.

But they've always supported me. I'm lucky, I guess. We don't have money to throw around like my aunt and uncle do, but we live in a pretty nice neighborhood and I go to Citrus Valley High, which is a college-prep magnet full of the "right" kind of kids, as Uncle Randall would put it. The kind of kids that parents love.

Kids like Shiri.

I reach the front of the room. The sickly sweet smell of the flower arrangements almost overwhelms me, but I step up to the coffin, trying to swallow past the huge knot in my throat. I force my eyes to stay open, force myself to look at her. At her body. This isn't really her, says a little voice in my head. She's still back at school, studying in the library or throwing a frisbee with her hair flying in the breeze. Not lying here, her lips artificially pink and her skin powdery and dull with makeup. Not dead.

—*dead. no no no—*

I grind my teeth. I don't want to remember the voice. The swim meet. Not now.

My limbs feel jerky, like they aren't attached to me, as I step down from the dais and stand near the end of the front row of seats. My dad is off to one side, talking quietly with Grandma and Grandpa Pryce, Mom's parents. Cassie's older sister Tessa is on a bench about halfway back, dabbing at her eyes with a tissue. She used to be one of Shiri's best friends in high school. It was because of Shiri and Tessa that I met Cassie, the summer before freshman year. Shiri brought me along to a swim party at Tessa's house, and there was Cassie, who loved swimming as much as I did and invited me to go shopping with her for first-day-of-school clothes.

I search for Cassie. She's in the very back, next to Spike, who's looking uncomfortable, and Marc, who's texting somebody. She's frowning at her mother, shaking her head, her arms crossed tightly over her chest. Some people might think she's being cold not coming up to me, but I know Cassie—she's not hard-hearted. She always remembers things like my birthday, like my *cat's* birthday. She's detail-oriented like that. But she's never been a touchy-feely person. She's not good with tragedy.

Who is, though?

Still, I have the urge to run over there. Rip the phone out of Marc's hand, put my head on Cassie's shoulder. Listen to Spike make a dumb joke. But I can't.

I move away, cross the burgundy-carpeted funeral parlor to the ladies' room in the back. There's a small cushioned bench in there, plush like the carpet, and I sit. I stare at the beige-painted wall but I can't bring myself to cry. I feel abnormal and disloyal, but I can't help it. I shake my head, almost violently. That's not her out there.

And she didn't commit suicide. *Suicide*. It's something that happens on TV. Not in real life. Not to *her*.

I can't grasp it. I may not be a religious person. I may not know what I believe. But I can't believe she's gone.

three

I go to school on Wednesday in a fog. I missed Monday and Tuesday. Of course, everyone knows what happened. Gossip spreads quickly at our school.

Failing that, there was always the local newspaper: "Suicide Suspected in Teen Overdose Death." Just in case you hadn't heard.

While I was gone, the school counselor held one of those excruciating assemblies where they talk about "what *you* can do if you think someone close to you might harm themselves." Today, everybody asks if I'm okay. I just nod, keep walking. I feel like they're all staring at me, at my disheveled hair and shifty eyes, trying to figure out if I'm "thinking of harming myself."

When I walk into my second-period Honors American Lit class there's a sudden uncomfortable silence, though I can still hear the clamor, the echo of voices in my head. I feel like plugging my ears. It's as if people were talking about me in their little pre-class groups and then zipped it the minute I showed up. Even Cassie won't quite look at me.

Eyes-Front—a.k.a. our friend Marc—does his usual chest-level stare. I automatically cross my arms. At least I know the world hasn't gone entirely nuts.

Mr. Patrick says, "Welcome back, Sunny. We all hope you're feeling better." He puts the emphasis on *feeling better*, just in case there were one or two people still left who didn't have a clue. I duck my head and slouch into my seat, but I'm sure they can all read it on my face. Still, I try to stuff down my emotions, swallow them so that I can get through the day and go home.

Lunch is even worse. I buy a bottled water from the cafeteria, trying to hide from the curious stares that seem to be everywhere. Then I go back outside to the table where I usually sit with Cassie, Eyes-Front, Elisa, James, Spike, and a few other people from swim team, at the west side of the quad near the popular crowd.

One table away is where Shiri always used to sit before she graduated. Before she left us all.

I try to pretend everything's normal, but Cassie can't resist talking about it.

"Oh, Sunny...we all miss her so much. It must be so awful for you." She flips her perfect straight blond hair back, reminding me that I'm a few weeks overdue to lighten my own hair. I could see the dark-brown roots in the bathroom mirror this morning when I was getting ready. "Dark Chestnut Blonde" is still sitting on the side of the tub, but I haven't had the energy.

"Yeah, everyone's been talking about it while you were gone," James says through a mouthful of fries. "Even some of the teachers were crying when they found out." He leans against the picnic table, his tall, skinny frame towering over the rest of us.

"At first all we talked about was how you freaked out in the pool," Cassie says. "That was totally weird enough."

"Mr. Lopez asked me if I was okay." I sigh heavily. "I've never even had a class with him. People I don't even know keep coming up to me and talking to me about Shiri." I stare at the ground.

"Doesn't that drive you nuts? I'd be so sick of it," Cassie says in an irritated voice.

I look up at her, curiously. "I guess so. They're just trying to be nice."

"Yeah, whatever. Like they care." She turns away, takes out a tube of lip gloss and starts reapplying it, casually, as if this is the kind of conversation we have every day.

"Harsh," Spike says, laughing. We exchange a wry smile. Classic Cass.

Like last year, when James took a spill that time we all went mountain biking at Lake Arrowhead. All she could do was stand there and pretend she wasn't freaked out by the whole thing, even though everyone else was gathered around James and fawning all over him to make sure he hadn't broken anything.

Still, Cassie's sister was one of Shiri's best friends. I saw how unhappy Cassie was at the funeral. And she knows how

I feel about Shiri. I expected she would have something more to say.

The last two classes of the day pass in a blur, all concerned faces and hushed whispers whenever I walk into a room. When the final bell rings, I leave campus gratefully. I get into the Volvo and start driving.

It's too quiet, so I turn on the radio. Dad or Mom must have been using the car last because it's tuned to a classic rock station. I hardly notice the music, just head for home on auto-pilot, until the Beatles song "Yesterday" comes on. Just like that, there are tears streaming down my face and I'm remembering Shiri's note. *We'll always have yesterday... Maybe one day you'll figure it out.*

Mascara runs down into my eyes, making them sting. It was one of Shiri's favorite songs. She loved the Beatles. Her other musical tastes came and went, usually according to whatever group of friends she happened to be hanging out with at the time. But the Beatles always stuck around. She was always trying to get me to listen to them, copying playlists onto my computer when I was out of the room: "Wistful Beatles." "Happy Beatles." "Funny Beatles." "Trippy Beatles." On and on.

I went to my first concert with her when I was thirteen and she had just turned seventeen. It was just a cover band playing at an all-ages beach party, but we spent over an hour getting ready, Shiri helping me with my makeup and brushing my hair until it shone. By the time she was done, I looked almost her age. Almost as pretty.

But, squished into the back seat, tall tennis-team guys

to either side of me, I still felt small. Shiri sparkled in the front passenger seat, smiling and laughing. I scratched at my eyeliner surreptitiously, pressing my knees together to avoid too much contact with the guys next to me. But it didn't matter. I was going to a concert with high school kids. When I went back to middle school the next Monday, my friends were in awe.

My stomach hurts. I'm having trouble concentrating on the road, so I pull into a Target parking lot halfway home. I drive to a space at the very back, where it's less crowded, and sit there taking gulping breaths until I finally calm down again.

I glance in the rearview mirror. My eyes are puffy and red-rimmed, with traces of makeup giving me raccoon eyes. I pull my hair out of its elastic and try to arrange it around my face so that my eyes don't draw as much attention. I look awful with my hair straggling down like this, like one of the stoner kids who hang around the convenience store near school, but at least nobody can see my face.

I start the car again and head for home. Traffic is heavy and I keep my eyes on the road ahead, the white lane-lines, the light turning from green to yellow to red.

At home, I eat half a small container of fat-free vanilla yogurt before feeling gross, my stomach turning over like I'm going to throw up. I toss the rest of the yogurt, go upstairs, and turn on one of the playlists Shiri left me: "Wistful Beatles." Then I lie down on my bed. The strains of Paul McCartney singing "Let It Be" whisper softly out of my computer speakers. Mom and Dad aren't home yet and the house is still. My tortoiseshell cat, Pixie, hops silently onto the bed, settles next to my shoulder, and starts kneading my upper arm, purring loudly.

I don't know what I would have done the past week without Pixie. That's one thing I always had that Shiri didn't. Her dad doesn't like animals in the house.

When we were kids, Shiri spent months asking for a pet rabbit. Uncle Randall smiled and said he had something special planned. When her eleventh birthday came around, she was positive she was going to get a rabbit. Instead, Uncle Randall gave her an investment portfolio.

Shiri burst into tears. Uncle Randall didn't get it.

"A rabbit only lives for ten years if you're lucky," he said, a frown creasing his forehead. "I'm planning for your future. Your college education. Maybe even a house, if the stock market goes up." Shiri cried harder. Uncle Randall got up and stomped out of the room.

"I can't believe he would say that," Shiri said, wiping her face with her sleeve. Auntie Mina hugged Shiri and whispered, "I know. I'm sorry." I just huddled in the corner of the couch, wishing I were somewhere else.

Later, that type of thing made Shiri frustrated, not sad. Last winter—after taking a women's studies class—she said her mother was still too traditional, that she wouldn't know what to do with her life if there weren't a domineering, paternalistic male in it.

Uncle Randall hadn't wanted Shiri to take that class. He was always trying to butt into her college life, telling her what she should be studying and interrogating her about her grades after every test, just like when she was in high school. I didn't realize this until I started reading her journal. She always acted so happy when she called or visited, telling me stories about late-night pizza outings and loud college parties with live bands.

But the stuff in her journal—she didn't tell me any of that.

The last time I saw her—just a couple of months ago, before she left for the fall semester—she was giving me advice about college applications for next year. I've gone over the conversation a million times in my head, wondering if I should have guessed something was wrong.

"Don't worry, you can always call me if you need help with the essay, but I know you'll do great," she said, her brown eyes lighting up. Then the light died and she broke into a brittle smile. "Just pretend you're trying to impress my dad." She shook her head. I laughed, a little tensely, and flopped back across my bed, eager to change the subject.

"So how about Blackwell Cliffs? What was the application like?" I asked. Her eyes strayed off into the distance and her smile disappeared.

"Blackwell's okay, I guess." She bit one fingernail unconsciously, though it was already down past the quick.

"What, do you not like it there?"

"I don't... No, it's great. I just think you'd prefer someplace else," she said, still not meeting my eyes. It sounded like she didn't want me there at the same college with her, and I felt confused and hurt. Then the moment passed and she pulled a smile back

onto her face. "I know you'll find the right school. You're popular and friendly. You'll fit in wherever you go," she reassured me.

Yeah. Popular. Friendly. Those were words I would have used to describe Shiri. So, why?

Why?

Why?

That one word pounds into my brain like a jackhammer. My lips, my jaw tense into an unfamiliar-feeling rictus, almost a snarl.

Suddenly I'm furious. I pound my fist into my pillow, over and over. I want to scream. I want to yell at Shiri. I had so much I still wanted to ask her about, to talk to her about. I thought she *cared* about me. Enough to stick around.

I should have known after she left us the first time.

I grab the pillow and throw it as hard as I can. It hits the glass of water on my nightstand. The glass falls. Water stains the beige carpet. I pick the pillow up and throw it again. The bedside lamp tips, crashes to the floor. Pixie streaks out of the room and runs downstairs. My face is hot and I'm breathing hard.

"Sunny, is everything okay?" My dad comes stomping up the stairs, rushing into the room with a look of panic.

"I'm fine, Dad," I say. Strangely, I do feel calmer. Dad picks up the lamp, puts it back on my nightstand, and replaces the shade. Then he turns to me and puts his hands on my shoulders.

"What happened here?" He squeezes a little, gently.

"Nothing." I look down, avoiding his concerned gaze. Water's still seeping into the carpet. What can I tell him?

I lost my temper? I'm mad at Shiri? No. I can't. I can't bear to have that conversation yet. "I scared Pixie. She knocked everything off the nightstand and ran out."

"Okay," he says, doubtfully, brushing his disheveled black hair out of his eyes. "If you're sure. I'll be downstairs if you need anything." He looks like he wants to say something more, but he just squeezes my shoulders again. I close my eyes. He must see something in my expression, because I feel his hands lift, hear him walking softly out of the room. Thank God. I just want quiet. I go over to my computer and turn off the music.

Usually I like the sound of voices and music around me. Sometimes when I'm home alone I switch on cheesy comedies about high school, the kind my parents hate. Cassie and I watch them while we're doing homework, cracking up at the idiotic one-liners and making fun of how the actors are obviously way too old to be in high school. We haven't done that in a while. Not since the beginning of the school year.

I pick up the now-empty water glass, wondering what Cassie is doing right now. Then I remember I'm currently missing swim practice. Ever since that disastrous meet and everything else that's happened, I haven't felt like swimming. After the funeral, I emailed Coach Rydell to tell her I needed some time off the team. I felt a little guilty, but it seems like too much energy to get my arms and legs to function in tandem.

My body is tensing up again, so I lie back down. Mom is always trying to teach me deep-breathing meditation techniques and I try some of those, inhaling slowly through my nose and visualizing my breath filling my body all the way from my toes to the top of my head. I hold it for a moment and then gradually exhale, trying to imagine the tension in my body leaving along with the used-up oxygen.

After a while, my mind drifts and I lie there in a stupor. Images swirl through my head, but I keep going back to one memory: Shiri and me as little kids, hiding in a backyard fort made of chairs and bedsheets, dressed like superheroes in pillowcase capes and safety goggles from the garage. She was Wonder Nerd and I was Super Dork, fighting to rid the world of "dum-dums." Alone and silent in my room, tears flow down my cheeks.

I can't handle this.

I suck in air, desperately at first, gasping, then more slowly and evenly. After a few minutes, my thoughts are quiet again. I focus on the catch in my breathing until it finally goes away, too.

That's when I hear the voice in my head.

Not her, no, no, why? I don't understand why she—

It bursts in like static and then fades away like a radio station, leaving me with only the surge of emotion that accompanied the voice, all grief and pain and loss. My eyes sting, and I feel a pain in my chest like my heart is breaking.

And then my mind is silent again, and I can hear the usual noises of the house and smell some kind of spicy re-heated chicken dish my Dadi sent over, and it's like I'm waking up from a bad dream. I almost felt disembodied for a minute—the voice in my head seemed so *not* me. But it sounded familiar. I must have been dreaming.

I open my eyes and flex my muscles stiffly. Arranging my sun and moon pillows, golden yellow and creamy white plush, I get up and change out of my school clothes, now damp from spilled water. Clean gray sweats are all I can manage before going downstairs. Gray fits the overall mood, though; dinner is somber, and mostly silent. I pick at my chicken biryani, pushing the grains of Basmati rice around my plate with a fork.

"At least eat some naan," my dad says, putting a piece on my plate. Normally, naan is comfort food, pure doughy goodness only available on special occasions or in restaurants, but I can barely choke it down. Dad, on the other hand, is wolfing down his food, tearing chunks of chicken away from the bone with little pieces of naan and scooping them into his mouth. His shirt is wrinkled and disheveled-looking, and he's got a five o'clock shadow of dark stubble on his chin and upper lip.

Like me, Mom isn't eating much. Her hair is sloppily pulled back in an elastic, one long, stray light-brown lock dangling unnoticed into her plate. There are dark circles under her eyes and she looks even paler than normal.

"Have some green beans, honey," she says quietly, passing me the dish. "And put some on your father's plate, too, please. He needs the fiber."

Dad looks up momentarily. "I ate some already." Usually he'd make some kind of dumb, inappropriate-for-the-table joke about having so much fiber in his diet he ought to be crapping bran muffins. But tonight he's just quiet.

I sit there, too, and eat green beans one at a time. I'm pretty sure this is the longest meal ever. I can hear the clock ticking in the living room and the sprinkler going outside. A rumbling feeling of frustration starts welling up inside me like an earthquake about to let loose, but I just clench my jaw and put my fork down. I take deep breaths and try to envision a calm ocean.

Calm. Ocean. Calm.

My mom coughs, takes a sip of water, and then says, forcefully, "I just wish she would have told us, that's all. We could have done something."

"I *know*, Mom," I say. "I know exactly what you mean." And I do. All of a sudden, I'm frustrated again, almost uncontrollably so; and sad.

Mom looks at me strangely, her fork halfway to her mouth.

"What was that?"

"What you just said. I was agreeing with you." I eat another green bean since she's looking at me.

"I didn't say anything, honey. You must have been thinking out loud."

But I *know* I heard it, loud and clear.

"No, you just said you wish we could have done something for Shiri," I insist. But she looks so surprised that I'm no longer sure.

"I was thinking something along those lines. Did I say it out loud, Ali?"

"Hm? Sorry," Dad says. "I wasn't listening." He goes back to cleaning his plate, still preoccupied with his own thoughts.

I try to go back to my meal, but it's hard. My head is spin-ning, confused. Full of static fuzz with bursts of coherence like a poorly tuned radio station.

"Poor girl," Mom sighs. "Poor Mina." And I'm not sure now if she's talking out loud or if I'm going crazy.

But as I stare at my mother, her words trickling to a stop, I know it in my bones: It's in my head. Her mouth isn't moving, but I can hear her voice *in my head.* Her bewilder-ment, her grief—they're filling me up, ready to overflow.

My jaw involuntarily clenches, and my teeth grind to-gether. I shove my chair away from the table and run up the stairs. I can hear my mom's questioning tone and a mumbled response from my dad. It makes me want to plug my ears.

By the time I get to the top of the stairs, I'm in a cold sweat and I'm shaking. I go into the bathroom, strip off my clothes, and duck into the shower, blasting myself with hot spray. I must have been dreaming. Or hallucinating.

I shudder, despite the warmth of the water and the suf-focating steam. The less-appealing explanation is that I'm somehow going crazy. That I'm cracking from the pressure of everything that's happened.

I get out of the shower and wrap myself in a fluffy towel. My mom's voice comes through the door, muffled, asking if I need anything. Tea. Aspirin. I say no, I'm fine.

Normally, I'm a perfectly functional person under stress. I even *like* it. Coach Rydell can tell you that. I'm the one she boasts about having ice in my veins before a swim meet. This kind of thing—it's not me.

I read something in Shiri's journal yesterday, though.

There was something unexplained happening to her, too, a mysterious "that." "*THAT happened again,*" she'd say, never quite saying what "that" was. But it got worse and worse until eventually she couldn't take it anymore.

Going back into my room and sitting on the bed, still wrapped in my towel, I glance at the desk drawer where I hid the journal away. I haven't been able to stop thinking about it. What if she was hearing voices, too? What if something was seriously wrong with her, and now it's happening to me? I can't even fix my mind on that idea—that what's happening to me isn't just stress, but something weird.

Really weird.

From Shiri Langford's journal, January 31st

Another "incident." I was hoping it would stop once I got back to school, far away from everything my dad says and does and how my brother gets everything he wants all the time and my mom doesn't say anything about it. I always thought it happened because of them, and so I couldn't stand being home. Couldn't stand hearing, knowing. Knowing too much. Feeling so out of control.

Yesterday Professor Macken talked about people who enable inequitable behavior by not ever protesting, people who imply tacit agreement with an unfair situation by never expressing their disagreement. And she said well-behaved women rarely make history.

My mother is definitely an enabler.
I don't behave. We'll see if I make history.

four

"Sunny honey," my mom says. "It's time."

I press my lips together and stare at a spot on the wall across the waiting area, unwilling to leave the holey vinyl chair. As long as I stay in this stupid, shabby little waiting room, I won't have to talk about anything. Not talking equals not thinking, and not thinking equals not driving myself crazy. Which I think I've mostly succeeded in doing this past week and a half, since ...

I pull my phone out of my pocket and start scrolling aimlessly through my contacts list. I could text Cassie, or Spike: TRAPPED IN THERAPY. PLS SEND REINFORCEMENTS. Spike, at least, would laugh. Cassie would get that smile she gets whenever I'm joking around and she doesn't think I'm all that funny.

"Honey, this is for your own good. I think you've been getting depressed the last couple of weeks, and Bettie can help you." My mom reaches out her hand and tilts her head at me with a coaxing smile, like I'm five years old, but her eyes are exhausted and shadowed.

"*Getting* depressed?" I say. My attempt at sarcasm only succeeds in eliciting the Stare of Pity. I'm no match for the Stare of Pity, so I give in and swing myself up out of the chair, past my mother, and into the therapist's office.

Halfway through the door, I hesitate. I wonder if I *should* talk to her. About all of it. But if hearing voices in my head suddenly means I'm a "troubled teen" or "debilitated by grief…" I have visions of my arms strapped down in a white straitjacket, a burly orderly standing by with my daily dose of chill pills before I spend the rest of the afternoon watching game-show reruns in the mental asylum rec room.

The worst part is, it doesn't sound all that bad.

"Sunshine Pryce-Shah! What a great name. Come *in*. I'm so glad you're here." Bettie practically leaps up from her swivel chair and shakes my hand, hard enough to make me flinch. "I have some readings for you about the stages of the grieving process. They're geared toward adults, but after talking to your mom I think you're mature enough to handle it."

I spend ten minutes listening to a spiel about the stages of grief, Bettie's curly blonde hair bouncing in time with every sentence, and I nod silently when she hands me a list of suggested books from the library.

After that, the questions start. How am I feeling? Is this the first time I've lost someone close to me? How do I feel about Shiri? Am I angry? Am I sad? Have I talked to my parents? I want to flee. Instead, I remain monosyllabic, hoping it'll speed things up and get me out of here. *Okay. Yes. I don't know. Kind of. Yes. No.*

There aren't any windows in Bettie's office, so I stare at a spot on the wall where the ghastly orange paint is partially scraped off, revealing a gray layer underneath.

Then she says, "I want you to start keeping a journal. I've already mentioned to your mother that I think it would really help you."

I groan, knotting my hands into the bottom of my sweatshirt. This is not exactly a time in my life I want to preserve for posterity. I'm tired of thinking about it. I've thought about it over and over and it still doesn't make any more sense.

"If writing a journal had helped Shiri," I say, as levelly as I can, "maybe she'd still be around."

Bettie winces, then sighs. "Just try it," she says. She takes off her cat's-eye glasses and cleans the lenses, looking tired. Once again, I consider telling her everything. But if they tell me something's really wrong, or put me on medication… Shiri was on antidepressant medication, and it didn't help her. And… what if that's what made her… change? What if they made her feel different? I read an article online about that, how some antidepressants actually make certain people *more* depressed. What if they try to give me the same medication? What if I—?

My head is full of my own thoughts, my anxieties. I don't say anything else.

———

In the evening, Spike rings the doorbell, ostensibly to drop off history notes from the days I missed. His eyes are sleepy like he just woke up, and his unruly hair is squashed down under an old beanie that he'd never be caught dead wearing at school. He gives me an awkward hug and hands me a giant baggie full of cookies from his mom.

We chat about school, and for a few minutes my life feels almost normal again. He lounges on the front porch, the palm trees in the street behind him blowing into graceful arcs in the Santa Ana wind. His hand brushes mine as he passes me a spiral notebook and a messy sheaf of papers in a blue folder.

For the first time in days, I'm not sad. I'm not crazed. I feel almost okay.

Then Spike grins like a fool, lopsided and cheesy, and invites me to one of his infamous barbecues at Corona Del Mar on Saturday.

"Saturday? Maybe," I say, hesitantly. I'm not sure I'm ready for a swim team barbecue even though I've been going to Spike's beach barbecues since we were kids, since way before the swim team. "I might have ... you know ... family stuff."

"Aren't we like your second family? Come on—you *have* to go." His grin gets even wider, crinkling the corners of his eyes. "James said he'll get his brother to bring us some beer. It'll be awesome."

And then, like it's a simultaneous track on a CD, a discordant harmony behind the lead singer—

it'll be awesome all right when those
swim hotties get all —
—drunk girls in bikinis
a real party for once, come on, come ON
don't let me down—

And that's what I hear. It's like overhearing something that's under the surface, whispering into my mind, low and urgent. *Under*-hearing. Unmistakable.

I stand in the open doorway in shock, my body frozen with one hand gripping the blue notebook, because this time I know it really happened. I know. And, for a moment, I'm completely caught up in his glee, his excitement, his urgent need for—I don't know what. Then it's gone. I sag against the doorframe.

Meanwhile, my mind is hyperactive, going over and over what I just heard until it all clicks into place. This is what happened before. It happened with my mom at dinner. It happened at the swim meet during my race; when I got home that day, Mom told me that Shiri—

No, I can't think about that.

I want to dismiss it as my imagination, but I can't. It sounds unbelievable to even consider, but it isn't just "in my head."

I straighten up; strain my ears trying to listen. But I don't hear anything else.

I'm *not crazy*.

I must have been giving Spike a weird look, because he

starts coming at me with his lips parted and tongue wiggling exaggeratedly, like he's going to French kiss me.

I raise my eyebrows, take a big step back, and tell him I'll see him tomorrow. Then I tell myself that if what I heard was really what he was thinking, it's no big shock. It's just Spike, through and through. I tell myself that despite that whole business about not letting him down—whatever that means—despite his excitement, he's not really going to mind if I don't show up to his stupid barbecue.

And I spend the evening trying not to think about it. Not just because it's freaky weird. Also because...I know he can't help being Spike and thinking that stuff, but I don't want to admit to myself that I thought I knew him better than that. That he's disappointed me. That *he's* let *me* down.

———————

The next morning I open my eyes to the insipid, crooning strains of some second-rate boy band. I pull my pillow over my head to muffle the sound. I don't want to get out of bed. I'd rather stay tucked in here. I try to ignore my alarm clock, but I can't.

I drag myself into a sitting position and reach out to shut off the clock radio, then withdraw my hand. I imagine hearing the echoes of the music die away, leaving the room still and silent but my mind burning with the sound of voices in my head. My stomach does a slow somersault, and I swallow hard.

I'm really losing it. Is this what schizophrenia is like? I

shiver a little, feeling cold even under the blankets. I reach my hand out again, slowly stretching out to touch my clock radio. Trembling a little, I crank up the volume.

When I get downstairs to the kitchen table, my mind is so paralyzed I can't even seem to make conversation.

My dad squints up at me, setting his spoon down in a bowl of granola. "You look tired. Are you feeling okay? Do you need to stay home?"

I jump at the sound of his voice. "I'm fine, Dad. Just… cramps. I have to go today. I have a test in Pre-Calculus." I don't really want to go, but I need to. I'm sick of my parents fussing. Dad goes back to crunching away at his cereal, but I can feel his eyes on me when I turn my back.

I start making myself breakfast, pulling things mechanically out of the cabinets and fridge. But I can't eat. I just can't.

I put away the banana, Rice Krispies, and milk I got out for myself and go back upstairs to get ready. In the bathroom, I try to style my hair, but I give up after squishing in a handful of mousse. I look at myself in the mirror, at my puffy eyes and half-wavy hair with an inch of dark roots showing, and I want to crawl right back under the covers. I try to pretend I'm Cassie, try to pretend I'm above it all, that nothing can touch me. But it doesn't help.

I randomly pull a hoodie out of the closet: gray with pink edging. It's late fall already, so the weather's been unpredictable. Today it's almost chilly. Only Spike could think that this was good beach party weather.

Spike. I clench my teeth. Every time I think about last night when I talked to Spike, I get a weird feeling in the pit of my stomach and I try to think about something else, anything else. I sing songs in my head. I do deep breathing exercises. I slip my earbuds in and turn the volume up to maximum.

This morning, in the car, I turn on some earsplitting aggro rock and the drive to school ends quickly. The math test gives me something to think about besides everything else. And nobody's giving me the Stare of Pity anymore. Still, it's hard to concentrate. During American Lit a sudden wave of exhaustion comes over me and I spend the period staring at the wall. At Mr. Patrick's yellowing poster advertising Banned Books Week from eons ago, at the tiny square window in the classroom door reinforced with crisscrossing wire. A prison window.

In history class, I stare down at my desk and doodle a few sad little spirals to nowhere in my therapist-endorsed journal. When I look at it, I'm reminded of the journal that Shiri left me, the one I can't bring myself to pick up again.

What if whatever happened to her is happening to me?

I put my pen down and resist the urge to slam the journal shut. I don't know what gave Bettie or my mom the idea that this would actually help, or that I'd have anything to write about. Seriously, what would I put in there? What I had for lunch? How many times Eyes-Front had his eyes on my front? There's nothing to tell.

Less than nothing, in fact. Because there are things that I *don't* want to say. Things I don't want to put down on paper because that would make them way too real.

———

I was looking forward to lunch, at least. To one part of my life getting back to normal. And it looks the same from the outside, the whole crew occupying one of the miscellaneous jock tables near the gym. Everyone's here, everyone's talking and laughing as we eat lunch. But James and Marc keep glancing warily at me like they think I might start acting crazy at any minute. Elisa's voice drops to a nervous whisper every time she talks to me. Spike just acts like the same old Spike, but I still feel like an outsider.

I wish Cassie would scootch up to me on the picnic-table bench and distract me with silly gossip, the way she always used to when I was sick or tired. I know this is different, but they didn't act this way when Elisa's Great-Grandma Nguyen died. These are the same people I've been friends with since freshman year—longer, even, for Spike—and it's like they're afraid I'm contagious.

"Lame, dude, I can't believe your parents are making you go to some *wedding*," Spike's saying, like this is the most disgusting thing he's ever heard.

"I know; it's like punishment. It's like hell in a tuxedo. It's like…" Eyes-Front trails off, staring at Cassie's chest as she takes off her jacket.

"Quit staring, Marc. You're such a perv," Cassie says offhandedly, but with a tiny smile. She never minds extra attention, even from him. "I, for one, will *not* miss you at the barbecue."

"You wound me, woman, you wound me," Eyes-Front says, putting a hand to his heart in mock anguish while still somehow managing to eye up Cassie.

"Sunny, are you coming?" Spike looks over at me from across the table. I'd almost forgotten I was part of the conversation.

"I'm, uh … I don't know." I can't picture being at a barbecue with them, with these people who suddenly feel like strangers.

"James's brother is going to be there, remember," he says, trying to sound persuasive. My cheeks get hot. Last year I had a humongous crush on James's older brother Evan, a junior at UC Irvine. Spike's argument might have convinced me once upon a time, but today I raise my eyebrows at him and shrug.

He keeps looking at me, expectantly.

I can't think of any conceivable way this barbecue will be fun for me right now, but I feel bad because I know Spike wants me to go. I squirm uncomfortably. I hate this; hate feeling guilty. I don't want to have to feel bad about not writing in a journal or not going to a party that I don't want to go to.

My neck is damp with sweat and I take deep breaths, trying to recapture a semblance of calm. After a moment, I can meet Spike's gaze again. I am fine. I am perfectly serene. I am—

Now Cassie is staring at me out of the corner of her eye. One second my mind is clear and uncluttered and Zen-like, the next second—

> *oh my god look at her eyebrows*
> *she hasn't even gotten them shaped since—*
> *she always wants all the attention and boy*
> *has she been getting it*
> *—sick of feeling sorry for her, what about me?*

It's Cassie's voice. I don't want to hear it. I want to pretend that it's not her and it's only my paranoid imagination. But I can feel her layers of confused annoyance, her frustration and anger and even loneliness, coming off her like waves of heat from a summer parking lot. Her expression is placid, one perfectly arched and penciled eyebrow slightly raised, but to me it looks like a smirk.

And I hear the rest of them, like a buzz in the background.

—never wants to party with us
feeling sorry for herself—can't she just get past—
—major downer, I wish she'd just—

I want to put my hands over my ears, but I know it won't help. My eyes prickle like I'm going to cry. It must be showing on my face, but nobody else's expression changes.

I swallow hard. How long has Cassie felt like this? Maybe we never had the deepest friendship, but we always had fun. I thought I knew her. But I guess I didn't.

I can't hold it inside. I stand up.

"Are you sure you even *want* me to go?" I say bitterly, directing my question at Cassie. "You don't seem that excited."

"What are you even talking about?" She frowns, cuts her eyes at me, but I know she's lying. For all I know, she's just been going along with our friendship, going through the motions on the outside when inside she's backstabbing me. Or maybe it isn't only inside. A horrible, unfamiliar feeling of suspicion begins to take shape. Bile rises in the back of my throat. Everyone at the table is looking at me. Spike looks confused, and Elisa looks worried, but the longer I stand there, the worse I feel. I grab my backpack.

"I, uh, have to check something in the library," I say, my voice weaker than I'd like it to sound.

"Sure, whatever," Cassie says, sounding perfectly casual, but I know what she wasn't saying and I saw her roll her eyes at Marc. And was it my imagination or was he grinning knowingly back at her?

I don't care. I start walking briskly away, backpack dangling heavily off one shoulder.

"Hey, wait," Spike shouts. "You coming Saturday?"

I wave noncommittally, not looking at him, and keep walking. Spike's beach party: James, his brother, lots of beer, the swim team crew, and Cassie. My so-called friends.

There's no way I'm going to that barbecue.

five

The texture on my bedroom ceiling has a funny shape like an evil clown's head, right above my bed. I never noticed it until tonight. It's amazing what you notice when you spend ten hours lying around staring at the ceiling.

It's starting to get dark, so I turn on the bedside lamp so I can see the evil clown more clearly. Next to it is a bunny with three ears. The better to hear you with, my dear. With three ears, that rabbit could hear a wolf just *thinking* about chasing it.

And, just like that, I'm obsessing again. No matter how hard I try, I keep going back to what happened yesterday at school, and even more than that, the fact that I've started hearing thoughts.

Hearing thoughts. Whenever I think about it, I get a nervous, gut-churning feeling inside. It's like a sci-fi movie. Except I'm no heroine, and I don't feel powerful. I'm just me, scared and alone. And angry.

I turn on my side and pull my knees up to my chest. I

can't get the image of Cassie's smirking face out of my mind. Or the faces of all my so-called friends, plastered with fake smiles while their real feelings hammered my brain.

It's like the first day of kindergarten all over again. I'm wearing an embroidered dress—my favorite dress, bright purple and sparkly with tiny mirrors, a dress that Dadi had brought from Pakistan. I was still a little pudgy with baby fat. At recess, a group of mean kids surrounded me near the jump rope area, teasing me. *"What are you wearing?" "You look purple like a grape." "Grape girl."* Back then, Shiri was there to step in, running all the way over from the older kids' recess area when she saw me being cornered.

If she were here, I wonder if she'd understand, if she'd rub my back like she did when she was nine and I was five, and comfort me. *"Forget it. They don't know anything. You look cute, that's all. They're jealous."*

A tear slides down my nose. They *don't* know anything. Cassie doesn't know anything about how hard this is. And obviously I can't tell her.

I used to just laugh it off when she'd make bitchy little comments. I'd always known she didn't really mean it, that she was trying to be funny when she didn't know what to say. But yesterday ... I heard what she was thinking, and somehow that made all the difference. Maybe she didn't say it out loud this time, but she *felt* it. She meant it.

Part of me wonders if I should call her, try to confront her about it. But every time I pick up the phone, I hear her words echo in my head. She texted me a couple of times, but I deleted the messages without reading them. Maybe I'm being too harsh.

—sick of feeling sorry for her—

No. I'm doing the right thing.

The door hinges creak a little as Mom peeks into my room yet again. "Okay, Sunny honey?"

"Fine, Mom," I mutter.

When she shuts the door, I sit up and fumble my feet into my fuzzy slippers. I took another day off school today, but it's time to make an appearance downstairs and pretend everything's normal, pretend I'm feeling better. I don't want to have to talk to my parents about this. How can I? How could I explain it?

Who tells their parents they might have ESP?

Whatever was happening to Shiri, she didn't tell her parents either.

Downstairs, I plop myself on the couch in front of the TV and try to lose myself in an hour-long hospital drama, hoping it'll keep me from thinking about how I'm either a freak or crazy, and how I probably don't have friends anymore. Instead, I have to bite my lip so I don't cry. I've had it with crying. It's not going to change anything.

After a little while, Dad comes in and sits next to me. He holds up the remote and gives me a questioning glance. I shrug. He changes the channel to an Angels game. It's utterly boring, and perfect. I lean back against the cushions and stare vacantly at the screen, my eyes half-closed, watching statistics scroll by and portly guys standing around in the outfield scratching their butts. Some guy with an ugly mustache hits a triple, and my dad says an "a-*ha!*" of approval. Mom is rattling pots and pans around in the kitchen, washing dishes and getting dinner together, but it's only background noise. Before I know it, an hour has passed.

Maybe this is why Dad watches so much baseball. You don't have to think.

After a late dinner I go upstairs to my room, then spend a minute debating with myself whether to turn on the clock radio or put in my earbuds. For now, I settle on the clock radio. I tune it to a rock station and turn it up loud. All part of the strategy so I won't "underhear" any more horrible nasty thoughts I never wanted to know.

I try to catch up on French homework, but my eyelids start to droop even though I slept a lot today. Then I realize it's Friday and I have the whole weekend to do it. So I put my notebook away and, on impulse, pull my laptop over and open a search window.

"What to do if you hear thoughts," I type, and click Go.

Big mistake. I give up after scouring five pages of results. Apparently my most likely scenarios are that God is speaking to me or I'm going crazy.

I can't accept either of those answers.

But I do find a website with tips to help people relax their minds and go to sleep, and I could really use that right now since I'm keyed up again. I skim the page, then open the top drawer of my nightstand and pull out a long teakwood incense burner and a package of lavender incense sticks that Mom gave me on my last birthday.

I turn off the radio and slip my earbuds in with the volume set to low. Then I lie back on my bed, trying to clear my mind and focus on the swirls of smoke, the feeling of my breath going in and out of my nose, the smoky floral smell of the incense, the sound of quiet, slow guitar music strumming in my ears. After a while the incense makes my throat scratchy and I have a coughing fit.

I reach for my water glass and wonder if I should try some of my dad's incense from Pakistan, the pungent-smelling *agarbatti* sticks; and just like that I'm thinking of Shiri again. Of how I used to escape from my parents' embarrassing Saturday yoga group in our living room and hop in the car with Shiri and Auntie Mina on a trek to India Sweets and Spices...hot samosas from the deli counter, the air in the tiny shop filled with competing scents of incense and cardamom and fried goodies and a million other things; the three of us pointing and giggling at all the melodramatic Bollywood movie posters on the walls. That's never going to happen again.

I wonder if Shiri ever thought about those times. If she did, she didn't write about them in her journal. But I can't stop thinking about them. Even if the memories make my heart twist every time I relive them.

I smile a little, bitterly. When we were kids, Shiri and I used to hide up in the big tree in her parents' backyard, our legs dangling off the biggest branch, and talk about what special powers we'd have if we were superheroes. The one thing we both agreed would be great was to know what other people were thinking.

Now that I've heard what other people think, I'm realizing it's not so great. My own thoughts and memories—those are more than enough. But I can't help wondering, in some deep dark part of me, what if I'd been able to hear Shiri's thoughts? Would I have been able to do something to help her? Or at least maybe understand?

———

Monday morning is grayish and overcast, but not too cold. Typical early November. My motivation for getting dressed for school is severely limited, so I throw on an old green Yosemite sweatshirt, then pull my hair back into a loose braid and cover it with a faded baseball cap of my dad's with some Led Zeppelin symbols on it. My wardrobe is the least of my worries today. Today is the first day of the rest of my life, as they say—the first day of sitting alone at lunch and watching my former friends having a great time without me. Clearly they haven't been having a good time *with* me.

Maybe I'm not being fair. But midway through my drive to school, I have a moment of sad epiphany. Nobody called me before the beach barbecue Saturday to see if I was going. Except for a drunk text from Spike late that night, nobody seemed to care that I didn't show up. No call from Cassie saying "Are you okay, Sunny Bunny? We missed you." No call from Elisa to fill me in on James and Eyes-Front's goofy exploits, or to tell me Evan still looked as hot as I remembered. Spike called yesterday to ask if I was feeling better—as if I'd come down with a virus and it would be gone next week.

As if. By the time I pull into the school parking lot, I'm fuming.

My first class is French. Eyes-Front is in that class, and at first I can't even look at him. Unfortunately, Mrs. Lam pairs us up for conversation exercises.

"Monsieur Marc avec Mademoiselle Soleil, s'il vous plait, merci," she chirps, tapping on each of our desks with a burgundy-painted fingernail as she walks by. *Soleil* is "sun," of course. Mrs. Lam tries to give everyone a French nickname. We normally hassle each other the whole time about "Soleil" and "Marrrc" when we're doing work in pairs, but today we hardly talk. Eyes-Front doesn't meet my eyes—or anything else, for that matter—for more than a second at a time, and there's no extraneous conversation. To me, this is confirmation that Cassie has been talking about me behind my back and that I shouldn't expect any of those dumb guys to jump to my defense. But it hurts.

I really thought they were my friends. Stupid me.

By the time lunch rolls around, I have a serious stomachache. Still, out of habit, I get in line at the pizza cart parked at the edge of the quad. When I glance behind me, the whole gang is sitting at our usual table, laughing and talking like nothing's out of the ordinary. I can easily guess what's going on: Elisa is wondering out loud which of her many club meetings to go to. Eyes-Front is staring at Elisa's chest. Spike is regelling his hair and teasing Elisa for being such a geek. James is not-so-surreptitiously trying to show off his latest pair of expensive brand-name sneakers, which his parents regularly buy for him. And Cassie...Cassie glances up and sees me looking at her. She quickly looks away again. She seems quiet; sorry. Maybe things will be okay. If I go over and sit with them and pretend nothing happened...a tingle of hope zings through me.

As I'm watching, Cassie says something. Suddenly, they all look up. At me. Cassie stares at me almost challengingly. Without breaking eye contact, she makes some other comment to the group. Then she starts giggling, a high-pitched, annoying sound that carries all the way to where I'm standing. The wanna-be gangster behind me in the pizza line turns his head, looking around. James and Elisa grin, and Marc even lets out his braying donkey laugh. My face goes hot, and I hope the people around me don't realize I'm the one being laughed at.

Spike is the only one not joining in. Feeling desperate, I try to catch his eye, but he looks away. He crumples up his empty brown bag, picks up his backpack, and heads off toward the volleyball court. My jaw clenches involuntarily. Why isn't anybody standing up for me? For an instant I have this intense wish, like an ache in my chest, to know what they said. Maybe it was something perfectly innocent, completely unrelated to me. Then I change my mind. I don't *want* to know what they said. Thinking about that moment with Cassie on Friday, I realize that knowing for sure is infinitely worse.

—what is her problem? we didn't do anything—

I flinch and turn away.

As I wait, it starts to drizzle, which is just perfect, but I don't even care if my hair goes flat. It's as hideous as it can get already. I'm surprised I didn't underhear Cassie saying something bitchy about *that*. Despite myself, I reach back to straighten my ponytail, then let my hands drop to my sides.

I've been part of that group for more than two years. The first day of ninth grade, Shiri and I met up with Tessa and Cassie near the back parking lot, and Cassie introduced me to her friends. I introduced her to Spike. That day at lunch, we were all so nervous that we tried to identify something weird, or goofy, or embarrassing about each person we saw so that we wouldn't feel so out of place ourselves. *"Look at that guy—can you believe he's wearing a Hawaiian shirt? Check out Tracie. She's had the same hairstyle since the fifth grade."* When I think back on it now, I cringe.

But I thought they actually liked me for *me*, not because I was cool Shiri's cousin or because we just happened to be on the swim team together.

I guess I was wrong.

I'm a big girl now, though. I can do without them. When I get to the front of the line I pay for my pizza, grab the little box, and brave the drizzle with a surge of angry energy.

I don't need them. I'll just find a new place to eat lunch, preferably someplace with nobody around to laugh at me.

I jam my dad's cap down further on my head and do my best to shield the pizza box with my arm as I make a quick, damp circuit of the campus. Everywhere seems to be already occupied. Even the bleachers at the far end of the football field are taken over by the stoners, who are sitting underneath smoking cigarettes and talking about some band they all saw over the weekend. When I peer in at them, they look at me like I've lost my mind. If they only knew.

I move on. The grass next to the auditorium is too wet for sitting. Inside the auditorium is where the drama geeks hang out. I peek in the side door and see a few people from my history class, two guys and three girls I don't like because they're always all over each other in public and oozing fake friendliness all over everyone else. Fake friendliness is the last thing I want right now. Instead, I try some of the open classrooms, but they're mostly full of students taking shelter from the light rain.

One of the science classrooms is nearly empty: just a group of guys playing Dungeons and Dragons. By now I'm kind of hungry, so I'm fully prepared to ignore them and sit down for lunch, but one of them leers at me through a shaggy fringe of hair and says, "*I'm* a seventh-level elf wizard" and looks at me expectantly. I beat a hasty retreat. I know it's a game, but I don't want to pretend I'm someone I'm not any more.

I'm about to give up and go eat in my car when I remember there's an awning at the back of campus, sandwiched between the decrepit little art building and the portable classrooms. I think there's even a lone picnic table back there.

The table is empty. I feel an amazing rush of relief, and I sit down. It's quiet back here. I can faintly hear some football players yelling out by the bleachers, and the strains of innocuous, principal-approved pop music drift over from the lunch area. But mostly I just hear the steady dripping of rain from the gutter onto the awning, and the hum of traffic on the street behind the school. It's nice. The orange paint on the bench is peeling and there's some black-marker graffiti on the table, but I think I could get used to eating here.

The rest of the day drags, though, and it's hard to pay attention in class. Images of Cassie and her mean laugh, of Spike walking away and not even bothering to defend me, keep floating into my mind. A vindictive little part of me wishes something bad would happen to one of them so they'd know how I feel. In sixth-period physics there's a pop quiz. I know I'm going to bomb it; I leave a fourth of the questions blank, but I can't bring myself to care. When I hand it in, Ms. Rabb takes one look at it and glances at me with concern—a watered-down version of the Stare of Pity—but I just give her a vague, fake smile and go back to my desk.

Finally, the day is over and I'm home. It's quiet, and nobody is here to laugh at me, or quiz me, or even talk to me. I toss my baseball cap and backpack onto the faded old Persian carpet on our living room floor, and switch on the TV. I try halfheartedly to do some history reading, but give up partway through and lose myself in a reality show in which people's friends set them up for tasteless pranks involving public humiliation.

———

The next day, fourth period, I'm staring out the grimy window of the library at the empty lunch area. Cassie and Marc ignored me in class today; even Elisa looked the other way when we passed each other between periods. Some friends they turned out to be. Maybe it's just as well. But there's a part of me that wishes nothing had changed.

Nobody shows up for chemistry tutoring. The clock over the librarian's desk ticks away the minutes way too slowly.

After stewing over everything a while, I get kind of mad. I'm not the one who needs to apologize, to make excuses. I'm not going to whine at them or beg them to take me back into the group. They're the ones with the attitude, not me.

At lunch, when I pass by their table on my way to buy a soda, I see their little identical-zombie clique and feel... less bad, anyway, than I did yesterday. At least today I'm not ready to run to the bathroom and barf. Spike even smiles at me tentatively, but I'm not quite prepared to smile back. Let them stress for a change.

After getting a cola, I quicken my pace on the way to my new table, far away from Cassie and the Zombie Squad. I set down my lunch bag and drink and plop down in the middle of the bench.

I'm about three bites into my turkey pita sandwich when I hear people approaching from the parking lot. The conversation grows closer. I can pick out a couple of female voices, a few male; none of them recognizable. Then a group of artsy goth types turns the corner of the art building and heads for the table. *My* table. My heart sinks.

"Hey," says one girl. "What are you doing at our table?"

She looks at me disdainfully, pouting from a mouth lip-sticked a dark maroon color. It strikes me that Cassie probably would have said the same thing if I'd tried sitting at my old lunch spot. My heart starts pounding and my ears get hot as I try to think of something to say.

Another one of the girls stares at me closely for a moment, and I realize she's recognized me as The Girl Whose Cousin Committed Suicide. Just what I need. I duck my head a little, trying to hide under my untrimmed bangs while I peer up at her surreptitiously. She looks familiar, and I realize I had English class with her freshman year. Back then she had really long brown hair, though; now she has short, spiky two-inch-long purple braids that poke out from her head like little coiled springs. I also remember her being quiet in class. Now she speaks up.

"No big deal," she says, flashing a look at her comrades. "It's cool. If she wants to, she can stay." I give her an uneasy smile. She doesn't smile back, but she takes the lead in sitting down next to me at the table.

The rest of the group starts filling in the bench around and across from me, haphazardly tossing an array of army-surplus messenger bags and black patent leather purses next to my baby-blue backpack. I stand out like a sore thumb in my swim team sweatshirt. My legs tense with the urge to bolt.

Mikaela Ramirez. I remember her name all of a sudden, randomly, along with the subject of her ninth grade oral report on *A Midsummer Night's Dream*: something about tricksters and fairies. Even that thin thread of connection helps me relax a little, and I sneak another look at her. Other than the new fashion statement, she's pretty much as I remember: short and sturdy, with light-brown skin a few shades darker than mine. Then one of the guys stares over at me, coldly enough to make me look down.

"Nice. We ditch one day of school and the Attack of the Clones moves in." He says it in a low voice, offhandedly, but with a hint of a snarl. For a minute I can't even bring myself to look up. My ears are hot, my eyeballs are prickling, and I wish I'd worn anything other than swim team sweats and my Citrus Valley Vikings hat.

I haven't been sitting with these people five minutes, and they're already judging me. How unfair is that? I guess it's karma coming back to bite me, after everything I used to say. A song lyric pops into my head, the one about instant karma. John Lennon.

Shiri loved that song.

"So, what's a clone like you doing slumming it back here?" the guy adds.

"Ex*cuse* me?" I look up at him. He'd almost be cute, in a goth sort of way, if he hadn't just annoyed the crap out of me: tall, a little skinny, but with a strong jaw and profile. His eyes are blue, he's got a silver eyebrow ring, and his hair is jet black, obviously dyed. His lips twist into a sneer. I shoot my fiercest glare back at him.

It doesn't seem to matter where I go; all anyone ever does is judge me by the way I look. I might as well still be five years old wearing my purple kindergarten dress.

I don't need this. I swallow my bite of sandwich and start gathering my stuff together.

"Hey, don't go anywhere," Mikaela says. "You can't take him seriously. He doesn't have a filter between his brain and his mouth." She turns to the guy. "God, can you stop being a bitch for one day? This is that girl Sunny; *you* know." She glares at him across the table, then lowers her voice. "The *assembly*, Les. Remember?"

I let out my breath as silently as possible in a long sigh and sit back down, mortified. This is going about as badly as I could have imagined.

"Quit calling me Les. It's Cody now," he corrects her, turning the sneer on her. She seems to wilt a little, momentarily, but then her face hardens to a glower again. "And yeah," Cody continues, "I remember the assembly. So what?"

"So nothing. So, shut the fuck up," she says almost good-naturedly, like she says it a dozen times a day. The group laughs and Cody flips her off, but he's smiling as he does it. Meanwhile, I'm just sitting there like an idiot without a single intelligent thought running through my head. And then

> —*jerk you always act like such a jerk,*
> *god just get a life and leave*
> *the poor girl alone.*
> *jesus I can't believe she's taking this so well,*
> *I'd be bawling already I'd be crying*
> *still from what happened—*

My body shakes a little, and I feel her anger almost as intensely as if it's my own. The anger hums through me along with a mixture of frustration and—not pity, but a feeling I can't quite put my finger on, something complicated like the flavor of spice cookies or the smell of anise. It takes a moment to regain my composure, but my eyes finally focus again and I drop the squished remains of my sandwich, blinking stupidly.

I have no idea what to think. All I know is, she defended me to her friends and she absolutely, positively meant it, too.

I inhale sharply, trying to calm down, then immediately regret drawing attention to myself.

"What, Little-Miss-Preppy-Pants is traumatized by the F-word? Do you want to wash her mouth out with soap—what's your name—Sunny? Is that for real?" He directs a mildly amused glance in my general direction, briefly making eye contact. Is he trying to flirt now? What a freak. I tilt my head, strain to pick up something, anything, but my brief moment of underhearing has stopped and I'm left confused as ever, without a clue what's going on behind his eyes.

"I had her in a class freshman year. It's for real, *Lester Cody Anderson*," Mikaela says scornfully. She turns toward me and, all of a sudden, her face lights up with a huge grin. Not another glare, not even the dreaded Stare of Pity. She has a truly gorgeous, thousand-watt smile, and sitting there basking in it, I can't help feeling a little better.

From Shiri Langford's journal, February 22nd

Dad said if I don't "shape up" he's going to have to "seriously reconsider his decision to send me so far away to such an exclusive college." I'm not even sure what that means. Is he going to make me move back home, just because he's paying for my housing? I can't let that happen. I'd run away first. He can't stop me. My tuition, at least, is paid for with my tennis scholarship, as long as I get my grades back up.

It's so unfair. Randall gets everything and I get nothing, I never even asked for anything, and what little I get is contingent on doing exactly what HE wants.

I hope Mom's holding up.

Some good news, though. Brendan. Every time I think about him, I think that maybe if things get bad… maybe we could run away together. The first time I met him, THAT happened and I knew he was the kind of guy who would understand how my family is, because he's had his own struggles. I admire him so much.

If I could just never go home again, I think I might be able to stay happy.

six

Breathe. In past my nostrils and filling my lungs; hold. Feel the breath leave my body and puff out of my mouth. Again. *Breathe.*

Again.

Breathe—there's another knock at the front door, and my eyes fly open.

It's Saturday, and I'm spending it on an unsuccessful attempt to meditate in my room while my parents lead the neighbors in their weekly session of Yoga for Aging Suburbanites.

Normally the last thing I'd do would be to follow one of my mother's wacky suggestions. She thinks meditation is the solution to everything except maybe actual broken bones. But I can't keep from hoping that somehow it'll help me. It's worth a shot. I don't know what else to do. Once or twice a day, without fail, I'm hearing somebody's thoughts in my head, feeling someone else's emotions sweep me away like the tide. And I don't have anyone to talk to about it.

I never asked for this … ability. My life was fine.

I never even asked for anything. It's almost like an echo, and I shiver. Shiri's journal. She said nearly the same thing. Only she said it about her own life. Her sad story, all the little hurts we never suspected but which added up somehow. The mysterious THAT. Shiri's life was anything but fine. And now mine feels like it's spiraling out of control, too.

I sit cross-legged on the floor next to my bed with my hands folded in my lap. What a joke. I'm supposed to be focusing on my breathing, clearing my mind. Instead, I keep *thinking*, nonstop. Shiri. Auntie Mina. Cassie. Spike. Even Cody and Mikaela. All of them going around and around my skull like animated bluebirds when a cartoon character gets whacked on the head.

This isn't working. I open my eyes and try a different strategy: I grab my journal. I might as well make it good for something, so I write down every incident of underhearing that I can remember.

I start with the very first time, the time I was in the pool during the swim meet and thought I heard screaming.

The day that Shiri died.

The first time it happened, it was during the phone call to my mom. THE Phone Call. Then I write the rest down: the incident during dinner at home, the one with Spike, the Cassie debacle, and everything else. I try to remember every detail I can. What I was initially doing. What the other person was doing. What I was thinking and what they were thinking. I make a chart, I draw arrows, I sort and re-sort the information. I make one more list, writing down what both parties were feeling at the time.

That's when it all starts to fall into place.

Emotions. Each time I underheard someone's thoughts, the other person was having strong emotions that I was able to sense, *feel*, at the same time that I heard their thoughts. And I was completely caught up in their feelings, my own emotions drowned out. If the moment of strong emotion was just a flash, all I heard was a few words. If the feeling was surging through, then I might catch as much as a few thoughts. It's as if their thoughts are the notes from a musical instrument, their feelings an amplifier. And the other person is always nearby; if not next to me, then somewhere in the vicinity.

But it's connected to *my* emotions, too. Like when I was sitting there with my old friends from the Zombie Squad, feeling guilty about not going to Spike's party. It was the minute I cleared my head, like I'd hit pause on my feelings, that I heard Cassie. Or my first day in Emoville with Mikaela and friends, earlier this week, when I got pissed at Cody. I tried to maintain composure, swallowing down my gut reaction, and suddenly I heard Mikaela's angry thoughts. It's a moment of clarity, but I've still got those emotions pushing at me below the surface. Something about that state of mind makes the impossible possible. At least for me.

I close the journal, put my pen down and massage my tired hand. Then I get up and stare into the mirror on my closet door. It seems as if I should look different. Have sparkles around my head or weird shimmery eyes like a character in a TV show. But I look the same as I always did. Just with worse hair.

Is my life going to change now? I can't imagine it changing more than it already has. I don't even know if my under-hearing is going to stay forever or just disappear one day. But I've figured something out about it, figured out *when* it happens, and that makes me feel a little less out of control. Less scared.

———————

The next morning, I'm lying on my stomach across the bed, Pixie purring next to me and my journal open to the page with the charts, when my mom opens the door without knocking. I turn my head, startled, and she breezes in, wearing one of her trademark long Indian-print skirts. She takes one look at the diary and a grin appears on her face.

"Oh, baby Sunshine, I am so happy to see—" I glare at her pointedly and she cuts her sentence short. "Anyway. Well. If there's ever anything—"

"I *know*, Mom," I say, hurriedly, and slam the diary shut. "Thanks," I add. I don't want her to get nosy, start asking questions I don't know how to answer. I mean, my mom is a little bit out there, but it's not like she believes in magic or ghosts or anything supernatural. At least, I don't think so. Not like some of her crazy dippy friends.

Mom paces over to the window and opens the curtains, flooding the room with painfully bright light. I squint. "Don't forget Auntie Mina's coming over this afternoon," she says, leaning against my desk and smiling a little. "We need to get her out of *that house* for a while. And I bought a vanilla chai tea blend I think she's going to love."

That house. I can't even remember when we first started to call it that. But when I got older, I could see for myself how Uncle Randall was when he'd get into his "moods." He'd have everybody walking on eggshells, hoping not to say the wrong thing. And it seemed like it got worse after Number Two moved out and Shiri started high school.

Maybe that's why she was such an overachiever back then, going out for tennis team and spending time in after-school study hall on days when she didn't have tennis practice. Going to as many SAT and AP prep classes as she could. Was she trying to make her dad happy, or just trying to stay out of the way?

"Sunny?" Mom says, looking at me. I shake myself a little. I know she asked me a question, but I have no idea what it was.

"Sorry. Guess I'm a little distracted." I sit up and try to look attentive.

"I asked if you'd like to sit with me later this evening and go through some family photos," Mom says, picking at a loose thread on her skirt. "I was hoping to make a scrapbook for Mina that we can give her, later, when she's ready, to help her preserve the good memories of—everything." Her eyes are shining. I can't deal with my mom crying, so I nod, just so we can end this conversation. But I don't know how I can bear to go through photos.

"Oh, good. I'm so glad you said yes. I've been feeling like I need some moral support these days," she continues, "with you and your father keeping everything so bottled up. You're like two peas in a pod."

I scowl and stow the journal safely in my desk drawer, on top of Shiri's journal. I love my mom, but she takes the touchy-feely thing a little too far sometimes.

She smiles a little and straightens up, wandering back toward the door. "Oh! And I invited Antonia to come over later tonight to help us with the scrapbooking. She's got such a fabulous collection of supplies—rubber stamps, glitter, rickrack, stickers... I thought it would cheer us up." Mom's voice fades as she cruises out of the room, and I slam the door behind her.

Antonia lives down the street and is even more touchy-feely than Mom. She comes to the weekend yoga sessions and has every corny new-agey hobby on the face of the earth—tarot cards, aromatherapy, crystals, you name it—and she's just so disgustingly nice. TOO nice, if you ask me. Spike's theory is that she was lobotomized. I think she probably just smoked too much pot in the '70s.

I can't deal with her right now.

"Dad, you have to get me out of it," I complain, tugging on his arm as he tries to grade Intro to Film term papers. He's slouching in the swivel chair in his home office with a stack of papers in his lap, his hairy bare feet propped up on a file box. Blues music is playing quietly through the speakers of his computer. "Antonia is coming over tonight and I'm supposed to help with scrapbooking!" I whine this last word right in his ear.

"Sunny, please," Dad says, sighing. He puts a finger in the book to hold his place and frowns up at me. "I know how you feel, but—"

"*Pleeeeease.*" I know it's no use, but I try anyway. "I'll do chores. I don't care."

"Sunny, be nice," Dad says, his tone sharper now. "This isn't a bargaining situation. If your mom wants to make a scrapbook, then I don't think it's too much to ask for you to help her. We need to be supportive of your Auntie Mina right now."

"We meaning *me*, you mean." I stomp out of the den, exasperated. I can hear Dad grumbling to himself, but I don't care. I go to my room, shut the door, and study with my earbuds in until the doorbell rings, when Dad comes up and marches me down to the dining room for our afternoon of vanilla chai tea blend with Auntie Mina. I'm ashamed to admit that I'm dreading it almost as much as the scrapbooking. My guts twist.

Mom is sitting next to Auntie Mina at one end of the dining room table. She frowns at my outfit. I'm wearing a light-yellow tracksuit that Grandma and Grandpa gave me for my last birthday; it's hideous, but it was the first thing I grabbed that was clean.

I walk in and try to put on a smile for my aunt, who is sitting at the dining room table looking small and lost. Her normally shiny dark-brown hair hangs limply down her back, more gray in it than before. She's staring at her full teacup, still and silent.

I feel horrible. And I don't know what to do.

When I approach the table, she looks up briefly with a wan smile. "Hi, Sunny. I'm glad you're here."

"Hi, Auntie," I say uncertainly. She doesn't look glad; rather, the moment I walked in, it was as if her face crumpled just a little more under the weight of memories. I want to hug her, like I usually do, but I'm afraid to.

Dad walks in behind me and sits on Auntie Mina's other side, leaning over to give her a quick, awkward kiss on the cheek. I sit across from her, feeling queasy and awful. Her eyes are shadowed and hollow, her lips dry and cracked. I can't imagine Uncle Randall and Number Two have been much comfort; Dad told me that Uncle Randall's been working late every day. Number Two, as usual, is doing his plastic surgeon thing out in Palm Springs, in the Condo That Dad Bought.

"We're all so happy to see you," my mother says, a little too cheerfully, putting a gentle hand on Auntie Mina's shoulder. I fidget in my chair and force another smile.

"Oh, pooh," my aunt says, her voice slightly tremulous. "You make it sound like I've been in seclusion."

"Really, Mina. We are," Mom says. "It feels like it's been weeks since we've really talked. I'm concerned that you've been too . . . alone with your feelings."

Way to be subtle. Mom tries to draw Auntie Mina out of her shell, encouraging her to vent if she needs to and not hold any emotions inside where they'll "fester." Despite my mother's well-meaning attempts, Auntie Mina stays quiet and listless, putting in a soft word now and then but nothing significant. Nothing that tells us how lost she must feel. Not that she needs to tell us.

At some point, after our tea has long gotten cold and Dad and I have reduced the zucchini bread to a pile of crumbs on the plate, the conversation turns to Shiri. It happens by accident. I'm finally telling my parents about how I've stopped going to swim practice, how I think I want to quit the team, and it just slips out of my mouth: how Shiri would have wheedled, badgered me, whatever it took to get me back on track because it would be a major plus on my college applications.

And after that, it's like an invisible barrier has suddenly disappeared. Auntie Mina starts to talk. And then we're all talking, remembering weird random things like how much Shiri hated mustard and how inordinately happy she got whenever she was able to find a cute pair of shoes in her tiny shoe size.

Dad says, "Remember that time the newspaper wrote about the Mock Trial case against Vista Hills?" Mom nods, a sad smile on her face.

"That's *right*," I said. "The reporter got her name wrong. He wrote 'Sherry.'" I snort.

"Sherry," Auntie Mina says with a shaky laugh. "I'd almost forgotten about that." One minute she's smiling; the next minute, tears begin to roll down her face. Abruptly, she dashes them away and apologizes, eyes downcast with—what? Embarrassment? I'm not sure. I pass the napkins. She dabs at her face with one and then crumples it into a ball. My mom fusses, putting an arm around Auntie Mina's shoulders and pulling the cup of cold tea closer, telling her she has nothing to apologize for.

Auntie Mina lets out a shaky sigh. "But I *am* sorry, because you've been so nice to do all this," she says, her voice thick. "I know I should be coping better, but I just—" She breaks off, looking down at the table, not meeting anyone's eyes.

I exchange a look with Mom. Auntie Mina lost her only daughter, for crying out loud, and it's like she's afraid we'll be angry at her. But I just feel bad. We all do.

I open my mouth to tell her that she has no reason to be sorry, that nobody has any right to tell her otherwise, when the doorbell rings. Auntie Mina springs to her feet and says, "I should really get going."

"Mina," my dad says, reaching a hand toward her. "Stay for dinner."

She grabs her purse from the back of the chair. "You have company. Plus it's roast chicken night, so we'll have company, too, one of the other VPs in Randall's department. I'll just let myself out the side door. I *loved* the tea." She gives Mom a kiss on the cheek and says, "I'll call soon." She hugs me and Dad, quickly, and hurries out the door before we can say more than goodbye. Dad scoots his chair back and rushes after her, looking as confused as I feel, and Mom is frowning, but the doorbell rings again and she hurries to answer it.

Poor Auntie Mina. I wonder what she's thinking, what was going through her head. Why she decided to run off. And I wonder why I didn't underhear anything.

I guess I didn't try.

For the first time, it occurs to me that I could have. Could have tried to find out what she was feeling, deliberately. What she was thinking.

No matter what was going through her mind, I know she's got to be hurting a million times more than I am.

I don't have much time to think about it, because who follows my mother into the room but Antonia in the ample flesh, wearing a yellow tracksuit nearly identical to mine, only hers is adorned with a giant quartz crystal pendant and a silver dragon pin.

"Sorry I'm early," she's saying to my mom. "I really thought you said four o'clock. I—" Then she catches sight of me.

"Sunny!" she exclaims in a bright, chirpy voice. "Look at us! We're twins." Her shoulder-length, curly, carroty-orange hair has a white streak in the front where it's starting to go gray, and it's bouncy just like her personality. It makes me ill. And I'm angry, too, because if she hadn't shown up so early, maybe Auntie Mina wouldn't have felt like she had to jump up and leave.

Dad walks back through the side door at that moment. He doesn't look happy, either, and he quickly retreats to his study with his stack of grading.

Antonia turns to my mother and plops a huge macramé bag onto the table.

"Oh, that's really thoughtful of you, Antonia. I hope it wasn't any trouble," my mom says. Mom looks pleased, but for me, the rest of the evening is a nightmare. I try to bury myself in my pre-calculus homework when I'm not helping sort through photos. Every time I look at any of the pictures—the ones of Shiri as a kid at tennis camp, dressed up for eighth-grade graduation, or even the horrible one with the two of us as little kids, half-naked in an inflatable pool—I feel my teeth clench and my eyes sting. All those moments are worthless now.

Mom is unashamedly weeping and smiling, sharing every stupid memory that pops into her head, and Antonia keeps doing her thing with heaps of glitter and paper doodads, turning the stacks of photos and digital printouts into a nightmarish scrapbook monstrosity. Mom wields scissors and a glue stick as the two of them chatter away about Shiri, about Mina, and then, after Mom cheers up a little, about other scrapbook ideas and goofy household decorating projects that my dad would surely veto if he were privy to this conversation.

The evening seems endless, but finally Antonia leaves. I try to find my dad to ask him what he talked about with Auntie Mina, if he was able to find out why she left so abruptly, but he's taking a long shower, so I give up and go to bed.

At least I didn't underhear anybody all day. I don't know if I would have been able to handle hearing Auntie Mina. On one hand, maybe it would have helped me understand. Or maybe it would have made me break down completely.

———

Monday is dismal. The sky is grayish with smoggy haze, and the trees on campus are starting to turn brown, except for the high, soaring palms out by the road. Eddies of fall wind whip a few dry leaves around and bend the palm trees into gentle parallel curves, and my nose itches with flying dust.

My mood feels just as dismal; fragile as the dry leaves. My head aches.

I get through my first couple of classes okay, paying the minimum of attention to get by. Then, in third-period Pre-Calculus, we get our tests back from last week. Scrawled in red on the top of my test is a C+. My stomach drops. The scrawled numbers go blurry as I stare at the page. I do my best to blink the tears back, but I can't seem to control them, so I hurry to Ms. Castillo's desk for a bathroom pass.

When I reach the bathroom, I lock myself into a stall and lean against the graffiti-covered orange wall, my jaw clenched. *It's just a test. No, it's more than the test. It's everything.* I stay like that for a few minutes, trying to regain control.

The bathroom door opens and I freeze, holding my breath, tears still sliding down my cheeks and onto my neck. I peek through the crack between the door and the side of the stall. It's Mikaela. She clomps in on huge platform-soled black boots and stops to rearrange her ripped, holey black tights.

Then she goes into one of the stalls to pee. While she's in there, I take a deep breath and go out to wash my face. Mikaela hasn't exactly been *friendly* to me, but she and her Emoville friends have put up with me sitting with them at lunch and have pretty much left me alone, which is what I wanted in the first place. Even the girl who first gave me attitude, Becca, has been pretty nice. Cody got on my case at first for homing in on their lunch spot, but he got over it surprisingly quickly. For a day or two after that, he ignored me; now we seem to have a tentative truce.

He even smiled at me a little when I passed him in the hall after first period today. His smile makes him look like a different person. Less like a conceited jerk. More like a normal human being. Which he is, I guess.

I'm the one who's not quite normal.

I'm still drying my face on a scratchy brown paper towel when Mikaela comes out of the stall. She washes her hands and then stays in front of the mirror to fix one of her springy little braids. My face is more than dry, so I give up trying to hide and, heart pounding, try to sound as casual and normal as possible.

"Hey, Mikaela." I carefully don't look at her, but stare into the mirror and pretend to squint at a zit on my chin.

"Oh, hey, Sunny," she says, glancing at me before going back to her braid. She doesn't stare at my red, teary eyes. She doesn't sound scornful. She doesn't sound like anything. Just regular. I mentally sigh with relief. She finishes wrapping the end of the braid in a silver rubber band and starts to head for the door. She passes me on the way, and slows, peering closely at my face. She looks like she's about to say something, but instead she just smiles and says, "See you at lunch." Then, just as she's gotten past me, her hand shoots out and tucks something into the pocket of my windbreaker. For a second I think I've imagined it.

"Um, yeah … see you then," I manage to croak out. When Mikaela's gone, I reach into my pocket. Inside is a tissue packet.

I almost feel like crying again. Cassie would have been all over me. She'd have been all "what's wrong, Sunny Bunny?" and "oh, no, look how red your eyes are; we need to get some eye drops in there," and "let's get you fixed up." The thought doesn't seem comforting to me anymore. It seems smothering. It seems superficial, like she cared more about how I look than how I feel.

Maybe she did.

Mikaela didn't even *say* anything—all she did was shove Kleenex in my pocket. But she cared enough to not press the issue, and left me alone to sort myself out, which is what I do. I have to.

Next period is tutoring in the library. As usual, nobody seems to require my services. I do notice that one of the guys from Emoville is sitting at a table in the far corner by the window, a guy with nondescript light-brown hair who I think is named David. He's scribbling in a notebook. It's funny; it's like I never noticed any of them before, but now I'm running into Mikaela and her friends all over the place.

It makes me feel less alone.

At one point he looks up and catches me watching. I give him a half-wave, and he kind of half-smiles back and goes back to writing in his notebook. I might as well be friendly since I'm sharing their table every day. I don't want them to drive me out. I don't have anywhere else to go.

———

"Oh, of *course* you want to read the *Citrus Valley Voice*! Everyone wants to read the *Citrus Valley Voice*! Your mom wants to read the *Citrus Valley Voice*!" Becca says in a high-pitched squeak, mimicking the overenthusiastic office aide who just forced copies of the school newspaper on us.

"We can always use it to start fires, I guess," this guy named Andy says, with a slightly insane grin.

"Pyro," I say, absently, playing with the lid of my water bottle. I always kind of liked the *Citrus Valley Voice*, but I'm not going to say so now.

"Just kidding. I won't burn it. But I'm not gonna read it."

"Seriously," Mikaela says. "Like we want to read school propaganda *outside* of school. Hey, we should totally start up a competing publication."

Cody smirks. "Yeah. We could do better. The *Voice* is so full of garbage. It's all about kids who think they're popular, written by kids who *wish* they were popular." There are sounds of general agreement, and he pretends to flip through the paper. "Hmm. The football team lost. Golly! If they're not careful they'll lose their cheerleading groupies to, like, the swim team." He puts one hand over his heart and makes a ridiculously pathetic face at me.

Becca snorts. Mikaela and Andy bust up laughing.

I fidget on the hard wooden bench of the picnic table. The reference to swim team makes me feel a little weird. But I know Cody's just trying to make me feel better about the Zombie Squad, so I force a laugh.

I end up getting a coughing fit. Embarrassed, I down the rest of my water and get up to refill my water bottle at the drinking fountain near the parking lot. I'm just turning the corner around the side of the art building when I run into Spike walking back from his car.

I don't feel prepared for this, but he still stops in front of me, running one hand awkwardly through his haphazardly gelled hair.

"Hey," he says. "How's it going? Sorry I haven't called. I've been ... you know."

"Yeah," I say. "Me too." There's a long pause, and I kind of stare past him, out at the cars in the lot, feeling a little guilty. "How is everyone?"

"Oh, fine. Same-old. We miss you on swim team. Coach has Cassie doing the 100-meter freestyle now."

I grunt. There's a small twinge in my chest when Spike gives me the news, but I try to keep my face neutral. I swallow past what feels like a rock in my throat and ask, "How is Cassie?"

"She's ... just Cassie," Spike says, looking nervous all of a sudden. "She's taking it a little hard that you haven't been hanging out with us. She's been kind of pissed about it, actually."

"She's taking it hard?" I burst out. "*She's* the one who—" I stop. Spike has no idea. He has no idea I can hear thoughts. He has no idea how angry she really is. Until recently, I didn't either. "I just—I know she's been talking about me."

"I know, I know. Say no more." Spike puts out a hand like he's trying to ward off the crazy-chick vibes. "Listen, you know how she says stuff ... stupid stuff. She doesn't mean it.

When she gets that way, I'm out." He pauses, smiling sheepishly. "I've been spending a lot of time at the volleyball court lately."

"She says 'stuff?'" I say skeptically.

He scratches his neck, not quite meeting my eyes, and changes the subject. "So you started hanging out over here, huh?"

"Yup." I don't elaborate.

"Um, are you sure you should be...that emo group is a little..." He trails off.

"A little what?" My voice gets a slight edge to it. I can't help it. "Spit it out."

"I've just heard things about that Cody guy. I don't know. You might want to watch yourself around him."

"He's nice," I say icily, even though it isn't quite true.

"Okay, whatever. You'd probably know better than I would," Spike says.

"I think I do." I give him a challenging stare. What right does he have to barge in and tell me my new friends are jerks? Who is he to judge? No matter what else he says to me, he hangs out with the Zombie Squad every single day.

"Well...anyway. I just wanted to tell you."

"Sure," I say. There's a pause, and then the bell rings. "I'd better get my stuff."

"Listen, take care, okay? If you get bored at lunch, come play volleyball with me sometime. I mean it." Spike gives me an awkward hug and saunters back around the art building toward the patio. I wave in his direction, but instead of retrieving my bag, I stand there for a minute, staring out at the parking lot.

I debate trying to underhear what he thought he was doing just now, but my mind is too jumbled to even consider it. I really don't know if it would work, trying to underhear somebody on purpose.

Anyway, it doesn't matter. I know Spike probably means well, but... I think about Mikaela putting the tissue packet in my pocket, about Cody making stupid jokes to try to make me feel better, and I just know he's wrong.

seven

I glance at Auntie Mina across the restaurant table, my hands twisting the cloth napkin in my lap. She looks like she hasn't slept in weeks, and she's lost weight. Her face is all sharp angles. It makes her look younger somehow, more vulnerable. It could just be the dim lighting throwing shadows across her face, but she looks like Shiri.

Her Caesar salad is practically untouched, the fork resting across the top of the salad bowl with a single lettuce leaf speared on it, as if that will somehow keep us from noticing the fact that the bowl is still full. *Eat something*, I will her silently. *Please.*

A dark-haired waiter in a crisp white button-down shirt arrives with our entrees, moves from place to place with a wooden pepper grinder and freshly grated Parmesan cheese. Everyone takes a few bites in silence as other voices murmur around us.

"Well, this is lovely," my mother says suddenly, with a smile I can tell is forced. She toys with her silver napkin ring absentmindedly. "Thank you again for suggesting this place, Randall." She doesn't quite meet his eyes, instead sliding her gaze over to Auntie Mina, who takes a tiny bite of bread under my mom's scrutiny.

Going out was my parents' idea. Nobody really wanted to face the traditional Thanksgiving turkey around the Langfords' huge oak table. Not this year.

"Angelini's is very classy," Uncle Randall says, taking a sip of white wine. "I have a lot of business lunches here. Outstanding service." He addresses all of this to my dad, who gives a noncommittal "hm" and a nod in response.

Auntie Mina pushes the linguine around and around her plate, the Florentine sauce congealing into a gloppy mess. I look down at my three-cheese ravioli, feeling a little ill. I should have just ordered soup.

I wish this dinner were over already.

"Don't just sit there, eat your food. You love linguine," Uncle Randall says to Auntie Mina, as if she's a toddler needing to be coaxed. "You don't want Chef Carlo to think you didn't like it." He smiles and puts a hand on her shoulder.

My fingers tighten around my fork. He really doesn't see his family as people sometimes, just as shiny trophies from which he feels compelled to polish every last speck of dust lest they make him look bad. Ironically, there is a tiny, circular droplet of pasta sauce on his otherwise immaculate gray shirt.

"I'm just not that hungry," she says with an apologetic smile.

"It's *Thanksgiving*," Uncle Randall says sharply.

"You can always take it home for later," my dad puts in.

Dad told me once that he never cared for Uncle Randall, but he puts up with him because Auntie Mina loves him. Because Dad wants to "keep the peace." He says that's what he always did when he and Mina were kids—he'd try to calm down Dada's furious bouts of temper, be the peacemaker, the appeaser, until finally the yelling would stop.

Right now I wish he would forget about keeping the peace.

"I'm not going to be able to finish all this either," I say loudly, into the awkward silence. Auntie Mina gives me a little smile, but nobody else says anything. Mom isn't helping either. She's got this pained smile plastered on, like she wants to talk but doesn't know what to say.

They didn't say anything when Uncle Randall told them what kind of house to buy, either. What kind of neighborhood to live in. The evening after the funeral, my dad sat on the living room couch and drank down three glasses of wine, and then he told me: Uncle Randall was the one who pressured them to move here. He was the one who found an amazing deal on a house for us. They'd always been so grateful, so glad I could grow up close to family. But to me it just seems like more proof that Uncle Randall likes to boss everyone around.

Yet if we'd stayed in Pomona, I never would have grown up with Shiri.

For just a second, I wish we had.

My chest tightens and I put down my fork. My mother and Auntie Mina both glance up at me, so I try to act normally. I swallow my feelings down with a bite of ravioli and force a smile, willing myself not to think. And then I realize my mistake, realize that clearing my mind is the last thing I want to do. But it's too late.

—*can't see why she doesn't eat*
   does she do this just to embarrass—public—
      everyone is looking at us
   and they all know who we are and what she did—

My head whirling, I feel a surge of anger, of furious emotion that isn't my own. And it doesn't stop.

aren't women supposed to take care of the family so this
      kind of thing doesn't happen—
   —*always rocking the boat, never happy with*
         what I provide—
—*when we get home she'll listen to me or I'll—*

Uncle Randall. I almost trip on my long skirt getting up, but I manage to choke out a quick "excuse me" and then I run. I barge into the empty one-person bathroom, lock the door, and hunch over the toilet, my stomach churning, but nothing comes out.

I stay there for a moment waiting for the dry heaves to subside, for the emotions that aren't mine to untangle themselves from my own fear and panic. My nails dig into my palms and I feel a jabbing pain, but I don't care. I'm shaking, and all I can feel in my mind is dizzying darkness and anger, like a whirling tornado. I felt it coming from Uncle Randall when I underheard his horrible, selfish thoughts. But even more frightening is that I can feel a terrible darkness in myself, welling up from some deep part of me that I don't even want to look at.

———————

The Monday after Thanksgiving the weather is windy again, scouring the sky to a raw blue. I have to put my Gatorade bottle on my lunch bag so it doesn't blow away. Cody has been talking to me more, being friendlier in his own abrasive way; today he razzes me about my choice of beverage, my mom's oatmeal cookies, my tuna sandwich, and my "trendoid mall wear."

"Seriously, it's like an A&F barfed on you." He and Becca look at each other and laugh.

"Sorry," Becca says, smiling, "but he has a point."

"Of course I have a point," Cody says loftily. "I always have a point."

"Whatever. Shut up." I flick cookie crumbs at him and force my beige Banana Republic cap over his head, grinning, until he finally cracks a smile.

"You're an honorary mall rat," I say.

"Great." Cody gives up and just sits there, glowering, but the smile fighting to emerge from one corner of his mouth ruins the effect. So does the girly cap smushing down the black tendrils of hair he'd so artfully arranged.

"Hey," Mikaela says, reaching for her purse. "We could put my lipstick on him. And that hoodie of yours. Then he'd really be a mall rat."

"No!" Cody hastily pulls my cap off and scrambles down from his perch on the edge of the orange picnic table. "God, no." He composes his face and then saunters over to me with his usual scowl plastered over his face, bushy eyebrows a hard line. "I shouldn't even give this hat back to you. You look better without it. Much less like a droid."

"Fine. Keep it," I say, feigning indifference. I guess he just gave me his version of a compliment, but I'm not sure how to react. I blink my eyes innocently at him.

"Maybe I will," he says. "I'd be doing you a favor."

Mikaela walks over and interposes herself between me and Cody, hands on her hips, and tilts her head at him flirtatiously.

"Are you dissing my friend here? 'Cause if you are, I might have to punish you." She pulls the blood-red lipstick out of her purse. Cody backs away, forcing a laugh, and turns to talk to David. Mikaela follows, brandishing the lipstick at him threateningly.

For some reason this annoys me a little. I can handle Cody myself. I don't need Mikaela to convince him to like me, as if it's some kind of favor.

And I set out to prove it. All week I find excuses to talk to him: making him eat one of my oatmeal cookies, trying to elicit a coherent explanation for his fervent adoration of Black Sabbath, listening to his surprisingly convincing rant against the destructive conformist culture of high school athletics.

On Thursday, I come up to him in the hallway between classes and shove the hated Banana Republic hat on his head.

He whirls around in surprise. When he glares at me and says "What the fuck?" I just give him my most innocent look.

"Aww, what happened? Did an A&F barf on you?" I can't help smirking a little.

He rolls his eyes, snatches off the hat, and shoves it in his backpack, taking a quick look around to make sure nobody saw his abject humiliation. When the hat is stashed out of sight, he turns away and stalks off, leaving me unsure whether to laugh or be furious. Ten feet away he turns his head and flashes me a quick, impish grin. His teeth are perfectly straight and white, and his blue eyes squint just a tiny bit as he smiles.

For some reason, the incident leaves me in a blissful mood the rest of the day. I finally cracked Cody's obnoxious exterior, and it feels like an accomplishment. If I'm honest with myself, it's a relief, too; it's a relief that his jerk act is just that—an act. Armor, like his black clothes and oh-so-superior smirk. And underneath the armor is someone I can actually be friends with, maybe. I drive home with music going full blast, singing loudly to whatever comes on the radio and not caring what I look like doing it. I haven't been happy like this in a long time. I park the car in the driveway with a slight jerking of the brakes and let myself into the house.

It's nice to have the living room to myself, just me and Pixie with a bag of pretzels, a few hours of sitcom reruns, and, less fortunately, my pre-calculus book.

By the time my mom gets home from her case manager job at Citrus Valley Community Outreach, I'm ready for a break. I head into the kitchen. Mom is already puttering around trying to scrounge dinner ingredients. There's a random assortment of vegetables already on the cutting board: three carrots, a potato with a small root starting to protrude from one end, half a bag of spinach leaves, and an onion. I open the fridge, humming a little to myself, and grab a sugar-free soda.

"You're cheerful today," Mom says, beaming at me. "I'm glad to see you in such a good mood. I've been worried about you."

"Me? I'm fine," I say. "Never better." Feeling unusually magnanimous, I pull out the vegetable peeler and start scraping the carrots. "What's for dinner?"

Mom's head is half-inside one of the cabinets as she rummages around, pulling spices off the rack.

"Oh, just trying a little creative cooking with leftover ingredients," she says, emerging from the cupboard. "Cut those carrots into strips, would you please? I think I'll sauté all the vegetables together and ... do you think it would be too weird if I cut the leftover roasted chicken into pieces and put it in? Like a stir-fry?"

I roll my eyes. "It sounds fine, Mom." It actually does sound pretty good, unlike some of her experiments with leftovers. Like the time she tried making shepherd's pie with two-day-old lamb *korma* as the base. Dad liked it, but it sat in my stomach like a spicy brick. Today's concoction might work out, though.

I don't realize I'm singing to myself until Mom mentions it.

"Good day at school today?" She turns to me, her expression curious and eager. Her long hair is falling halfway out of its bun. "You haven't brought home much news lately. How are Cassie and Spike doing? I don't think I've seen them in weeks. Not since you quit the swim team," she adds pointedly.

I wince. "I . . . haven't been hanging out with them much lately. They, uh—" I try to think of something that sounds innocuous, that won't put her into interrogation mode. I'm positive the grief counselor gave her a spiel about "warning signs" and "troubled teens" because it seems like whenever I catch her looking at me lately, she's got little lines of worry between her eyebrows. Even now, when she's smiling.

"I've been making some new friends." It surprises me a little as it comes out, but I realize it's true. "But Spike's fine. His usual self."

"Oh! Good." Mom pretends to be scrubbing the potato, but she's looking at me sideways. There's a long silence. "So tell me about these new friends. How did you meet them?"

I slice carrots for a minute, not sure what to tell her. That I heard Cassie's thoughts and decided I needed a new place to eat lunch from now on? That I couldn't handle Cassie's anger, her scorn? I skip that part, but I can't help starting to smile as I tell my mom about Mikaela, about how she went from being just some other freshman girl to this way-too-cool chick with springy little braids and an attitude. Then I catch myself babbling about Cody.

" . . . And he dresses in black, which accentuates his eyes, and his teeth are really, uh, straight," I conclude, trying to wrap it up. But it's too late.

"He sounds adorable," Mom says, winking at me.

Ugh. "Yeah, he's a real hottie," I say flatly.

"Why don't you invite him over sometime so your dad and I can meet him?" She dices the potatoes into home-fries-sized bits. "He could come over for dinner. I won't even cook with leftovers, I promise."

"Mom! It's not like we're going out. I just met these people. We're not best friends or anything." The funny thing is, the minute I say that, I realize they pretty much *are* my best friends. At any rate, right now they're all I have. Them and Spike, who isn't very discriminating.

That gets me thinking. I can't help comparing them in my mind to Cassie the Pod Queen and her loyal zombie subjects, and I wonder, not for the first time, what I was doing with them in the first place. We had good times over the years, but when I try to remember one real moment of deep conversation with Cassie, I can't pinpoint anything. All my memories with her involve swim team, bad TV, and hair dye.

But somehow, I still can't help missing those times. Just a little.

Thinking about hair dye reminds me that my highlights have grown out at least two inches, something Cassie would have gotten on my case about ages ago. But not one of my new friends has said a word about it. Cody even said I looked better without a hat on. I smile to myself.

"What are you so happy about, little girl?" Dad walks in

the kitchen and drops his keys and wallet on the table, coming over to hug me and kiss Mom. "Debby, what's cooking?"

"Just leftovers. And Sunshine's happy *because,*" she pauses dramatically, "she has some new friends at school who sound like a fun and creative bunch." And just like that, the entire house knows my personal life. I frown at the onion before cleaving it in half.

"That's great, Sun." Dad smiles at me and leans against the table. "What happened to those other guys? Cassie and everyone?"

"They must have had some kind of falling-out," Mom answers for me. "Sunny, I'm not going to be nosy, but I hope you know you can talk to Dad or me any time. And I'd like to meet your new friends."

"Mom! Okay." I chop onions furiously, my ears hot. "I'll bring them over sometime, I promise." I don't need their approval every time I make a new friend, but I'm trying desperately to end this line of conversation.

I continue chopping in silence, and Mom finally gets the hint. But later on, when I'm sitting next to my bed trying to meditate, my thoughts start whirling uncontrollably and I think about how much things have changed. I'm happier now, a lot happier. Sure, I miss the pool like crazy. But I couldn't face going to practice, seeing my former friends every day. I'm truly done with that. I've been jogging in the morning instead.

All part of the new me. Trying to stay grounded. Literally.

I draw a shaky breath and clear my head of everything from my old life.

For a minute or two, I'm successful, and I focus on my uneven breathing, feeling my arms and legs getting heavy and relaxed like after a long swim. Then Shiri's face shimmers into my mind's eye and I get a creeping feeling of total aloneness, like everything that used to mean anything to me has floated out of reach, somewhere untouchable, sealed away forever.

I wonder if this is what it feels like when you're dead: being able to see everyone, so clearly, who used to be a part of your life, but knowing you can never be with them again.

Then I think of Auntie Mina and my shoulders slump. If it's this hard for me, I can't imagine what it's like for her.

I open my eyes and blow out the thick, black-cherry-scented candle, then crawl under the covers. For a while I lie there wide awake, listening to the water run in the pipes while my dad takes a shower, and then feeling the silence of the house press in on me. My muscles tense up again as I huddle. Pixie hops up, settling herself at my feet. Her purring makes the quiet a little more bearable. I try to let go of my thoughts enough to sleep, relaxing each muscle one at a time like my mom tells her yoga classes to do ... taking her advice willingly for once. After an hour or so my mind finally stops running in its hamster wheel and I start to drift off.

Before I fall asleep, though—while I'm still in that strange almost-dreaming, free-associating state—I think of Cody. I think of his smile first, and a small part of me loosens.

But it's not only his smile that's so compelling. There's something else about him ... something deeper. Like he understands what it feels like to be lost, to be drifting like me, not sure where I'm going to end up or if I'm even going to be the same person at the end of it.

It's just a feeling I get when I'm around him. Like that whole too-cool-for-you act he puts on. I see his anger, his scowl, but rather than pushing me away, it seems like proof that there's something more underneath, that he struggles with his emotions, too, and he's vulnerable like the rest of us.

Maybe I'll have to ask him, one day soon: Do you know what it feels like to have your world come apart at the seams?

From Shiri Langford's journal, March 28th

I love Brendan so much. I never thought I could feel this way. I can't explain it without sounding maudlin, without channeling the Romantic poets or sounding like a sentimental movie. It's the most amazing feeling.

I've told him all about my family, how screwed up my dad and my half-brother are, and how frustrated it makes me that my mom just can't seem to see it. He doesn't think I'm crazy or messed up, he just smiles and kisses me and then eventually we seem to end up in bed, and later we lie there and talk and he tells me about how he worries about his little brother, who's mixed up with a bad crowd of kids at home.

Sometimes, after he talks about Neal I end up worrying about Sunny, but I know I shouldn't. She always seems so secure, so sure of herself. Unlike me.

eight

The next day at lunch, Mikaela and I are sitting next to each other at the orange picnic table, on the bench nearest the building wall. It's raining, drumming lightly on the awning. An occasional droplet blows in on a gust of wind and catches me on the face, or on my hands clenched tightly in my lap.

Cody, Becca, and the rest of the goth crew just took off for the lunchtime pep rally in the gym—to "ridicule the conformist masses," or so they claimed. I asked Mikaela if she'd stick around so I could ask her about something. She agreed, saying she doesn't like watching anorexic cheerleaders waving their stick-limbs around anyway.

Once everyone else is out of sight, we both scoot down so that our shoulders and heads are resting on the wall behind us and our legs are up on the table. Trying to work up the nerve to talk to her, I stare at my plain white canvas sneakers lying there next to her vintage knee-high purple Doc Martens. Typical Mikaela: outrageous. Typical me: blah. I might as well still be part of the Zombie Squad.

I let out an explosive sigh.

"What?" Mikaela nudges me.

How can I explain it to her? I'm incredibly lucky, I know that much. I could have been spending the rest of the year eating lunch on my own, wondering if I'd done the right thing. But Mikaela and her friends—they let me stay. Why did they even care? I hate to feel suspicious of everybody, but I need to know what I'm doing here.

And yet, I worry that if I question it, it'll all fall apart, like a dream about flying where you suddenly realize hey, people can't fly.

"Nothing," I say. She stares at me. "I just hate these shoes. They're boring."

"That's *it*? You're bumming out about having boring shoes?" She snorts a laugh. "Okay. On the scale of life's major problems, that's one we can easily address."

"Yeah, but..." I make a frustrated noise. This isn't happening how I imagined it. I blurt out, "Why me?"

"Are we having a philosophical discussion now?" She grins.

"No! What I meant was..." I take a deep breath. "Why are you guys okay with hanging out with me? You didn't have to humor me when I just showed up here uninvited." I stare at my knees, afraid to look at her face. "But you didn't kick me out."

There's silence for a moment. I bite my thumbnail anxiously and listen to the rain dripping off the awning.

"Listen," Mikaela finally says. "I will freely admit that at first, I was driven by morbid fascination." Her voice is a little sheepish, and I glance up. She's staring into the distance with a tiny, embarrassed smile. "I know, I suck. But trust me, I got over it. I can now truly say that I find you a worthwhile person. Regardless of your footwear."

Still not looking at me, she flicks one of my tennis shoes with a black-painted fingernail. Just like that, the tension is broken. My clenched muscles relax a little.

"Okay," I say, a little warily.

"Okay," she says, and sighs.

I try a tentative smile. "My shoes still need help, though."

"I'm not arguing with that," Mikaela says, shifting a little to turn toward me. "You know, there's this thing called a shoe store. You may have heard of it before."

"Yeah, but I need serious help. My closet is full of cute pink hoodies. I can't be trusted to shop for myself."

Mikaela laughs.

I'm trying to make a joke out of it, but inside, my heart is breaking because I'm remembering one of the last times I saw Shiri when she was alive. It was August, right before she went back to college, and we were at South Coast Plaza together, combing the stores for new school wardrobes. Or, more accurately, I was following her around and trying to emulate her as best I could with the limited budget my parents gave me.

"I'm really going to miss doing this with you, Sunny," Shiri said, throwing her arm conspiratorially over my shoulders, her Macy's bag flapping against my arm. "It's been fun."

Then I do cry. Tears slip out of my eyes as I sit there silently, aching.

Mikaela looks over at me, her dark eyes worried.

"I'm fine," I manage to croak. "It's just—God, I'm sick of being such a mess. Everything reminds me of her."

Mikaela's voice is soft. "She meant a lot to you." It's a statement, not a question.

"Yeah." I wipe my face with one hand and stare upward, at the rusty metal roof of the awning, and listen to the light clatter of the rain until I feel more under control.

"Hey," Mikaela says suddenly. She's not staring at me anymore but messing with something in her purse. "Are you busy tomorrow? Want to go shopping?"

I turn and look at her stupidly.

"Like at the mall?"

"Sure. Or, if you want, I know some cool stores in Santa Ana. Or even Grovetown. Ever been to Thumbscrew? Over on Fifth?"

"In Grovetown?"

"Yeah, I know, Grovetown, right? But it's the best. The 16 bus stops right there. Come on, we should go." Mikaela swats me on the arm. "You were complaining about your closet. We have to replace those hoodies with *something*."

"Okay. Sure. I just have to let my mom know." I pause awkwardly. "You know, she wants to meet you now. She's all excited that I have 'creative' friends." I roll my eyes. "So maybe you can come over afterward and stay for dinner or something?"

The minute the invitation slips out of my mouth, I regret it. I squeeze my eyes shut, press my lips together. She's going to think I'm trying too hard.

I try to backtrack. "I mean, only if you're not busy. Either way is cool."

"Yeah, why not? My mom works a late nursing shift on weekends, so I'd just be doing a whole lotta nothin' anyway."

My shoulders unknot a little.

Mikaela finishes rummaging in her purse and, with a flourish, produces a black marker. I frown at it.

"Uh, what's that for?" I have this horrifying vision of having to stand watch while Mikaela tags the picnic table.

"This," she says with a grin, "is for your boring sneakers."

———————

As I walk into the house admiring my feet, I have to admit that Mikaela's embellishments are a major improvement. Where I once had plain white low-top sneakers whose only adornment was the all-important brand-name logo, I now have shoes that swirl and vibrate with amazing designs, intricate mind-bending spirals and thorny-tattoo-looking black branches. Mikaela has serious talent.

I hope her talent extends to improving my wardrobe. Pastel tops and swim team swag—they just remind me of my old life, and I'm more than ready for a change. I can't keep getting bogged down in memories, can't deal with crying every time I'm reminded of the past. I'm done.

Later, when my mom gets home, I make sure she gets the message as if it's a top story headline: "Reclusive Daughter Finally Ready to Leave House, Be Sociable." I slide off the bed, run down the stairs, and start burbling about Mikaela like I'm five years old and just made my first friend at school. The funny thing is, I *do* feel that excited.

"A shopping trip? Oh, honey. That's great." Mom closes the front door behind her with a tinkle of the chimes hung on the back.

"Not only that, there's a vintage clothes store over in Grovetown, and Mikaela wants us to go there tomorrow," I say all in a rush. "And look what she drew on my shoes!" I show them off, tilting them one way and then the other so my mother can get the full effect.

"Oh, how *cute*," she says. "How creative!" She smiles at me distractedly and hangs up her blue sweater in the front closet. I'm a little dismayed. I could pierce my chin and my mom would just say "How unique! How creative! I wish I were your age so I could do wild stuff like that!" It takes the appeal out of just about anything.

Swimming was one of the few things that was mine, and mine alone. Mom would come to my races whenever she could, but she always stepped back when it came to the whole swim scene, when it was me and my friends. And she knew that I was a different person then—not just when I was in the water, but whenever I was with Cassie.

I miss swimming. But I don't want to be that person anymore.

And . . . now I have something new that's mine, whether I want it or not.

"So is it okay if I drive to Grovetown with Mikaela tomorrow?" I take off my shoes and stash them on the shoe rack in the front hall closet. Mom thinks about it for a minute while she brings a paper grocery bag into the kitchen, depositing it on the counter.

"I'm a little nervous about it," she says, giving me a direct look. "I haven't met Mikaela yet."

Anxiously, I clench my hands behind my back. "Well, I asked her if she wants to come over for dinner after we go shopping. You can meet her then. I hope that's okay. You know I'm always careful." I stop, press my lips together.

"Oh, honey, I know you're always careful." She smiles. "I wish you'd asked me first, but I'll be happy to meet your new friend. I've been hoping you'd invite her over—you've been so unhappy and you could stand to have a little fun."

I resist the urge to cringe.

"Well, great," I say. "Thanks."

Mom beams at me, reaches into her purse, and presses a few twenties into my hand. "Just call me when you're leaving Grovetown, okay?"

I nod and turn back toward the stairs.

"Oh, and don't forget we're having dinner at Uncle Randall and Auntie Mina's on Sunday."

That sounds like a barrel of laughs. I try to muster up something enthusiastic to say, but I can't think of anything. Auntie Mina will sit there like a ghost; Uncle Randall will criticize her in between praising Number Two's latest achievements in the world of plastic surgery; Mom and Dad will nod and smile. And I won't be able to leave.

Forget it. I'm not going to worry about Sunday. I have Saturday to think about. I paste a smile on my face and trudge back upstairs. By the time Sunday rolls around, there will be a new and improved Sunny in the house. I think about the diary entry that Shiri wrote, the one about me always seeming so sure of myself. That's the Sunny I want to be. Someone who can always handle things. Not someone who's too scared to even give her fears a name. Not someone who holds everything inside until it leaks out anyway, until something breaks.

I know my fears. And I'm not going to break.

Not cool enough, not fun enough, not quirky enough. The litany torments me as I ransack my room the next afternoon for something bearable I can wear out with Mikaela. After tossing aside lots of khakis, skinny jeans, and other remnants of my old life, I decide on a "transition outfit"—something I can tolerate being seen in while I shop for clothes that fit the new Sunny.

Whatever that is.

I pull on a pair of baggy old tan cargo pants that are splotched with green from when we painted the dining room, belt them with a black scarf, add a plain black V-neck sweater, and top it off with an Indian-print kerchief in maroon and tan. Under the kerchief, my hair hangs loose past my shoulders. A little weird, but passable.

I head for the bathroom and rummage in my makeup drawer, hardly touched since the funeral, and put on a trace of dark eyeliner pencil and some ChapStick. As I'm leaving the bathroom, I change my mind and decide to put on red lip gloss. You never know who you might run into. *Maybe Cody*, I think, surprising myself a little. But the truth is, I wouldn't mind running into him.

When I glance at the clock I realize I'm going to be late. I hope Mikaela's not the punctual type. I rush downstairs and pull on my newly adorned sneakers.

"Mom!" I shout in the general direction of the living room. "I'm going. See you around five."

"Have fun," she says, poking her head into the front hall. In one hand she's holding the scrapbook we're supposed to be finishing up for Auntie Mina. For a moment I feel guilty that I'm leaving Mom with the rest of the project, but mostly I'm glad that just this once I don't have to be reminded of the way things used to be.

When I get back today, I'll be a new Sunny Pryce-Shah. Not a member of the Zombie Squad. Not the Girl Whose Cousin Committed Suicide. Not that sad little kid who followed around a false idol. I'll be someone else.

———

When I pull up in front of the apartment complex where Mikaela lives with her mom, she's waiting there already, bouncing a little on the toes of her heavy black platforms. The iron entry gate she's standing near is bent and dented, and the dull tan paint on the buildings is dirty and weathered.

Most of my former friends live in gated communities with fancy cars and security guards, or in newer tract houses like my family does. I haven't really hung out before with anyone who wasn't from an upper-middle-class background. Not deliberately. It just seemed to work out that way.

I kind of want to say something, but I'm not sure what to say. I just don't want to say the wrong thing.

"Aren't these apartments nasty?" Mikaela slides in on the passenger side and slams the door, letting her purse fall to the floor at her feet. "My mom divorced my dad a few years ago, but she didn't have enough money to buy a house after we moved here. I've been house hunting with her forever, but everything is either too expensive or too pre-fab. Like they're cloning houses."

"I know what you mean," I say. My stomach unclenches a little. "We live in a tract house. *Definitely* the Land of the Clones." We both laugh. Then there's an awkward silence. I just drive, following the occasional "turn left here" or "go that way" from Mikaela. Finally, I open my big mouth.

"Sorry about your parents getting divorced," I blurt, in lieu of something intelligent. At the same time, Mikaela says wryly, "Nice Volvo; is it yours?"

"Kind of. My dad bikes to work most of the time, so my parents are letting me use it," I say, blushing furiously. Now I *really* don't know what to say, so I just sit there for a minute, clutching the wheel tightly.

"Uh, anyway, sorry about your parents," I finally manage.

"It's cool," Mikaela says. "My parents used to argue all the time, and my mom was sick of my dad being such a tightwad asshole, so it's definitely a good thing."

"Oh." I fidget uncomfortably. The extent of my knowledge about divorce comes from people like James, whose parents seem to be in a constant competition to buy his love. I'm starting to feel hopelessly sheltered. "Do you, like, have to visit him on weekends, or what?" It's probably a stupid question, but she doesn't treat it like one.

"Nah, not anymore. Right after the divorce, I was supposed to visit every other weekend, but since we moved here I only see him once every couple of months or so."

"Oh," I say again. "Where did you live before?"

"Near San Francisco."

"Wow," I say, stupidly. I can't seem to give her anything but robot answers. My nervousness starts to come back, and I fiddle with the rearview mirror unnecessarily.

"It was pretty cool," she says. "But my dad's there, and he bugs me, so I'm glad I'm down here, hundreds of miles away." She turns to me and smiles. "So where do you want to go first?"

"Uh…" I haven't really thought about it. "You're the guru for the day. You tell me—where do I get my preppy dweeb makeover? I'm ready for anything."

"Well, why don't we start with Thumbscrew and then go to the vintage place? If there's anything else we need after that, we can try the Orangewood Mall on the way back. I know this little shop there that has cheap Manic Panic hair dye and stuff."

Manic Panic hair dye? I gulp nervously, wondering what I'm in for.

It turns out I have very little to worry about. Mikaela doesn't try to tell me what I should or shouldn't wear—unlike some people—but instead just pulls a bunch of clothes off racks and lets me accept or veto items for the dressing room. At first I'm a little weirded out by Thumbscrew, whose patrons all seem to be of the nose-ring-and-tattoo persuasion, but very few of them give me attitude. When they do, Mikaela is quick to glare at them from her full five-feet-one-inch height, and amazingly, they back off.

I look at her. "Good thing you're here. Otherwise they'd probably bite my ear off."

"It's all in the way you carry yourself," she says, looking me up and down critically. "Your new wardrobe will help—trust me. Although you should keep that head scarf around; it's very retro."

By the late afternoon, I have three new T-shirts and a pair of black jeans from Thumbscrew; a gauzy black top, a long silk skirt, and a pair of slightly worn black Converse hi-tops from the vintage place; some shoelaces from a mall store, which are printed with Japanese cartoon characters; and hair dye that matches my natural dark-brown color. And I still have twelve dollars left from the money my mom gave me.

"These Afro Ken shoelaces are *so you*," Mikaela says, examining our hoard as I pilot us back to my house.

"Yeah?" I feel a surge of happiness. "I really like that crocheted sweater you got from Vintage Alley. And all the stuff you helped me pick out is … I love it." I concentrate on turning the corner onto our street. I can't help seeing it as though I've never really looked at it before, wondering what it looks like to Mikaela.

To me, now, the houses seem huge and ostentatious, like giant stucco boxes with identically trimmed lawns and squeaky-clean cars parked in front. It's dusk, so they look even more identical than usual. Of course, there's *our* house. Mom painted a huge rock in our front yard with our house number in bizarre colors. You can't miss it. She had a huge fight with the neighborhood association about it, but she didn't back down, and, as usual, somehow she got her way.

"This is you, huh?" Mikaela looks at the place appraisingly but doesn't say anything. I know she must be thinking about what a homogenous McNeighborhood I live in. Maybe she even thinks I'm spoiled. But I'm glad she doesn't say it.

"Nice rock."

"Uh, yeah. My mom did that," I mumble as we carry our haul up the front walk.

"Cool. My mom just knits crap." Mikaela follows me through the front door. Clinging to my shopping bags like a shield, I introduce her to my parents.

Dad actually manages to act pretty normal, considering he wasn't too pleased about me putting dibs on the car at the last minute. He asks her how our shopping went, what we bought, and whether she thinks a film professor like him needs to make a dramatic fashion statement. I should have guessed that Mom would fawn all over Mikaela, and she does, exclaiming over her "adorable little braids" and offering her every nonalcoholic beverage under the sun. Mikaela seems to be okay with it. I'm surprised. I'd have expected her to be—I don't know. Uncomfortable, or disdainful. Instead, she grins at my mom and sits down at the kitchen table like she's been here a million times.

I drop into a chair next to her, letting Mom's chatter wash over me. My breathing slows a little and I start to relax. At the same time, I feel something open in my mind, like a sliding door, or like a television turning on, and I realize this is the first time I've known beforehand that my underhearing is about to happen.

What I hear almost makes me drop my bottle of orange soda. This time, it's not my mom. It's Mikaela.

> *—this THIS is what we deserve mom I wish we could*
> *have this a house a new life something better*
> *because we should have it and it wasn't right of*
> *dad to take it away but I guess we have to deal—*
> *but—still—I want this—*
> *for us—*

The words—barely coherent—are accompanied by a wave of profound sadness tinged with a whole array of other emotions. Regret, frustration, anger, determination. And, shockingly, nervousness. My own stomach does a slow somersault in response; my forehead breaks out in angry sweat.

It's dizzying, and I put a hand to my head involuntarily. Mikaela glances at me. My face gets hot.

I shouldn't have heard that. It's not something I should ever know, unless she chooses to tell me. But I *do* know.

I shift uncomfortably in my chair and force a smile. She smiles back wryly, as if nothing strange happened. As far as she knows, nothing did. As the lingering emotions subside, I steal another glance at her. She isn't showing any of what she feels on the outside.

Dinner goes quickly. Mom and Dad serve spinach lasagna, salad, and garlic bread, and Mikaela tells them how great everything is and thanks them for having her over, just like my parents are always reminding me to do, so I know they'll be pleased. They're all smiles, actually. They don't even blink when Mikaela asks if she can stay for another hour or two.

After dinner, we go upstairs to my room. She looks appraisingly at my posters of the Olympic swim team and the sun and moon pillows that I got for my thirteenth birthday, but she doesn't say anything about them.

"Ready to go brown again?" she asks, shaking the bag with the hair dye in it.

"Yeah, I think I am," I say. "It's been a while." I try to remember the last time my hair was its natural color. Probably freshman year, like Mikaela. "It's going to feel weird."

"Are you kidding? Your natural hair color is gorgeous." She rips open the cardboard container and pulls out the plastic squeeze bottle of dye. "It's just sad that we have to approximate it with this crap."

Funny; I never thought my hair was that exciting. And Cassie never really had any suggestions other than to highlight it. I assumed that meant it was hopeless.

It takes us about half an hour to work the dye through my hair. Once it's finished and goopy with brownish crud, we stuff it into a shower cap and go into my room to wait for the dye to set. I debate whether to turn on some music, and if so, what kind of music Mikaela would want to listen to.

"This is cool," Mikaela exclaims, picking up an incense burner sitting on my bookshelf. It's a small brass cone burner in the shape of a genie lamp that my grandparents brought back from Pakistan.

"Yeah, I guess so," I say. "But the incense kind of makes me sneeze."

"Oh, that's too bad. Hey, we should light this candle." She points at my black-cherry meditation candle. She pulls a plastic cigarette lighter out of her purse and sets the wick alight. "Smells good. Where'd you get this?"

"I found it at the drugstore." I avoid meeting her eyes. "I, uh, use it when I'm trying to meditate."

"You meditate?" She sounds genuinely interested. "Is it hard?"

"I don't think I'm very good at it," I admit, sitting on the floor next to the bed. Mikaela sits down next to me, leaning back and staring at the ceiling.

"I wish I could meditate," she says. "I heard you can really reach a different state of mind."

I let out a sigh. "I don't think I'm there yet. I just spend the whole time obsessing about lame stuff."

"It can't hurt," she points out. "Trying is better than nothing. More than I'm doing, anyway," she adds under her breath, like an afterthought.

I'm not sure what to say to this, so I just sit there and let the hair-dye fumes and the cherry-candle smoke have a little war in my nostrils. It's making me lightheaded.

"Why do you meditate?" she asks suddenly. "If you don't mind me asking." She still looks curious.

I hesitate. "I started after my cousin … died. My mom suggested it. I guess it's helping with the—with being depressed." I stumble over my words awkwardly, my stomach increasingly queasy. I feel so stupid. "I mean, I'm not *that* depressed, not like my cousin was—she was on medication and … but it's been so hard, I …" I suck in a breath, but I can't seem to stop babbling. "I haven't had anyone to really talk to and I'm tired of holding it all in, and tired of these stupid thoughts in my head and of being scared all the time." I look down at my lap, my breath trembling in and out.

"Whoa, wait—what do you mean, you're scared all the time?" Mikaela's voice is gentle and soothing. She's been so nice to me, and I desperately want to trust her, and I must be loopy from the hair-dye fumes because my mouth opens and I start to tell her. Everything.

"Okay, this is going to sound crazy," I begin, my voice shaky, "but after my cousin killed herself, I started being able to—" I swallow, repeatedly, and continue. "To hear other people's thoughts. Not all the time," I add hastily. "But every once in a while." I stare at my bare feet, my long toes with dark-red polish peeling off the nails. It sounds so ludicrous. But just having told someone makes me feel so much better, lighter, that I'm not sure I even care if she believes it. And maybe, if I tell her about this, it'll make up for the fact that I know something about her—something I really shouldn't know.

She's staring at me open-mouthed; I can see it out of the corner of my eye.

"No *way*! Are you sure?"

"Um, pretty sure. I thought I was going crazy for a while. But…" I pause for a minute, trying to choose my words carefully. "Some things happened that convinced me it was real." I pick at the nail polish on my big toe, scraping it off in little flakes that settle on the beige rug.

Mikaela goggles at me, like she's not sure what to believe. There's a long silence where I can hear my uneven breathing and the tiny *skritch* of my fingernail against my toenail polish. Then, finally, Mikaela takes a sharp breath and seems to come to some kind of decision.

"Are you—I mean—can you really hear what people are thinking?" Her voice is almost a whisper. "Like, could you hear what I'm thinking right now?"

"No, it's not all the time. Not even that often. I can't really control it. It just happens." I explain how it started, during the swim meet; how I heard my mom's voice at dinner but her mouth wasn't moving; and all the other times. Except what I heard tonight, from Mikaela herself. I'm not ready to tell her that.

The timer goes off for my hair. We walk to the bathroom in silence. As we rinse the dye out under the bathtub faucet, I tell her about how I've been trying to meditate so I can get some kind of control over it. And I tell her how it scares me to death and makes me want to vomit at the same time, and that I never asked for this. That I keep wondering, why me?

I wrap my wet hair in a towel and we leave the bathroom, stopping in the hallway outside my room.

She looks at me gravely. "Have you thought about what it means? Do you think it's, like, a gift? You could probably really help people." One corner of her mouth turns up, wickedly. "Or annoy the hell out of them."

I go into my room, wait until she follows me in, and shut the door.

"Help people?" I say miserably. "How can this help *anybody*? And it's not a gift. I didn't ask for it. I don't even know how to control it. I don't even want it! I'm scared," I say in a hoarse whisper, my nails digging into my palms.

Mikaela doesn't say anything. I'm still not sure she believes me, but at least she's sympathetic.

"You'll figure out what to do," she says finally, and she gives me a quick, hard hug. "You've survived a lot. You can survive this."

nine

The next morning I stay in bed, in my pajamas, reading, until Mom walks in, opens the curtains, and blinds me with daylight.

"Pretty hair," she says. She gives me a pointed smile and waves a can of cleanser at me before taking it into the bathroom.

I get the hint and drag myself up to scrub the brown dye splotches out of the tub. The light glooming in through the bathroom window is grayish and the sky is overcast. Only two more weeks until winter break.

I scrub briskly at a dark-brown stain on one of the turquoise shower tiles. Since spilling my guts to Mikaela, I've had second thoughts, over and over, wondering if I can expect her to be my friend after what I've told her. If it were me, I'd definitely think I was nuts. And she hasn't even met my extended family.

My family. I sit back on my heels, the sponge in my hand dripping sudsy brownish water into the tub. When I think about the upcoming dinner, I'm filled with a cold queasy dread. What if I hear Uncle Randall's thoughts again? What if I can't act normal? I'm not even sure I'll be able to look him in the eye, let alone allow him to hug me.

If I shrink away when he touches me, I wonder if anyone will notice.

When the time comes to get ready, I flip through hangers in my closet, lingering on the new clothes I bought with Mikaela yesterday. It's not like anybody at the dinner will care about what I'm wearing. But I pull on my long dark-blue skirt from the vintage store anyway, along with a brown V-neck sweater and sandals.

I'm staring critically at my pores in the mirror on the back of my closet door when my phone rings, a vibrating rattle against my nightstand. I grab for it distractedly.

"Hello?"

"Sun, it's Mikaela." She sounds fuzzy and far away, like it's a bad connection.

"Hey," I say. "I was just putting on my new skirt."

"Cool," she says absently. There's a long pause. "I just wanted to make sure you were feeling okay after … you know, last night. You seemed kind of upset."

"No, it was okay." I swallow nervously. "It felt good to talk to someone."

"Yeah, but then I was worried I might have said something wrong after you told me about, uh … your power thing. But I wanted to say I had a good time shopping and everything."

"I had a good time too," I reassure her. After a pause, I

say, "Sorry if I was a bummer. Or if I, you know, freaked you out."

"*Chica*, it takes a lot to freak me out." She laughs, but it sounds a little stiff to me. "But like I told Becca, I like living dangerously."

"Becca?" I repeat, confused. A suspicion starts gnawing at me. "You didn't tell her about my underhearing?"

"What? No, of course not. What kind of jerk do you think I am?"

"I don't. I'm sorry. You guys are friends. I thought maybe— it sounded like—" I clench one hand around the phone, knot the other into a fist.

"Nah. Believe me, I wouldn't tell Becca about that," she says with a cynical chuckle. "I can't tell Becca anything. You know she can't keep her mouth shut."

My hands relax. "Okay." I pause awkwardly. "Sorry. I didn't mean to jump down your throat. I'm just stressed about this dinner at my aunt and uncle's house."

"Oh!" Mikaela says, her tone changing to disgust. "The ones you told me about?"

"Yeah. Uncle Randall and Auntie Mina. My parents are making me go." I glance out in the hallway to make sure they're not listening. "I told you about what happened the last time we had dinner with them. God, it makes me nauseated just thinking about it."

"Well, if you get nauseated enough to puke, make sure you use his bathroom. Or his closet. Ooh, or his shoes." That brings a small smile to my face.

We say goodbye and hang up. On impulse, I take one

of the anime shoelaces we bought yesterday and tie it in a floppy bow around my ponytail. Kind of like a good luck charm. Tonight, I could use a little boost from luck, God, karma, or whatever else regulates the universe.

———

Uncle Randall ushers Mom, Dad, and me through the tacky white-painted cement columns flanking the front door. Compared to our house, their place is huge, and it feels too quiet. The heels of my sandals click alarmingly loudly on the gray marble tile of the front hallway. My mother fills the silence with some small talk about how nice their yard looks, and Uncle Randall praises their landscaping service. He seems tense and distracted. I manage to avoid his one-armed hug.

As we pass the entryway to the living room, I try not to look at the formal family photo hanging above the fireplace, but my eyes wander over to it anyway. Shiri is thirteen and smirking. Randall Junior is haggard, in his last year of medical school. Auntie Mina is glamorous in a flowing burgundy dress. Uncle Randall stands behind her, smiling proudly, one hand on her shoulder.

I used to think he was dashing, and that they lived in a palace. When I'd spend the night with Shiri when we were kids, I'd pretend I lived here too. I thought she had everything.

It was only recently that I found out I was wrong. Of course she didn't have everything. And some of the things she had, nobody in their right mind would want.

The oak table in their formal dining room is already set, but we pass it by and go into the den. Or, as Shiri called it, her dad's man-cave. The décor is all dark wood and forest-green leather with mounted fish on plaques on the wall. Dad eyes the fish but doesn't make his usual whispered joke to Mom about how they probably came out of an overpriced catalog. Instead, he jams his hands into his pockets and quietly whistles the first few notes from "Under the Sea." Mom shushes him, but one side of her mouth is twitching. I stare at my feet, terrified that Uncle Randall's going to notice and figure out the joke. Say something snide, even nasty. But he doesn't seem to pick up on it.

"Have a seat, guys. Ali, Debby, can I mix you a drink?" Uncle Randall strides to the bar at one end of the room, where Auntie Mina is setting out bowls of nuts. With an unnecessary flourish, he pulls out a shiny metal tumbler and lid, and a matching ice bucket and shot glass. Show-off.

I try not to think about the fact that as a kid, I used to love watching him do that.

"Sunshine? I could mix you a Shirley Temple."

I nod. I'm mortified, but I'm not sure whether it's because Uncle Randall just called me by my full name, which I hate, or because I've just been offered a beverage suitable for a five-year-old.

Mom and I sit on two of the chair-backed stools next to the bar, and Dad stands behind Mom. I take a token sip of my cloyingly sweet Shirley Temple, remembering how Shiri and I used to pour them into martini glasses, sipping at them theatrically and pretending we were rich people at a fancy party. We'd spin around on the barstools until we were dizzy, but we only did that when Uncle Randall wasn't there.

Everywhere in this house is choked with memories.

Suddenly I realize the room has gone silent. When I look up, everyone's still—staring at their drinks, the floor, everywhere but each other. The tension feels almost tangible, like fog filling the air.

Auntie Mina is crying. She's holding the scrapbook we gave her, the one I should have helped with more, and tears are flowing down her cheeks and staining her green blouse. I clench my jaw, not wanting to watch but unable to turn away. Mom's sniffling a little herself, helping Auntie Mina flip through the decorated pages of photos and handwritten memories. Uncle Randall peers over the bar for a closer look. I don't want to see his reaction, so I get up, walk toward the nearest wall, and pretend to be very interested in a freeze-dried marlin. I try to focus on the fish, staring into its reflective, laminated surface.

I do a little meditation breathing, in and out, deeply and evenly, until for just one moment—a perfect moment—I'm not really there in the room, but simply a body and mind existing in space. Just me.

In that silent moment I hear someone, and it's Auntie Mina this time.

oh, Shiri, my baby—

With the words comes a burst of incoherent emotion. Anguish, like a scab accidentally ripped open. Pain that makes my heart race in sympathy. And, for some reason that I don't want to think about, can't think about—fear.

I come back to myself, shaken, and find I'm staring at the reflection of the room in the glassy surface of the fish. There's sweat on the back of my neck and I feel uncomfortably warm.

I turn my head. Mom is looking at me a little strangely, but everyone else is still absorbed by the scrapbook or lost in their own thoughts. I give my hair a little pat as if I was just settling it back into place, try to smile reassuringly at Mom, and make a beeline for my Shirley Temple. On the way, I look at the clock on the wall and sigh. Sliding back onto the barstool, I reach for my drink with a trembling hand. Two hours left. No way out of here. And that scared feeling still hasn't fully gone away, but seems to have settled between my shoulder blades like a cold hand.

———————

We all race through dinner in relative silence, as if we're in a hurry to get somewhere. The only real "conversation" consists of Uncle Randall trying to convince my dad that he should have voted for some congresswoman because of her sense of fiscal responsibility, my dad nodding but obviously not listening and my mom butting in to say "fiscal responsibility begins at home," looking pointedly at the imported Waterford crystal vase in the middle of the table. That effectively kills the mood.

I try to imagine being Shiri, sitting here, having to deal with this every day of her life. Even after she moved away, it didn't seem to help. But why not? I press down my mashed potatoes with my fork as if I can squeeze an answer out.

After we finish eating, the table is a disaster zone of crumpled white linen napkins, silverware sitting on empty china plates, and bread crumbs on the tablecloth. With a satisfied smile on his face, Uncle Randall starts regaling my parents with the story of how Randall Number Two met his latest piece of arm candy, some convoluted misadventure involving a blind date and mistaken identity that sounds completely exaggerated. I jump up to help Auntie Mina clear the scraps of prime rib and curried mashed potatoes from the dining room. We both try to move through the kitchen doorway at the same time, and jostle one another.

"Sorry!" I back away and let her through ahead of me with a stack of dirty plates. As I follow her through the wooden saloon-style doors, my eyes fall on an oval bruise, nearly an inch long, yellowing the brown skin of her left shoulder.

"What happened?" I point at the bruise, wincing a little in sympathy.

"Oh, that?" Auntie Mina deposits the plates on the marble countertop next to the sink and pulls her green cardigan back up so it covers the bruise again. "I was cleaning the den yesterday and one of your uncle's silly fish fell while I was dusting it. Can you believe it? Is that stupid or what?"

"Ouch," I say. I drop my load of dishes next to hers and start pouring tea into the cups sitting ready on the kitchen island. Something feels weird about this conversation. The tension in my shoulders returns full force.

"Those fish are such an eyesore," she continues, running water on the plates and raising her voice to be heard over the garbage disposal. "It's not as though he caught them himself—the CFO of our company goes fishing in Ensenada every year. Randall goes with him sometimes, but he's not much of a fisherman." Uncle Randall is the Vice President of Finance at an investment firm, and Auntie Mina works there doing something in financial data analysis. I can't picture either of them on a fishing boat.

"Randall's dream is to make the den look like a fishing lodge." She rolls her eyes. "A fishing lodge!" Suddenly, she slams a cup down on the marble countertop with such a clatter I'm scared it's going to break. I jump, nearly spilling boiling tea.

"And Randall Junior just encourages him." There's a note of exasperation, of outright hostility, in her voice that I've never heard before, and it's shocking. Auntie Mina's always been the mild one in our family, even when compared to Dad. Shiri and I, and Number Two, were the loud mischief-makers, climbing up a tree onto the patio roof and hiding out or trying to spray passing cars with silly string.

Until slowly, imperceptibly, Shiri changed.

I don't know what to say. I stand there uncomfortably, shifting from foot to foot, wishing I hadn't asked about the bruise. It seems far-fetched that one of the fish would have just fallen off the wall, but I have no reason not to believe her. It's hard to believe Uncle Randall could have hurt her.

Except … I've never heard her angry like this. And after Thanksgiving, I can't help wondering.

I still haven't deliberately tried to use my underhearing. But I feel terrible for her, and maybe if I find out what happened, I can help.

It's frightening—frightening enough to make my hands tremble and my armpits sweat—but I close my eyes and still my mind. I take my confusion and worry and terror and try to channel them into a tiny boiling point in the middle of all the stillness, like a laser of emotion that can cut through the layers and let out Auntie Mina's secret anger and fear.

But somehow—maybe because I'm trying so hard, digging my fingernails into my palms and squeezing my eyes shut—somehow it just doesn't work. Nothing happens. It's only me inside my head. Auntie Mina is still *out there*, still standing at the sink rinsing dishes with an unhappy frown on her face.

Maybe I can't figure this out after all. The anxiety feels like a hand clutching at my intestines as I stand there, powerless. I slowly, carefully start to carry out cups of tea on a tray, composing my face into a smiling mask.

———

At lunchtime the next day, I pull Mikaela away from the group, hustling her around the corner from the picnic table where Cody and everyone else is gathered. We sit side-by-side against the wall and, once again, I tell her about everything. The embarrassing Shirley Temple. The scrapbook.

The underhearing and my strange conversation with Auntie Mina. I even tell her about my growing suspicions that Shiri might have had some kind of ability too.

"Man." Mikaela makes idle marks on the back of her hand with a blue ballpoint pen—a teacher saw her black marker and confiscated it. Now she's drawing angry little blue faces over and over. "That is really intense. I'm glad I wasn't there. But..."

"What?" I say, after she's quiet for a minute.

"I keep thinking about how you said you tried to listen to your aunt. 'Underhear.' Whatever. And nothing happened?" She peers at me sidelong, her expression unreadable.

"I *wanted* to," I say miserably. "I wanted to help her somehow. But I couldn't do anything. I tried so hard, Mikaela!"

"If you actually could have seen into her thoughts," she says, "maybe it would just be something you didn't want to know." She looks down again. It's a good point, but today, she sounds like she's not sure if she believes me. Not that I blame her.

I feel a stab of intense loneliness. Shiri might have understood, at least if her journal entries are anything to go by, but journal entries are a poor substitute for the real thing.

Mikaela gets up, gives my ponytail a tug, and walks back to the picnic table. I spend a minute composing myself before I stroll back to rejoin the group. When I arrive, Mikaela is saying something to Cody with an impish smile, giving his cheek an affectionate, granny-like pinch. Then she heads to the other side of the table to chat with Becca.

Cody looks up at me intently. I feel warmth flood my

cheeks and travel down to my stomach. I've tried to be aloof, but my physical reaction to him catches me off guard.

"Hey, Cody," I say, trying to sound casual.

"Hey. Did you see what Mik did to me? So uncalled-for." He rubs his cheek. I try not to smile, but I can't seem to help it.

"At least she didn't try to give you a makeover this time."

"Like you forcing your Banana Republic hat on me. Again, uncalled-for," he says, grinning for a second. "At least I relieved you of that nasty piece of bland, sweat-shop-produced, corporate ... *clone-itude*."

"Yeah, I got rid of all the rest of that stuff, too," I lie—I shoved it all into the back of my closet, including the hat, which he eventually gave back to me. I gesture vaguely at what I'm wearing today: black jeans and a burgundy T-shirt I got from Thumbscrew printed with a Brian Froud painting of evil-looking fairies. My hair, now dark brown again, hangs down in two sleek braids on either side of my head.

He'll have to say something. I don't look like the old me at all.

But Cody just smiles a little and turns abruptly to Andy, saying exactly nothing else to me. I'm surprised at how disappointed I am, but I try not to let on. I just grab my lunch out of my backpack and sit down as if nothing happened, as if I hadn't said anything to him or expected him to respond. But my cheeks burn.

From Shiri Langford's journal, April 13th

Friday the 13th! Lucky me. Because of course THAT happened again. It always seems to come when I least expect it, when I'm thinking about something else or nothing at all. It made me angry this time because I was with Brendan and spaced out in the middle of our date. What I heard—it seemed like he was irritated, but I couldn't be sure if he was annoyed with me or someone else. I was so scared he was angry at me, but I couldn't figure out why, and although I kept trying and trying, I couldn't hear anything else.

I just wish I could understand why it happens. And why me.

I was little, maybe nine, the first time it happened. My brother was home visiting from college. He told me he'd brought me a present, but it was up in the oak tree in the backyard. I climbed up there— higher, he said—and then suddenly I was so high I was too scared to climb back down. I clung to the trunk as tightly as I could and screamed, but he just thought I was joking. He must have been drunk or on something, because he just laughed and laughed. I stopped panicking and clenched my teeth, trying to steady myself enough to figure out how to get down, and that was when I heard it.

Not out loud. Not anywhere but in my head.

"Stupid kid."

ten

"Okay," says Mikaela, facing me cross-legged on my bedroom floor. "Let's try it without the candle this time."

I open my eyes, sigh, and blow out the tiny flame. My right foot is falling asleep. I flex it a few times and rearrange my legs into a more comfortable position.

"We've been trying for half an hour," I say. "I think it's hopeless."

"Come on. One more time, for shits and giggles." Mikaela smiles at me coaxingly.

"*Fine*," I say, and sigh again. Just once more. I close my eyes.

"Relax, and clear your mind," she says in a smooth, drawn-out voice. She sounds like an easy-listening radio DJ or my mom when she's leading weekend yoga. Somehow, I suppress a snort of laughter. "Focus on your breathing...in...and out..."

I keep the sound of Mikaela's voice in the back of my mind as I inhale and exhale as calmly as possible. I hear a bird trill suddenly, flying past the window, and my parents moving around downstairs. I can even smell remnants of the candle smoke. The carpet fibers are making my ankles itch. I'm extra-aware of my five senses. But it's not those senses that I'm trying to tap into.

"Okay. Now, remember your Uncle Randall and how *angry* you are at him," Mikaela says, in a flat and hard tone. "How sexist he is, how insensitive."

My nostrils flare and my breathing quickens.

"He never understood Shiri. He probably makes your Auntie Mina cry. Poor Auntie Mina."

I inhale sharply, thinking of Auntie Mina, of her bruised shoulder and her bruised feelings. I'm angry, but mostly I just feel sorry for Auntie Mina, and sad.

Maybe that's enough.

The plan was to try to hear Mikaela, though, not Auntie Mina. Mikaela would induce intense emotions. Then I'd calm myself and try to hear ... something. That's how it seems to work.

Come on, Sunny, I tell myself. *Ocean waves. Whale songs. Sunsets.* My mind wanders. Then everything gradually morphs into Shiri's face the way it looked the last time I saw her alive. A little too thin; sharp-featured, smiling, but with eyes full of something deep and unfathomable.

That's when I do get angry. Angry at how hard it is to move on with my life. Angry at myself for not being able to control the underhearing. Angry at Shiri for leaving me, for giving up on herself and on us. Rage condenses into a hard little ball inside my stomach, like a bubble of tar.

I squeeze my eyelids closed tightly and breathe in, out, in, out, until the knot in my gut slowly begins to ease. Then I feel it. That moment, the calm inside the storm. My stomach leaps in anticipation, and in that second I feel it slipping away again.

I sit as motionless as possible, trying to calm myself.

I don't hear anything.

I open my eyes. The sun is setting and a ray of orange light reaches a finger through the gap in the curtains. Mikaela is looking at me expectantly, searchingly. I shake my head and draw an uneven breath, resting my head in my hands for a moment. My eyes fill with tears of frustration.

"For a second—Mikaela, it was happening. I'm positive it was. But I lost concentration." I quickly look down at the floor, but not before I see a flash of disappointment cross her face. My jaw tenses. Without looking up, I say halfheartedly, "We can try again tomorrow. Maybe at your house?"

"It's okay. We don't have to." There's a short, uncomfortable silence.

She really doesn't believe me. As sympathetic as she's been, she just can't understand. I stare at the carpet some more, the frustration building again.

"Anyway," she says after a minute, "my mom will never leave us in peace."

I feel like arguing. "Your mom's sweet. She offered me and Becca soda like eighty times yesterday."

"Yeah, but she worries all the time. God. I hate it." Mikaela grabs her black purse with the elaborate silver buckles from the top of the bed and fishes out a bottle of nail polish so dark red it's almost black. I sigh loudly, get up to switch on the CD player, grab some silvery blue polish, and start painting my toes.

"When is she going to get it through her head? I *don't care* if she only makes a third of what Dad makes," Mikaela continues. "She's a nurse and she actually helps people. Meanwhile, Dad's a collections lawyer and feeds off people's broken dreams." She shakes her head. "I'd rather be here, with her. Even if it is suburban hell. Sorry."

Some friend I am. I never even knew until now what her dad does for a living. I want to be a better friend; better than Cassie was to me. I want to do something to help Auntie Mina. I want to underhear at will because I'm tired of feeling like a victim of some weird fluke of fate. But when it comes to any of those things, I'm a failure.

I breathe raggedly, trying to keep my face composed. Finally I settle down and just sit there, painting my toenails and not thinking about anything for once.

And then:

—no Mina it can't be true this can't be happening
this is the kind of thing that happens to other
people, not to us, not to YOU
I can't believe he—
not again—

A wave of exhaustion, of despair and anger, washes over me with the words, and the smell of burning autumn leaves sears my nostrils. The energy seems to drain out of my body.

For a moment, I can't breathe, and then my stomach does a slow flip-turn.

It's happening. But it's not who I expected to hear. It's my mom.

I draw in a sharp breath, coughing on imaginary smoke, and brush silver-blue lacquer across the top of my foot.

"Whoops," Mikaela says, holding out a tissue and the nail polish remover. I don't take it from her; instead, I strain to hear something more, anything. But my mind is silent. All that's left are sticky wisps of my mother's shock and horror. I squirm uncomfortably. I don't *like* having such an intimate glimpse into somebody's head. I feel invaded, like I'm the one who's exposed.

I have to get some kind of control over this.

"Hey, what's going on?" Mikaela waves the tissue at me. "Are you okay?"

I manage a nod and lean back weakly against the bed.

"You look pale." She looks at me in concern. "Like *really* pale."

Mikaela puts her hand on my forehead. "You know, some people spend an hour trying to get their faces that white. Becca did it for a party where she wanted to hit on this one mega-goth chick. Hey, you're all clammy!" She brushes my hair out of my face.

"Yeah." I slowly lever myself to a standing position. "It finally worked." I grab the glass of soda I left on the dresser an hour ago and gulp down the flat, warm liquid in fast swallows.

"What worked?" Mikaela looks at me blankly for a second. Then it dawns on her. "Oh! Oh, my God! Are you kidding?" She sounds like she thinks I *am* kidding. But I'd never joke about this. I tell her so.

"Wow," she says, over and over. "No way. Wow. What did you hear?" She carefully caps her nail polish and slips it back into her purse, looking back at me with large, intense eyes.

I hesitate. But I can't keep it inside. I'll burst. I start getting that sick, stomach-flipping feeling again.

I have to trust someone. Shiri didn't trust anyone. She didn't even trust me.

Mikaela says, "You know, if you don't want to tell me, that's okay." I can hear the skepticism in her tone.

"It was my mom," I say heavily. "It was something about Auntie Mina, something really bad." The memory of that awful burnt smell twines into my nostrils and I start trembling.

"What's really bad?" Mikaela scoots closer. She reaches one hand out, then pulls it back, watching me as I sit there and shake. "If you hold it in, you'll just feel worse."

"I don't know what happened." I let out a frustrated noise. "I felt all this shock and disbelief and—it just *felt* wrong." I tell her how I heard Auntie Mina's name, how my mother said something about a "he."

"'He'? Like who?" For a second, her eyes widen and she looks scared. Then her face relaxes. She leans in and hugs me. "It could be nothing. She's probably fine."

I sit there stiffly. What if she's just humoring me? I want to prove that I'm not making it up, that I'm not crazy. But even more than that, I have to know what happened.

"Let's go downstairs," I tell her. I slip out from under her arm and stand up, still a little shaky. "I have to know. I need to ask my mom."

"Okay," Mikaela says, eyeing me.

She follows me down the stairs and into the kitchen, where my mom is sitting at the table in semi-darkness. I flip on the kitchen light. In the sudden brightness, I can see the tracks of tears on her face. She glances at me but doesn't say anything.

I start to get a creeping feeling of dread, and I stop in the doorway, Mikaela lurking in the hall behind me. *Stay here*, I mouth to her, and walk in.

"Mom, what's wrong?"

"Oh … " For a minute it looks like she's going to tell me, but then her face closes off and an unconvincing smile appears. "No, I'm fine, baby. I was just thinking." She trails off, getting up to refill her water glass at the sink.

I *have* to know. I take a deep, shaky breath.

"Mom, can I ask you something?"

"Of course," she says, but she won't stop staring out the window at the darkness outside. I swallow hard.

"Is everything okay with Auntie Mina?" I hesitate, then continue. "After Thanksgiving, and … that dinner. And the time when she came over to have tea. She looks awful."

My mother stands in front of the sink, as still as a stone, her face unreadable. I can hear Mikaela fidgeting around the other side of the doorjamb. I wish I'd told her to stay upstairs.

"Mom!" I say insistently. "If something was wrong, you'd tell me, right? Is she—did something happen?" I *know* she's hiding something. I stare at her hard. Finally, she turns back toward me.

"Sunny, I need you to listen to me now," she says in a low, tense voice. "I don't want you to mention this to your dad. Not yet. Mina says everything's fine, that this is all just going to blow over. She says it's really not a big deal. She doesn't want your father worried."

"Um, okay," I say. "But what—?"

My mother rolls her now-empty water glass around and around in her hands, then puts it back on the counter. "Well, I don't know how to sugarcoat this, so let me tell you. Your Auntie Mina and Uncle Randall got into a big fight last night. She wants to quit her job, wants a change of pace—teaching instead of working in the corporate world."

"That sounds okay." I shift uncomfortably from one foot to the other.

"Well, Randall hasn't been in favor of that. He wants her to keep working at Jones & Gonzalez. They've been arguing about it for weeks. I don't know if you've noticed, but things haven't been going so well in their relationship since . . . "

Mom clears her throat, her eyes troubled. "Anyway, she just called me on my cell phone and was nearly incoherent. She told Randall today that she thought they should go to a marriage counselor. Apparently he really lost his temper and . . . " She lowers her voice to nearly a whisper. "He grabbed her."

"Grabbed?" I feel like the wind has been knocked out of me. "What do you mean, grabbed?"

"She's fine, Sunny. She just left the house for a little while so he could cool off."

I pace across the kitchen angrily, thinking about the bruise on Auntie Mina's shoulder. That word "grabbed" is utterly inadequate and wrong. Words bubble up to the surface of my mind, furious words that I stuff back down. I stop in front of my mother, my fists clenched at my sides. "This has happened before, hasn't it? And you didn't tell me."

"Sunny, I'm sorry," she says miserably. "But you were so young. We thought they worked it all out. Randall had lost his job, and he just wasn't himself back then." She pauses, and I stop breathing for a moment. "He had a breakdown. He pulled every dish out of the cabinet and slammed them to the floor one by one."

"I don't remember that." I glare at her, even though I'm not really angry with my mother.

"Like I said, you were just too young. You were only six. Mina calmed him down, though. They talked it all out. He found his new job, he found her a job there, too ... they were so happy." She reaches a hand toward my shoulder but I duck. I start pacing again.

"So now what? I'm just supposed to pretend nothing happened? Pretend he didn't hit her?"

"Nobody said anything about hitting," Mom says, but she looks uneasy. "Mina doesn't want to tell Dad because she's worried he'll do something drastic. You know how he feels about Uncle Randall."

"Yeah, but—"

"I wanted her to let me tell him," she continues, "but she

insisted Randall just needs to cool off, that's all." She smiles at me worriedly. "I hope she's right."

"I—okay." My shoulders slump, and all of a sudden I'm exhausted. "I guess I'll go upstairs and finish studying with Mikaela." I peer at my mom, but she seems to be pulling herself together.

"She's still here? You should probably take her home before it gets late." Mom starts loading the dirty dinner dishes into the dishwasher with a clatter.

"I will." I back out of the room and flee up the stairs, Mikaela at my heels.

"So, did you *hear* all that?" I say, once we're safely behind closed doors. "I knew something happened to Auntie Mina. I *heard* it. I just didn't know what." My voice gets a little shaky and I try to stuff the fear back down, try to keep myself calm.

"Yeah, but... don't take this the wrong way, but are you sure it wasn't just a good guess?" Mikaela picks at a loose thread on her black blazer, not meeting my eyes. "Or maybe your subconscious was noticing the signs at dinner on Sunday, and then manifested them in the form of, like, your mom's voice?"

"Mikaela, believe me!" My voice takes on a pleading note. It seems like the more evidence is in front of her, the more skeptical she gets. "I've thought exactly what you're thinking now—until it kept happening."

"That doesn't necessarily mean—"

"Mikaela, do you remember the first day you came over to my house, after we went shopping?" She nods warily, her dark eyebrows drawn down into a hard line. "You came in and met my parents, and I wasn't sure if you maybe would hate my house and think we were these rich snobs or McYuppies or something. But you were so cool. And then..." I take a deep breath. "I heard you. You wished you and your mom could have a new house and a new life to replace what your dad took away, and I just was so—I really admire you, Mikaela. You're a lot stronger than I am." It takes an effort, but I meet her eyes.

She just stares at me, her expression blank. My heart races. Maybe she's going to say she doesn't recall ever thinking that. Maybe she's going to finally admit she doesn't believe me and thinks I'm making it up.

"I remember that," she says slowly, tugging on one of her many tiny silver earrings. "I thought you must have the perfect life." She gets a wry little smile on her face and shakes her head, making all the tiny braids bounce around.

"I know you *don't*," she says after a minute, in a bleak voice. "Nobody does. But at least you have your underhearing—something that gives you a clue about what's going on and what things mean. I don't have anything like that." She sits on the bed, a dejected look passing across her face for second. Then her expression slides back to normal and she's tough, cynical Mikaela again. We clean up our nail polish mess and our American Lit homework, and I drive her home.

She doesn't mention underhearing again, or talk about her situation with her mom. In fact, she's quiet the whole drive back to her apartment. Distant. Almost like she's scared by what happened.

Or like she doesn't want me to know what she's thinking.

eleven

"So last night I helped my parents decorate the 'interfaith tree,'" I tell Mikaela as we pull away from her apartment complex the following Sunday.

Slurping on her coffee, she almost does a spit-take. So I explain: golden Stars-of-David hang next to crucifixes; a fat Buddha dangles above a small ceramic tile with intricate Islamic calligraphy. Mom's idea. All the yoga geezers love it. The tree's even made from recycled materials.

By now, we're already downtown. Citrus Canyon's fake-old-timey Main Street slides past through the window, complete with wreath-festooned lampposts and windows sprayed with artificial snow.

"You're just full of surprises," she says. "Can you imagine having one of those in the Orangewood Mall? That would be *great*."

"It would not," I say. The interfaith tree is our one concession to the holiday season. My dad doesn't put up lights; my mom doesn't bake cookies. It disappoints Grandma and

Grandpa Pryce, who always send us wreaths and garlands we never use. Meanwhile, my dad's family tries to wheedle my parents into celebrating Eid and observing Ramadan. My parents just don't do religious holidays.

In contrast, Uncle Randall and Auntie Mina hire a decorator every year to encrust their house with twinkling lights. Once, when Shiri and I were little kids, they even set up fake snow in the front yard with light-up plastic reindeer. We were climbing on the reindeer's backs and Shiri kept telling them to giddy-up. I laughed so hard I fell off. Uncle Randall got mad at Shiri for not watching me more closely, and his yelling made us both cry. Of course, it was Number Two who was supposed to be watching both of us.

"Ever wish we could just skip Christmas?" I sigh, glancing at Mikaela.

"What? No," Mikaela says, surprising me. "But I would skip certain things, I guess. Visiting my dad. Today's mall trip." I nod in agreement, even though Christmas shopping is easy in our house. I get my parents a couple of token presents and they usually give me a goofy gag gift and a check.

When we get there, the mall is swarming with moms and kids. Mikaela and I forge our way along like salmon swimming upstream. There's an ear-blistering cacophony of screaming kids waiting in line to visit Santa, and we go past the midpoint of the mall almost at a run. Just on the other side of the big central atrium is a store called Fresh, one of those places that sells an assortment of weird crap—T-shirts, posters, gag gifts.

I wander toward the back wall and start browsing through

a selection of plastic and wooden beaded curtains in boxes, looking for one my mom might like. She could hang it up during yoga classes, add some authentic hippie atmosphere. Mikaela is checking out the T-shirts for something to send to her brother, who lives with her dad. I'm just stuffing the end of a horrible pink plastic beaded monstrosity back into its box when I sense a presence standing over me.

"Hey," someone growls, practically in my ear, making me jump. Someone male, who smells faintly of clove cigarettes and soap. I turn around. It's Cody. My stomach lurches, and I can't control the smile that spreads across my face.

He looks good. He's wearing black, as usual—a long coat, a ratty old Pixies T-shirt, and black jeans—and he flashes me a quick grin as he leans back against the shelf of Magic 8 Balls behind him.

"So what's up?" He just stands there, one corner of his mouth quirked up as if he's trying not to laugh.

"Not much. Just shopping for my mom," I say, grimacing. "I mean, for a Christmas present."

"Yeah?" He cocks an eyebrow.

"Well, we don't really do the Christmas thing at our house. Just family stuff. My parents aren't religious or anything. You should see their so-called interfaith tree. It's *so* lame." I'm blathering. My cheeks get hot, and I turn around for a second under the guise of deciding on a beaded curtain. In a fit of nervousness I grab the first box I see in front of me and turn back around.

"Interfaith tree? I'm scared to even ask," Cody says, laughing.

"Yeah, they've got some weird hippie habits. They used to live in Santa Cruz," I say, as if that explains everything. Embarrassed, I change the subject. "So, what'll you be doing over the break?"

"Haven't decided yet. Trying to figure out how I can get out of the family thing. I probably haven't told you yet, but my parents are ... " He makes a cuckoo gesture next to his ear. "The holidays just make it worse. My mom is a total Martha Stewart." He lounges against the shelf, one hand unconsciously ruffling his hair back into its usual messy black spikes, which are tipped with blond today.

"I like your hair," I tell him. He looks at me and smiles a little, not saying anything. I'm conscious of how close together we're standing, and it's almost like I can feel an aura of warmth filling the aisle between us. There's definitely something here ... I think. But he's always giving me mixed signals.

"Let's see what's in store for my winter vacation," he says, picking up a Magic 8 Ball from the shelf behind him and giving it a brisk shake, still staring at me. I can't read his expression at all. And I haven't once underheard anything from him. Not yet.

One more reason to try to gain control over my ability, learn to use it somehow.

He looks at the little triangle in the 8 Ball window and swears.

"What?" I finally ask, nervously. He has a strange, almost wild look in his eyes. Reflexively, I clutch the beaded curtain box a little tighter.

"Oh, just … 'It doesn't look promising.'" His voice is scornful. "These things are such garbage."

"Well, what did you ask it?"

There's a long pause. A kid pushes past, wearing a pirate hat from the display at the front of the store, and disappears around the corner of the aisle.

"You know, I bet Mikaela would love one of these things." He glances over his shoulder and, at the same time, I see him casually slip the Magic 8 Ball into the large inner pocket of his coat. I inhale sharply. Cody must be crazy. I mean, security cameras? Guards? Even Cassie nicking makeup from the drugstore used to make me super paranoid, and that was tiny stuff—lipstick or nail polish.

I peer around the aisle. It's nearly empty except for one really stoned-looking guy at the other end who looks mesmerized by a glow-in-the-dark Led Zeppelin poster.

"Shh," Cody says with a secret smile. "It's fine." He steps closer and brushes a sweaty lock of hair out of my face. "Want one? I have another pocket." I shiver a little at his touch, but I shake my head mutely. My thoughts are racing, and most of them involve us being ushered to a mall-basement holding cell and interrogated by security goons. What if they blame me for something? What if they call my parents?

My breath is coming in quick pants. Is it panic, or is it because Cody's standing so close? I stand there, the beaded curtain box almost crumpling in my clenched hands, and try to slow my breathing down to a reasonable pace. Finally I succeed, and the panic begins to dissipate.

Then I feel the hush inside me, and I know what's coming. I look up at Cody. I can feel the goose bumps rise on my arms. And then I hear—

I don't know what I hear. Maybe it's because the mall is so loud, or because there are so many other people around, but his thoughts are a turbulent murmur that I can't quite catch, like voices underwater. I try to listen hard, but I can't make out any words.

But I do *feel* something. A flash of intensity—anger and determination followed by a rush of exhilaration—and then suddenly there's no more emotion, *at all*, and I see Cody do his little smile thing again. It's over. All that's left is a faint smell of cloves in my nostrils and that feeling of exhilaration, lingering, surging through my veins.

I just about pee my pants when Mikaela comes up behind me.

"Gotcha," she says, and then she sees Cody. "Oh *hey*, Cody, can't believe you're at the *mall*," she scoffs, giving him a mock glare and a burgundy-lipped pout.

"Come on, let's get going," I say, hustling toward the front counter so I can pay for my mom's present. I'm a nervous wreck, convinced that the clerk is going to notice the giant lump in Cody's coat pocket. What would happen if he got caught stealing a Magic 8 Ball? *You could ask the 8 Ball*, I think, a little crazily, as I pay the cashier. Grabbing the bright green Fresh bag, I walk as nonchalantly as possible toward the front of the store.

"Time to go, guys," I say breezily, but inside my stomach is Jell-O. I can't help feeling oddly guilty about our encounter, like we were conspiring together. And it feels... exciting. Like he trusts me to keep this secret for him. Like we shared something that nobody else knows about. Not even Mikaela.

The three of us walk as far as the atrium with the screaming kids and exhausted-looking Santa. Cody says, "Well, I'm off like your prom dress," and splits for the nearest exit.

"Yeah, nice talking to you for five seconds." Mikaela rolls her eyes and stomps toward the Bath and Body store. Before following her I glance back at Cody, strolling right past a security guard like he's wearing a halo. He looks back at me for a second and winks.

By the time we've bought bath stuff for Mikaela's mom and a desk set for my dad, my head is pounding.

"Christmas shopping sucks, huh." Mikaela gives my shoulders a sympathetic squeeze as we flee the mall and walk back through the packed parking lot to my car.

Despite my headache, I smile a little to myself.

———————

The next morning, I don't feel quite so much like a happy little co-conspirator anymore. The more I think about it, the more I don't like what Cody did. It's not so much the stealing, but the fact that he's put me in an awkward position where I'm expected to keep his secret for him.

Even more than that, I feel unexpectedly jealous. I keep thinking about how, when he swiped the 8 Ball, Cody thought of Mikaela first. It's an awful feeling, because I know it's completely unfair.

I'm supposed to give Mikaela a ride to school, and, when

I pick her up, it's hard to even meet her eyes. After she slides into the car, I clench my hands around the wheel and gun it out of the apartment parking lot, almost peeling out as I turn onto Main Street.

"Jeez Louise, what the hell is the matter with you?" Mikaela clutches at the oh-god handle, staring at me like I've gone completely nuts.

"Sorry." I ease my foot on the gas pedal. If Cody's asking me to keep this a secret, that means he trusts me. Sees me as a friend; maybe more. But Mikaela's my friend, too, and I'm being pretty harsh about something she doesn't even know about.

"If you keep driving like that..." Mikaela finally lets go and rests her hands in her lap. She gazes steadily at me. "Oh, I get it. Did something happen?"

"No," I say, but I don't sound very convincing.

"Is it your aunt?"

"No!" I lower my voice. "No, it's not that."

"Yeesh, okay. You don't have to talk about it if you don't want. It's cool." She turns her head and stares out the window.

After a few minutes of tense silence, I relent. "You'll probably think I'm just being stupid. Did you know Cody stole something from Fresh?"

"God, not again," Mikaela says. She looks back over at me and smiles a little. "And it's bugging you, isn't it? You're so cute."

"Well, yeah, it's bugging me a little." I remember the casual way he did it, how he didn't even look at what he was doing, just hid the 8 Ball away in his pocket in one smooth gesture. It should have been obvious that he'd done it before. "Cassie used to steal stuff, but never anything big. Nail polish, eyebrow pencils. That kind of thing. I just hate being put in that position. I kept worrying he'd get caught."

"Ah, he's an old pro," she says sarcastically. "I wouldn't worry about it. Just think of it as part of his mystique." Mikaela looks at me intently for a moment. "Did *you* ever steal anything?"

My ears get hot under her stare, and I focus on the road. "I—no. I guess I was too much of a chicken to ever try it. Cassie always wanted me to steal makeup with her, but I couldn't do it."

"Yeah, I really can't picture you doing that," Mikaela says. "Anyway, I probably wouldn't have as much respect for you if you were the shoplifting type."

I can't help wondering if that means she has less respect for Cody because he steals stuff. I'm pretty sure he wouldn't care if the shoe were on the other foot. He's actually pretty tolerant of people's weird little habits, like Becca's tendency to be hyper or David's constant drawing in his sketchbook. It's conformity he can't seem to deal with.

"Like I was telling Cody the other day," she continues, tapping her dark-red fingernails on the dashboard to the beat of the radio, "you're just a totally sincere person. I don't think you could be dishonest even if you wanted to. The only illicit thrill you get is driving us around unsupervised."

"And there's still two more weeks until I'm law-abiding," I put in. "My birthday's on the 20th."

"Ooh, you're such a rule-breaker." She smiles. "Come on; it's a good thing. You being nice is a good thing."

"Huh." I'm not sure how I feel about that assessment. "I guess."

"Seriously, you're not like most of the other people we hang out with at school. It's one of the reasons I like you."

I'm flattered, but I feel weird at the same time. Am I the token goody-goody friend? I try to change the subject.

"So Cody does this on a regular basis?"

"Yeah." Mikaela says it sourly, like she's sick of talking about it already. "He's just lucky he didn't get caught this time."

"This time? What happened before?"

"Oh, he ended up owing a big fine because he tried to steal an iPod." She makes a derisive noise. "What an asshole."

"That's … major." I'm trying to picture him getting caught, but my mind's eye keeps replacing it with an image of him reaching out, brushing my hair back, that secret smile on his face.

"Not really. His mommy and daddy paid for it. They always bail him out. They must be in total denial."

"You make him sound like a petty criminal." I turn into the driveway of the school parking lot, swerving around a group of students congregating on the sidewalk.

"No, but he seems to attract trouble. Like on purpose. It's like he wants attention or something. I don't know. Last year his parents found out he'd been ditching school a lot and told him to clean up his act, but it just turned him into the cheerful bundle of joy you see today."

"Oh." He said his mom was a Martha Stewart clone, but I wonder if he's exaggerating. His parents are probably perfectly normal. I could see him being annoyed by that factor alone.

"And then over the summer he got drunk one night and got caught out in public by a cop, reeking of rum and peeing in an alley."

"Where'd he get rum?" All too easily, I imagine Cody shoplifting from a liquor store, slipping a bottle into his pocket as effortlessly as the 8 Ball.

"He stole it out of his parents' liquor cabinet. They never notice."

"That's weird."

"Yeah, well, you'd understand if you met his parents." She leaves it at that, since I've just pulled into a parking space. The bell rings as we walk past the art building, so I wave and head to my French class.

I feel a little better after talking to Mikaela. Even so, I can't help feeling a tiny bit guilty about what I didn't tell her. I didn't tell her about the almost-underhearing incident. And I didn't tell her about how Cody smiled at me, touched me.

I didn't tell her how he makes me feel. I wonder if I should have.

———

Thursday, the last day of classes before Winter Break, Mikaela is absent. She left early to visit her brother for a couple of days, despite what she'd said about not wanting to spend time at her dad's over the holidays.

I sit with David, Becca, and Cody at lunch. David opens up a little and talks about a painting he's working on, showing us a few drawings in his sketchbook. Becca goes on and on about music and clubbing and veganism and how her parents went "batshit" when they saw her tongue piercing. I space out after a while. I wonder how Auntie Mina is going to cope with Christmas this year. I hope she doesn't have to spend the holidays alone with Uncle Randall.

"Thinking deep thoughts?" Cody slides in next to me on the bench, mocking me with a sculpture-like "Thinker" pose.

"Nah. Just stressing about holiday family stuff."

"I know all about that," he says. Then he abruptly changes the subject. "Hey, I need some food. Come with me?"

"I already ate," I say, poking my half-eaten turkey sandwich. "But I'll keep you company." I don't want to seem over-eager, but I'm intrigued by Cody. Maybe even more so after finding out about his nasty little habits. I haven't forgotten that Spike warned me about him, but somehow it just makes him more compelling. Something completely different than what I'm used to.

We walk over to the cafeteria and I wait in line with him while he buys a Viking burger and fries. He grabs four tiny paper cups of ketchup, then we leave the crowded line and make our way outside again, threading through the sea of tables under the awning.

"I wanted to ask you something," Cody says finally, toying with his burger, taking out the pickles and throwing them in the first garbage can we pass. He seems almost nervous. That must be a first for him. I get a little edgy, too, and look at the picnic tables, the groups of people, anywhere but at him. As we walk, I catch a glimpse of Cassie over by the pizza cart. I feel a twinge, and I'm not sure if it's anger or sadness. I hope she sees me with Cody. I hope she sees how I don't need her.

We're heading back toward the art-building patio, but before we turn the corner, Cody stops and looks at me.

"I don't know if you're into this kind of thing, but I have this group of Wiccan friends who are having a celebration for the winter solstice on Saturday." He looks at me kind of weird.

"What's a winter solstice celebration?" I refrain from adding that it sounds like something my mom would go to.

"Well, it's really just a regular meeting of the local Wiccan group, but with food," he admits. "They're into like, nature and being in touch with your inner energy. There's nobody too freaky, if that's what you're worried about."

"Who said I was worried?" I feel like he's issued a challenge. What's with him and Mikaela thinking I'm so innocent, so easily shocked? "Sure, I'll go. Whatever."

"Mikaela already said she's up for it, so you guys can hang out if you're nervous." The funny thing is, *he's* the one who looks nervous. He's being all ADD, eating fries one at a time and pacing back and forth in front of me, tugging on his eyebrow ring.

His fidgeting is kind of cute, though. Is he really that anxious about asking *me* to a party? I can't help a tiny smile. For once, I feel like the one who has the advantage.

"I said I'll go, jeez. Just stop doing that," I say.

"Okay, cool." He stops pacing and gives me a lopsided grin. It makes me a little wobbly, so I duck my head and start walking back to the picnic table.

"Wait a sec," Cody says mushily, his mouth full of fries. "I just wanted to say... it's cool you can make it. I think you'll really enjoy it. " He gives me another odd smile.

I'll get a kick out of the Wiccan winter solstice? I did tell him about our interfaith tree, but it still seems like a weird thing to say. He doesn't even really know me that well.

But then, he did ask me to a party. Maybe he wants to know me better.

I can live with that. Even if I do kind of wish we were going to be alone together instead.

From Shiri Langford's journal, April 20th

I called Mom on Thursday and started crying over the phone. I felt so stupid, but I couldn't help telling her everything, not about THAT but about my mediocre grades, about how I feel like such a failure and how I'm never going to be able to get into law school, about Brendan and how I'm confused about him and how I just don't know what I'm going to do.

She was giving me advice, and telling me I needed to do this, do that, keep taking my medication and just try to ride it out, that it'll all work out somehow. I wanted to laugh and weep at the same time, because she really doesn't understand that all I want is for all of it to just GO AWAY.

twelve

The pile of clothes on my bed is about a foot high and growing, but I have yet to find the perfect combination.

"So, what does one wear to a winter solstice party?" I
hold the phone to my ear with my shoulder as I toss possible shirts onto my bed from the dresser drawer.

"Black," Mikaela says. I hear her switch on a faucet on
the other end of the phone line, her voice muffled by running water. "With black shoes."

"Figured."

"And a pointy little witch hat."

"Riiiight." I smile. "Plus green makeup. You can't forget the green makeup."

"I think I've got some of that green facial goop." We both
laugh. My mom walks up and stops just outside my open
doorway.

"Sunny, honey, you're going to put those away before
you go, right?" She glances pointedly at the pile of clothes
on my bed, then sighs. She's still moping, but I don't want

to spend every second of my seventeenth birthday hanging out with her and Dad. "I don't know why you can't just wear that nice blue blouse you had on at dinner."

I resist groaning with disgust. "Mom! It's a party. I'm not wearing a 'blouse' to a party." I roll my eyes, then relent. "*Yes*, I'll put it all away." Once she clears the doorway, I toss the clothes into the back of the closet.

"*Sunny honey…*" Mikaela teases in a syrupy voice. "Sunny honey, can you please help me make a yoga scrapbook?"

"Shush," I tell her with an embarrassed laugh. I switch the phone to my other ear. "It could be worse."

"Sunny honey, you should wear something long and flowing, the better to dance euphorically around a bonfire with."

"Okay, do you know something I don't?" I dig around in the closet, pushing some of my old trendy duds to the back. "Seriously. I hope there's not a bonfire. I'm not doing any naked frolicking in the forest."

"Oh, jeez, can you imagine? Cody frolicking naked in the forest with a bunch of witch wanna-be's?"

"Hmm." Take out the witch wanna-be's and it's not an entirely unappealing image. "Hey, I've got a long skirt here. It's black with a lacy edge at the bottom."

"Sounds perfect," Mikaela says. "Really. It's just a party. They aren't going to cavort around in capes or anything. Hurry up and put it on so you can pick me up. I have to go finish my eyeliner."

It only takes me a few minutes to finish getting ready.

I put on the black skirt, a tight dark-green sweater, and my black Converse hi-tops, and I leave my hair down except for a black beaded clip on one side. I check my phone. It's seven thirty, fifteen minutes before I'm supposed to pick up Mikaela. I put on dark-red lip gloss and a quick spritz of vanilla body spray, grab her Christmas present and Cody's—a snowman ornament that I "goth-ified" with black marker—and rush out the door.

The air is cool and perfect; the sky is clear and full of stars. Happy birthday to me—and it's my first night of being able to drive Mikaela around without technically breaking the law. No more worrying about every passing cop car whenever I have friends in the car. I'd always pictured this moment differently—Cassie in the front, maybe, with the rest of the swim crew in the back—but I'm glad it's not like that.

Still, I really should call Spike. Not tonight, but maybe later.

Mikaela's ready and waiting when I pull up in front of her apartment complex. She gets in, wearing a long black velvet dress and knee-high burgundy Doc Martens and smelling faintly of sandalwood. Her eyes look huge, lined thickly with black eyeliner and some kind of smoky gray shadow.

"I've got something for you, Sunny honey," she announces, plopping a little package in my lap. It's wrapped in the Sunday comics. "It's your birthday *and* your Christmas present. Two for the price of one."

"Thanks!" I'm embarrassed and pleased at the same time. I'd told her not to worry about my birthday. "Your present's on the back seat."

"Well, I'm greedy. I want it now." She grins and unbuckles her seat belt so she can turn around and fumble in the back seat for her gift. I focus on driving and try to imagine Cody's reaction to my goth snowman.

Mikaela picks at the elaborate ribbon, which my mom tied artistically around the little package. "It's too pretty," she complains. "I'm going to wreck it."

"Just open it." I turn the car down a side street next to the Orangebrook shopping center, following Cody's directions to a strip mall I've been to a few times with my parents.

"Oh!" Mikaela draws a sharp breath. "Oh, Sunny, you jerk."

I smile. I can hear her tearing off the plastic backing attached to the bracelet I found at a funky import store. It couldn't be more perfect for Mikaela: a silver chain, inset with bits of onyx and burgundy-colored stone in jagged, irregular shapes.

"It's no big deal." I pull into the strip mall parking lot, maneuver the car into a spot under a bright lamppost, and kill the engine.

"It is. I love it. But I thought we agreed—no more than fifteen bucks." She glares at me.

"I got a discount."

She keeps looking at me. "You can't buy my love with a bracelet. I don't swing that way, anyway."

I laugh. "It was cheap. I promise. One of my dad's friends owns the store. Khan's Bazaar on Seventh, okay? Jeez. Can I open my present now?"

"Yeah, okay," Mikaela says. I can see her eyeing the bracelet, now glinting off her right wrist. "Just get it over with."

"Shut up." I tear off the newsprint wrapper. Inside, I find a small blank book with an intricately filigreed cover design, all silver spirals and knots on the black cloth cover. I turn it this way and that. The patterns glitter and twist in the dim light of the streetlamp.

"Mikaela. You drew these yourself, didn't you?"

"Little old me," she says. "And my silver marker."

"It's gorgeous!" I run one hand over the notebook reverently. She put so much thought and care into her gift. Meanwhile, I just got her some store-bought bracelet.

"It's no big deal," she says, and smiles at me. She always seems to know what to say when I freeze up. She doesn't even need to read my mind. I smile back, relaxing a little.

"Oh," she says, like an afterthought. "Cody asked me to give this to you." She rummages in her purse and throws a small paper bag in my lap, folded down at the top and stapled. "I told him it was your birthday."

I open it, curious, my stomach doing a little flip. Inside is a necklace, a slender silver chain with a tiny sun-shaped charm dangling on it.

"I pointed it out to him, but I didn't know he went back and bought it. It's cute."

It's beautiful. Too beautiful. My stomach flips over again. He probably didn't pay for it. At the same time...he was thinking about me. I fold it back inside the little bag, and slip it into my purse.

"So where's the party again? Cody didn't specify."

There's only one business still open besides the Vietnamese noodle house, and Mikaela points at it.

I look. Immediately, I cringe.

"What?" She swats my arm gently. "Let's go."

I sigh and get out of the car. "Krishna Bookstore? *Really?*"

"What's wrong with Krishna Bookstore?" She smiles at me wickedly and gestures at the hand-painted sign, complete with the Sanskrit "om" symbol in gold paint. "C'mon. It's *groovy.*"

"I know it's 'groovy.' I've been here with my parents. They bought a batik wall hanging." Not to mention the ceramic bong that my dad keeps insisting is a vase, as if I have no idea what goes on when they're laughing in his study late at night. It's horrifying. They think they're still in college.

I lock up the car and we head for the square of light spilling out of the shop window. The window display has all these crystals and geodes artistically arranged around a bunch of books with titles like *Today's Witchcraft* and *Your Psychic Potential*, and CDs of whale songs and sitar music. My dad always makes fun of that kind of crap. Never mind the fact that he's been known to shop here.

I hesitate outside for a moment. Mikaela turns back and puts her arm through mine.

"No need to be shy. I'm sure they're perfectly nice people. Even if they are friends with Cody," she says with a smirk. "Besides, you never know. You might actually like them."

"Have you even *met* them?"

She gives me a worried look. "No, but…give it a chance, huh? Cody's going to be there. I'm sure he's already here."

"Okay, okay." I slip through the door as she holds it open. A sign in elaborate loopy handwriting, taped to the glass, says "If you are here for our special event, proceed to the Gathering Room." The shop is empty, but I can hear voices wafting from an open door at the back.

"Must be where the party is," Mikaela says, gesturing toward the rear of the shop. "After you."

I start walking, see who's standing behind the counter, and stop dead. I can't believe I forgot this crucial piece of information.

"Oh, shit," I mutter. "Antonia."

"Huh?" Mikaela is distracted, fingering a crystal of smoky quartz. "Who's that?"

"She's friends with my mom," I whisper. "She works here. I totally forgot." I try to duck behind a shelf and sneak by.

It doesn't work.

"*Sun*shine! Well, look who it is! Are you here for the solstice? I never knew you were interested in witchcraft! Have you heard about our Mother Goddess Group?" She has a huge smile on her face, and, oh god, she's wearing *glitter eyeshadow*.

"Hi, Antonia," I mutter. I have to get out of here. I don't know what a Mother Goddess Group is and I don't want to. There's glitter all over her red hair, too, and she's wearing a silver sweater that clings too tightly to her ample bosom.

"We're just here because a friend invited us," I say, trying to cross the room as quickly as possible.

"Well, it's a lively little group; you'll love it. I have to mind the store during the party, but you go right on in! Have a glass of champagne—I promise not to tell your mom!" She winks at me. Mikaela gives me this cross-eyed look and I almost lose it, so I grab her arm and we flee for the back room.

We stop in the doorway. About twenty people are standing in little groups around the room, and they're all staring at us like we have horns. Or maybe like we *don't* have horns—who knows what these people are into. Most of them are older than we are, in their twenties or thirties. The walls are painted an unnerving orangey-red color, with posters of nature and diagrams of people's chakras. I recognize one of the chakra diagrams from my mom's weekend yoga sessions. Thick white candles are burning here and there throughout the room.

I feel like I'm having a very surreal dream.

There's a folding table against the wall to our left, laden with chips, vegetables, and store-bought iced Christmas cookies. Mikaela heads straight for the food, ignoring a few lingering stares. Her eyebrows are mildly raised as if she's the one in charge, as if everyone else is beneath her notice. I envy her for that; I feel like diving under the table.

Then Cody saunters in.

"Sunny, Mikaela. Hey," he says casually, as if this is all completely normal.

"Hi," I say. He flashes a sly smile in my direction and I get a not-unpleasant lurch in the pit of my stomach. Still, I'm not sure what I'm expected to do, so I join Mikaela at the food table and pour myself that glass of champagne.

"Hey, people," I hear Cody say in a louder voice, "these are the friends I was telling you about. You know, Mikaela and Sunny?" I'm not sure if it's my imagination, but it seems like he puts a little more emphasis on my name. He meets my eyes, and my mouth goes a little dry. I search his face; I want to know what he's thinking. But his expression is mild, unreadable.

Mikaela strides confidently over to one of the groups. I follow more slowly, and sip my drink. People shuffle around on the threadbare, institutional-gray carpet, making room for us.

A thirtyish woman in a dark-blue gauzy dress introduces herself as Rennie. "Welcome to the Canyon Wiccan Circle's annual solstice party," she says. "We're just chatting and enjoying the food before we officially get started." Her gaze lingers on me for a second, her eyes the artificial dark green of specialty contact lenses, and I fidget uncomfortably. Cody hangs his black raincoat on a chair in the corner and stands next to me. The soft, dark fabric of his button-down shirt brushes the bare skin of my wrist. I can smell his clove cigarettes.

I take a bigger swig of champagne.

There are a few perfunctory introductions, and then people start talking again. Obviously they all know each other, and Cody is nodding and smiling at whatever Rennie's saying like he totally gets it. I wonder if he hangs out with these people a lot.

I wonder if he hangs out with *Antonia*. The thought makes my brain want to implode. Rather than pondering the Cody-Antonia connection, I tune back in to the conversation.

"I know, I *know*, I saw him on Saturday. He totally gave me the brush-off," says this tall guy—Jake? Jeff?—in a loud voice. He's wearing a purple cloak, pinned at the neck with a silver pentagram. Underneath, he's wearing a T-shirt and jeans, an ensemble that strikes me as goofy. Nobody else is dressed that way, not even Head Witch Rennie, or whatever her official title is.

I elbow Mikaela and whisper, "I was told there would be no capes." She pinches my arm surreptitiously. I can tell she's trying not to laugh.

Jeff/Jake continues his rant. "He thinks he's all cool because he works at the Ren Faire, but it's really just an excuse to act like a snob."

"Well, you know that guy he's always hanging out with? The one who goes to Faire in black leather armor?" Rennie says this in almost an undertone, leaning forward. The rest of the group leans in eagerly. "I think that's his *boyfriend.*"

"Nuh-uh, I could have sworn he was straight!" Jake/Jeff shakes his head. There are gasps all around. I sneak a sideways glance at Cody, who looks a little bored. Gossip: not what I expected out of the evening.

I don't know what I thought would happen, though. Reciting odes to the passing of the seasons? Mixing potions out of eye of newt?

I nudge Mikaela with my left shoulder. "Hey," I whisper. "Check out Antonia." Antonia is standing in the doorway, watching the party and beaming. She's holding yet another platter of cookies, and after a minute of standing there with that inane smile, she approaches the food table and sets it down.

"Here's my contribution to the evening. I'm so glad you decided to hold your celebration here! Let me know if you have any questions about solstice traditions. We have some wonderful books in the store about—"

"Thanks *so* much," Rennie butts in, stopping the monologue. Obviously she's dealt with Antonia before. "It's great. Really. I'll let you know if we need anything."

"Okay, well, you have a beautiful time, and I wish I could join you but I have to watch the store—oh, and don't forget to try my vegan solstice cookies," Antonia chirps, her voice fading into the distance as she bustles out of the room.

Cody goes over and closes the door after her. Everyone else gradually sits down in a large, irregular circle on the carpet. Rennie produces a huge green candle from her bag and lights the four wicks before placing it in the center of the circle, then lights a stick of Nag Champa incense, which makes the room smell like my Pakistani grandma's house. She puts a few more items down: a prickly branch of holly complete with shiny red berries, a wilted sprig of mistletoe, a fragrant pine bough.

Rennie stands. Everyone else does, too. Mikaela and I look at each other, then at Cody. He gives us this serious look, almost concerned, then turns his attention back to Rennie, who spreads her arms wide and strikes a dramatic pose. Maybe things are finally going to get interesting.

"We are here at today's Yuletide solstice," she intones, "to celebrate the rebirth of the God to the Goddess, in this darkest hour of winter. O God and Goddess, see our sacred fires and bless us with peace and prosperity in the newly reborn season!" She continues in the same vein for another minute, and then there's a moment of silence, in which everyone except me and Mikaela has their eyes closed and seems to be swaying slightly. Then Rennie opens her eyes and says, "Blessed be your solstice and fertile be your spring-tide." I hide a smirk. This is more like what I expected, but it still seems kind of hokey.

Soon, everyone is standing up, smiling and hugging each other and saying "Good Yule to you." It reminds me of the time I went to Catholic mass with Grandma and Grandpa Pryce in Phoenix and everyone was shaking hands and saying "Peace be with you," only this time there's a lot more black clothing and pentagrams.

"She writes her own ritual invocations," Cody says quietly to me. "Pretty cool, right? I've been asking her about joining a real coven somewhere, a bigger group like the one in L.A. that doesn't have so many posers."

"Wow," Mikaela says. She seems impressed, or at least she's pretending to be. I don't even know what a coven entails, so I just nod and smile.

A few minutes pass, and the party fragments into small groups again. Rennie and the older, more serious-looking Wiccans are hanging out by the food table. Cody, Mikaela, and I are standing with two girls and three guys who look about our age, hovering near a back door that's been propped with a book so it's slightly ajar. An icy breeze drifts through the opening.

The guy standing on Cody's right pulls out a leather drawstring bag and rummages around in it.

My heart starts beating a little faster. Now what? The more imaginative part of my mind pictures some kind of weird bloodletting ritual with candles, a stained silver knife, and people chanting. Apparently, though, I've been watching too many bad movies. The guy pulls out a pipe made of blown glass shot through with swirly colors. As if it's no big deal to be doing this with Antonia right there in the next room, he starts packing it with really pungent-smelling pot. Out of the corner of my eye, I see Rennie glance over and frown, then shrug at Jake/Jeff and the other guy she's talking to.

I shift uneasily, wondering if Antonia's going to notice and if she would tell my parents. I don't even know what would happen if she did.

The pipe makes its way around the circle. Part of me is cringing at how lame this is, how much it reminds me of something my parents might do. But another part of me can't help feeling an illicit thrill.

By the time the pipe makes its way to Cody, it's gone out. He relights it with a Zippo he whips out of his pocket, and takes a long drag. He holds it in for several seconds, and then breathes a huge, stale-smelling cloud out of the six-inch gap in the doorway.

"Nice one," the guy who brought the pipe compliments him. And then Cody is looking at me, holding the pipe out as if he expects me to take it. I just sit there, frozen, my palms going clammy.

Am I the weird one here? I suddenly don't feel prepared for this moment. I don't actually care what my parents would say, but I don't feel comfortable with these random strangers, with Rennie and her weird eyes. I just can't do it.

Mikaela says, "Earth to Sunny. If you're not partaking, you can pass it over here."

I gingerly take the pipe and pass it to my left. Mikaela takes a puff and passes it on in turn. Nobody seems to think anything's strange about me not taking part, so I try to relax.

After a few rounds of passing the pipe around the circle, the corner of the room is hazy with smoke despite everyone's attempts to fan the evidence out the door. Someone on the other side of the room lights another stick of incense to try to mask the smell. Even though I didn't participate, I feel light-headed and strange. The swirling haze makes everything surreal, and the candle flames dance, casting flickering shadows.

I'm not sure how much time has passed, but it's been at least an hour, maybe two, since we got here. Rennie gestures for everyone to come together again, and motions for quiet. "Now," she announces, "it is time to honor someone special who is here with us tonight, one who has been truly blessed by the Goddess."

Everyone goes quiet, expectant. They're all smiling. Even I can't help being a little curious. Rennie stands tall.

"We have a true power in our midst, my friends, someone genuinely touched by the mysteries of nature. Who granted these blessings?" Rennie waves her arm, her diaphanous silver scarf billowing from her shoulder and trailing through the air as she paces back and forth before the group. "Was it the great Horned One? Was it the Threefold Goddess in her infinite wisdom?" There's a dramatic pause.

I have to resist the sudden urge to laugh hysterically.

But I'm unaccountably nervous again, too. My heart races. Maybe it's a contact high, or too much champagne.

"What is the true purpose of those who are chosen?" Rennie is looking right at me, as if I have the answers she wants. The moment stretches out for what seems like an hour. I shift my legs uncomfortably. The more she stares at me, the more I'm getting this creepy feeling like I want to run out of the room.

Finally, Rennie continues. "Perhaps, children of the Goddess...perhaps tonight we will find out."

In that minute I realize that not just Rennie is looking at me. *Everybody* is looking at me.

thirteen

"Sunny?" Rennie asks, leaning in closely, her green eyes boring into mine. "Will you be favoring us with a demonstration of your ... ability?"

I stand up. My head spins, and my throat is dry and scratchy. I swallow uncomfortably.

I look around the circle, my eyes falling on face after eager face, all looking at me expectantly, almost hungrily. There's a sick feeling in the pit of my stomach.

Somebody told them about my underhearing.

And Mikaela is the only one who knows.

I look at her, but she doesn't meet my eyes. She just looks miserably at the floor. I look at Cody. He smiles at me almost earnestly. Suddenly, everything becomes crystal clear, and then I really start to feel like the walls are closing in. I don't want to be around any of these people any more, these strangers who know my secret.

"I have to go," I manage to whisper, and I run out of the room. Rushing through the store, I hear Antonia say something questioningly, but I don't stop, I just push out the front door and keep going until I'm almost at the other end of the strip mall. I stand hidden in the shadow of a dark storefront, gulping in breaths of cold night air. A chilly breeze blows my neatly brushed hair into whorls and tangles, but I don't care.

I bend forward, my hands on my knees, until the cold air starts to clear my head. And I realize this:

One—these so-called Wiccans know about my underhearing and want me to be some kind of freak show for their personal amusement. Two—the only person I told about my underhearing was Mikaela. Three—Mikaela has never hung out with the Wiccan group before. She couldn't have told them. But Cody could have.

Since I doubt Cody has mind-reading powers of his own, that means Mikaela told him.

I squeeze my eyes shut, turn toward the wall, and press my forehead against the rough stucco. This explains a lot of the strange things he's said over the past week, like him having a "feeling" I'd really be interested in the solstice party.

I can't believe her. She had no right to say anything to anyone, not even Cody. I might have told him myself, eventually. But it's my secret to keep or give out. And I don't want to be put on display for a roomful of random strangers.

Then I realize another thing.

There's only one reason I can see for Mikaela breaking my trust. One reason why she'd tell Cody, even when I told her not to say anything to anyone.

Mikaela *wants* Cody. So badly she'll tell him anything to keep his attention.

I feel sick, and stupid. It seems so obvious to me now. All the little looks, the teasing, the play-fighting. She's completely hopeless when it comes to Cody.

And, says a tiny, mean voice inside me, *she was there first.*

When the door of the bookstore opens and Cody comes out alone, I can't even look at him. My jaw tightens. I try to stay still, hidden in the shadows. I hear his footsteps, though, and I know he's seen me. He leans against the wall next to me in his ripped, patched black blazer and puts a hand on my arm. I pull away with a jerk, but I can still feel the heat on my skin where he rested his hand.

"Are you okay?"

I look up and stare at him, hard.

"No," I finally respond, forcing the answer out through gritted teeth. I turn away.

He sighs and leans back against the wall. "Look, I'm sorry about what happened in there."

"Whatever." I start stalking toward my car, my head down. "You and Mikaela can have each other."

He follows me, a few paces behind. "Oh, come on—it wasn't that big a deal, was it? I thought Mikaela was joking, like you knew some kind of fun party trick. Like the 8 Ball. I figured everyone would get a kick out of it."

I walk faster. "She told you my one big secret, you guys talked about me behind my back, and now *everyone* knows my secret. Yeah, no big deal," I say caustically, my voice getting louder. "But you don't know. You don't know what it's been like." I stop; turn to face him. "It's real, and it's horrible, Cody."

"Hey," he says softly. "Shh. I didn't know." There's a long pause and I clench my car keys in my hand. "Listen…if something weird *is* happening to you, maybe you could use some backup, you know, in trying to figure it out. Rennie and her friends are into that kind of thing. They might be able to help. She understands more than you think. She can see people's auras. She says it's a gift."

I look at him again, not sure what to believe. He looks sincere now. Serious.

"It's none of their business," I say. "It's nobody's business." But there's a tiny doubting part of me that wonders: maybe if I'd been honest with him from the beginning, I wouldn't be in this situation. And maybe Mikaela wouldn't have decided to blurt out something exciting in order to impress him. Or if I hadn't told her? What then?

I don't know what to do. I don't know what I should have done.

I duck my head and take a step backward, away from him, toward the car.

"I just think you should think about it, is all," he says, insistently. "Maybe do some practicing on your own, try to figure out how it works." He takes a step toward me, his eyes glittering in the reflected light from the street lamp. "I know if it was me, I'd feel a lot better having some control over what was happening to me."

I feel a surge of anger. Even though part of me wants to tell him everything, he seems to already *know* everything.

"Like I said, it's my business." I face him with my arms crossed. We glare at each other silently for a minute, and then I'm not angry any more, but deadly calm. In that next moment, I see something in his eyes that looks like hurt, and I *feel* something—some kind of burning intensity of emotion that I don't know how to interpret.

—have to—
if I could just—she has to understand—

There's a bitter orange-rind taste on my tongue. Then, as quickly as I felt it, the flash of emotion is gone. Like his expression, all I get is a blank. He smiles. It doesn't reach his eyes.

I shiver. Suddenly I'm freezing, and I pull the sleeves of my sweater over my hands. But I continue staring daggers at him, because it doesn't matter what he's thinking, or even what he's feeling. It matters what he *did*. "You owe me an apology."

"I know," he finally says. "I'm sorry. I should have asked you before telling Rennie about it. I didn't know they'd put you on the spot like that." He puts his hand on my shoulder for a second and then lets it fall back to his side. I don't jerk away this time, but I'm still angry.

"Yeah, you should have asked," I say. And Mikaela should have asked before telling *him*. "Let's just drop it. I'm going to go. Can you give Mikaela a ride home?"

"Yeah, but she wants to talk to you first. She feels bad."

She should feel bad. I'm almost too furious to talk to her, but I guess I should give her a chance to explain herself.

Cody goes back in to get Mikaela. I linger outside, wishing I'd caught more than that momentary glimpse into his mind. He's always so guarded. And I'm never a hundred percent calm around him, can never quite focus properly, no matter how hard I try.

"Sunny!" I turn slowly. "Leaving without telling me?" Mikaela's falsely cheerful tone gets on my nerves. I stand there, not moving, keys dangling in my hand.

"You don't mind me staying a little longer, right?" Mikaela says, tentatively. "I can hitch a ride back with someone. I always wanted to ride a broomstick."

I don't laugh.

"Sunny, talk to me! I know it was kind of a weird scene in there, but it wasn't that bad, was it?" She sounds hopeful, like she wants to hear me say it's all okay. But it isn't okay. I want to hear her apologize, want to know that she feels bad. My hands ball up into fists.

"You told Cody," I say, my voice shrill. "I trusted you. How could you think it was okay to tell him? You didn't even ask me." There's total silence for about a minute, while I stare out at the darkened parking lot and Mikaela looks down at her feet.

Finally, she looks up. "I don't know why you're making such a big thing out of this," she says. "It's not like anything bad happened."

"A big thing?" I look at her in shock. I can't believe *she* has the nerve to sound annoyed. My head throbs.

"Yeah, a big thing! It's just Cody, for Christ's sake. I didn't think you'd care if I told *him*. But hey, I'm sorry. It just kind of slipped out."

"I didn't want you to tell anybody! Not Cody, and definitely not anyone else. This isn't just a 'fun party trick.' It's serious, and I'm scared." I cross my arms tightly across my chest. "I didn't ask for any of this. It's a problem I might have to live with for the rest of my life!" I feel an eerie echo of Shiri's voice in my words, and I take a breath to calm myself down.

"I already apologized. I don't know what more you want." Mikaela says. She stares sullenly out at the dark parking lot.

"I want tonight to have never happened. I don't want anyone to know! I don't want Cody to think I'm a freak." I pace back and forth, gritting my teeth.

"He doesn't think you're a freak," she says, exasperated. "Who even cares what he thinks, anyway? This is all his fault."

"Yeah, but..." She's right—this is his fault. Not all of it, but some of it. I think about the warm feeling of Cody's hand on my arm, his distinctive smell of clove cigarettes and soap, his smile. Then I think about how he told the Wiccans about me; how he stole the Magic 8 Ball without even thinking twice about it. How he brought me into a totally uncomfortable situation without even telling me what was going to happen. Maybe Spike was right about him. I sigh heavily.

"You *like* him, don't you?" Mikaela says suddenly. Her voice goes hard and flat. "That explains a lot." Her shoulders sag, and she leans against the lamppost behind her.

The silence stretches on for what seems like an eternity. I'm not even completely sure how I feel about Cody, but I still can't help feeling drawn to him. I don't know what to tell her. And her accusatory tone isn't helping. "*You LIKE him, don't you?*" Like she's one to talk.

"We're just friends. It's not like anything's going on."

"Yeah, whatever," Mikaela says. "You're mad at *me*, but you're all worried about what he's going to think of you? It's so obvious." She picks idly at the bracelet I gave her earlier that evening. "You know, you could've told me you like him. Isn't that what friends are supposed to do, share important feelings and bullshit like that?"

"I don't know how I feel, okay?"

"Sure you don't." Her voice is bitter. "I told you about my mom. My family. I don't just tell that to everyone. That's important to *me*. I shared that with you." I hear her take a deep, shaky breath. "The least you could do is be straight with me about liking Cody. If you can't even be honest about that, how do I know you told me the truth about anything else? How do I know you didn't just make it up for attention?"

I jerk my head up to glare at her. I know she's just angry, that she can't possibly mean it, but I can't seem to control myself.

"I don't need attention," I say in a furious whisper. My voice is raw and rough. "I don't *want* attention. That's why this whole night was such a disaster. You don't understand what it's been like for me. Nobody does! Those stupid people at the party have no idea. Obviously you don't, either."

"Are you saying I'm stupid?" Her voice is dangerously quiet.

"I'm not saying you're stupid. I'm just saying you don't understand."

"Oh, I understand. I understand a lot. I understand you want other people to feel sorry for you and all *your* problems. Well, other people have problems, too, and if you really could *read minds* or whatever, you'd know that."

I stand there, stunned. Mikaela almost flings herself back in the direction of the bookstore and disappears inside.

I don't watch her go.

I don't sit there wallowing in my problems.

I don't even think about what's going to happen now that Cody knows my secret.

Because all of a sudden, I understand something, too. Confusing and messy and impossible as my life has been, as envious and even threatened as I've felt by Mikaela's confidence, her individuality, her artistic talent, her interesting friends … *she's* felt threatened by *me*.

Mikaela is scared of me.

And it feels terrible.

From Shiri Langford's journal, May 2nd

I only have a couple more weeks to bring my grades up before the end of the semester. I was able to talk Professor Macken into giving me an extra-credit assignment, but the rest of my classes are depending on finals. I have to keep my grades high enough to keep my tennis scholarship. I have to.

When I talked to Mom on Friday, she said something

really weird, something that made me wonder about THAT and why it's happening and whether she knows more than she's letting on. I didn't exactly tell her everything, but I told her that sometimes I feel like I know what other people are thinking, and it makes me sad, and she said this: Shiri, sweetie, there are a lot of grim things in this world, a lot of unpleasant people. But no matter what's happening, you can't control what other people think, even if it makes you sad; you can't change them. You can only change your own mind and your own life.

It made me cry. And it made me wonder: does THAT happen to Mom, too? Or something like it? Is it genetic? If it is genetic, how, WHY does it happen?

I don't think I'll ever understand. I'm not sure I'll even pass undergrad biology.

fourteen

Hot tears are running down my face before I've even pulled out of the parking lot and onto the main road. I can't face my parents right now. I don't even want to face myself. I've been so stupid, so naive.

Instead of going back across town, I get on the freeway and drive.

The road winds between rocky dark hills covered with the lights of tract houses, and all four lanes are busy with holiday traffic, but I can hardly focus on any of it. I can't stop thinking about the party, with all those eager, hungry faces staring at me; about Mikaela's anger; about how I'm back where I started, alone and friendless.

After about twenty minutes I get to the cutoff for Pacific Coast Highway. I drive for another mile or two, then I pull my car onto a short dead-end street with bungalows on either side, get out and lock the doors, and climb past the guardrail that separates the road from the sand. A chilly, salty breeze cuts through my sweater, but it feels good.

Cold sand filters into my shoes as I walk. I drop down into a crouch, my breathing ragged, and hunch over, listening to the sound of the waves and trying to understand.

The half-moon is bright. I see the silhouette of a couple walking along the sand, close to the water. A dog runs after them, dashing in and out of the waves. I look down, waiting until they go past, and then stare back out at the ocean.

The reflection of the moon breaks along the water's choppy surface. It's what my heart feels like—scattered in a million confused pieces.

Mikaela shouldn't have told Cody. That's what makes me angriest. But Cody's the one to blame for blabbing to a bunch of strangers. He must not know me very well if he thinks I would *want* people to know about this. And me—I should have been more honest from the beginning, or I shouldn't have said anything at all.

My phone vibrates. It's probably my mom, wondering where I am. I ease myself into a seated position and dig my fingers into the cold, damp sand, feeling the grit work its way under my fingernails, trying to delay the inevitable.

I should never have told Mikaela. There's only one person in the world who might, just might have understood what's happening to me. One person I'll never be able to talk to again. My jaw muscles tighten; my fingers dig more painfully into the sand. I'm convinced that Shiri went through what I'm going through now. And she might have been able to help me or comfort me, but instead she left me alone on this earth, alone with nothing but this—this curse of a "power."

Stupid. I'm angry at someone who's dead. There's something mean about it, too; something petty and small. Guilt takes over, and I wrap my arms around my knees, feeling completely miserable.

We'll always have yesterday... and today, and tomorrow, her note said. Whatever that means. The truth is, I was left with an awful lot more than that. This... aloneness, this horrible knowledge, is something I never would have asked for.

Something occurs to me then. What if she somehow did "leave" me this ability? The first time it happened was the day she died. What if her death triggered it somehow?

I can't imagine how that could even be possible, scientifically speaking. But somehow, something did happen. Even Shiri thought it could be genetic; she said in her journal that her mom was always unusually sensitive to the emotions around her. If Auntie Mina could underhear, there's no way she'd ever have married Uncle Randall, but if her sensitivity is related somehow... it's a theory, anyway. Nothing else even comes close to making sense.

After a while, I finally relax a little. Periodic snatches of laughter reach me on the breeze, wafting by from someone's patio and interrupting the quiet rustling of the waves. The moon is bright, and the cold of the sand seeps through my thin skirt, making my butt numb. An occasional car roars by on the highway.

My phone vibrates again. I pull it out of my purse to check. Another call from my mom, even though it's only nine thirty. I start to get a horrible feeling that she might have heard something from Antonia about the party, so I reluctantly haul myself up and walk back to the car.

I drive home with the radio off, and soon my angry circling thoughts return. I can't believe Mikaela thinks I'd be self-absorbed enough to assume I'm the only one with problems. I know she's got family issues and doesn't get along with her dad. And I know she trusted me, confided in me. But I don't know why she's so threatened by the idea that I might like Cody when they've been friends for so much longer; why she's so angry at me for not saying anything about it. I *did* confide in her—I told her the biggest secret I've ever had in my entire life. Whether I like Cody or not is nothing compared to that. I told her about my underhearing—and look what happened.

I try to relax my clenched muscles, and I take purposeful, deep breaths in and out as I signal for the freeway exit and merge onto Citrus Valley Boulevard. I can't stay furious like this. My mom says that anger builds up inside you if you let it and it can cause all kinds of health problems. My stomach hurts, so I think she's probably right.

Breathe in. Breathe out. I turn the corner onto my street. In. Out. In. Out. Almost home. I pull into the driveway.

Then my mother's voice shatters the silence in my head.

—you can't go there you can't don't please Al please listen! please come back—

Overwhelmed with an urgency I'm not sure is even mine, I slam on the brakes, kill the engine, and run for the front door.

By the time I've rushed inside, my parents are already halfway down the hall leading to the garage. My mom has hold of my dad's arm, tugging at it, and they're talking over each other in frantic, urgent voices—my mother hushed as if someone might overhear, my dad uncharacteristically loud.

"Just let me do this," my dad says, almost in a shout, trying to pull away. "Mina needs me right now."

"You *can't* go over there!" Mom's voice is desperate. My dad's face is red with anger. Obviously Mom told him about what happened to Auntie Mina, her arguments with Uncle Randall. Or maybe she didn't. Maybe something else happened, something awful. I shiver, and goose bumps raise the little hairs along my arms.

Dad says in a ragged voice, "All I know is, Randall cannot keep doing this." I've never heard him sound like this before.

"Please, just wait until tomorrow," my mom says, her face drawn and tired. She tries to pry the car keys out of my dad's hand, unsuccessfully. "I don't want you trying to talk to that man until you cool off a little."

"There's no cooling off about this. I have to do something." He yanks his hand back out of my mom's reach and takes another step toward the garage. "He could be hurting her again right now. God, I tried to tell her from the beginning what a mistake it was to marry him."

I quickly move past them and lean against the door to the garage, my arms crossed so I don't tremble, until they notice me standing there. My mom gives me this complicated look of apology and anxiety and frustration.

"Sunny," she says. "I tried to call you. I was worried. You

were supposed to call when you left the party. Instead hours go by, and what do I hear from you? Nothing."

My mouth opens, then closes again. I can't even force out a perfunctory excuse because I'm still focused on my dad, his thunderous expression, his uncharacteristic anger. It scares me. It makes him look like a stranger.

"Dad," I finally force out, my voice raw. "Don't go over there. Please. We'll figure something out. We'll help Auntie Mina." I reach one hand back and block the doorknob, as if that will help. Tears are spilling down my cheeks. "Just tell me what happened."

He sighs heavily and leans against the wall, letting his keys drop to the ground. "Sunny, I don't know . . . I'm not sure we should involve you in this."

"I'm already involved!" Suddenly I'm exhausted, too exhausted to stand, and I sink to the floor. I look down at my crossed legs. "I know she called. I know about him 'grabbing' her."

"Oh, really?" Dad looks down at me, frowning. "Funny; I only heard about that tonight, myself. Why? Because your mother talked to Mina again today, and she said Randall hurt her *again*." He straightens up, starts pacing the hallway. "He twisted her wrist and threatened to cut off her access to their bank accounts. And you know why? Because she told him she wants them to spend some time apart to work things out. It is not a healthy environment for her in that house, I'm telling you."

"Al, listen," my mom begins, in her calmest, most soothing everything's-going-to-be-just-fine tone. "I'm sorry. I should have told you right away the first time she called. But Mina said it would blow over." Her voice is pained now. "Honest to God, I believed her. She made me promise not to say anything."

"Oh, is that right." Dad's voice is bitter, and I cringe. "But you still told Sunny? You told her and not me? No guys allowed?" He looks at Mom steadily.

"I guessed about the phone call," I blurt out. "Mom didn't tell me."

"That's a pretty uncanny guess." Dad glares at me.

"It's true! I..." I hesitate for a moment, then realize I have something to say. Something important. I stand up again. "That Sunday, when we were over at their house for dinner, I helped Auntie Mina clean up. When we were in the kitchen..." I swallow, hard, past a lump in my throat. "I saw a bruise on her shoulder. She said it was an accident, but..."

"Oh, God—" Mom chokes off whatever she was going to say. My dad stands up straight again, his face dark with rage, and clenches his fists at his side as if he's trying not to hit something. I shrink back, despite myself.

He'd never hurt anyone. I don't *think* he would. Maybe he's planning to make an exception for Uncle Randall.

"Deb." Now he sounds deadly calm, despite the expression on his face, his tense body language. "You're right. If I go over there now, I might make things worse. Or I might just kill him outright," he adds in a not-very-quiet undertone. "But—"

"Dad!" Now I'm yanking his arm as he starts to walk purposefully back toward the kitchen.

"I'm not going anywhere, Sun. *But*," he says, shaking me off, "I am going to pick up that phone and call my sister."

Mom follows us into the kitchen and sits at the table, massaging her temples. "Fine. But if Randall picks up, you are *not* going to yell at him, you are *not* going to threaten him! Please promise me you're just going to talk for now."

Dad stops. He sighs, then nods.

I don't say anything, but I pull up a chair next to my mom and press the heels of my hands into my forehead. Since the moment I ran through the front door, nothing has seemed quite real. Just when I was getting used to everything that's changed, my life feels strange and unfamiliar again. Even our kitchen, with the same green-striped curtains and boring beige countertops we've had since I was a kid, seems like someone else's kitchen. I hunch over, picking at a shoelace. Then my new shoes remind me of Mikaela and I don't want to think anymore.

I snap back into focus at the soft beep of the phone's "talk" button. My dad is holding the cordless, pacing back and forth as he waits for someone to pick up on the other end. I lace my fingers together and twist them tightly until my knuckles pop.

"Mina," my dad finally says, his whole voice a sigh of relief. My hands instinctively relax. "You're okay?" It's a question, not a statement. Mom and I sit there waiting. I hold my breath and sit as quietly as I can, though there's no way I can hear what Auntie Mina is saying on the other end.

"Okay, well, we were worried about you." My dad's voice barely hides his tension.

"Why? You know why!" He sounds incredulous now. "You called Debby again. And Sunny said—" He breaks off after my mom shoots him a warning glare. There's silence on our end for a moment. I don't know if Mina is talking to him or if they're both just sitting there saying nothing.

"But, today when you talked to—okay," he finally says, quietly. "Well . . . " He seems at a loss, lost, his eyes sad now instead of angry. "Just—if anything else happens—if you— we're here, Mina." I look away, stare at the patterns of texture on the ceiling, confused. It seems like Auntie Mina is blowing him off, telling him nothing's going on. But we all know that isn't true.

"Are you sure there's nothing we can do? Do you want me to come get you? You can stay here until . . . as long as you want."

There's another long pause.

"Okay. Oh . . . Okay. Call if you need to. Yep. Bye."

"Oh, honey—" Mom jumps in as soon as Dad hangs up. "There's something very wrong here. It doesn't take a genius or a psychic to know it." I fidget. Tears pool in the corners of my eyes. "I think Randall must know she said something to me," Mom continues. "I'm so sorry I didn't tell you the first time she called."

"He'd better not hurt her again or he'll have me to answer to," Dad says, as if he's an action hero who can solve everything with a good kung fu scene: *Dorky South Asian Professor Man! Beware his hairy knuckles of fury.*

"Oh, honey, really. But I'm at a loss. She asked us not

to interfere. Even though we can *see* how bad things are," my mom says grimly.

"But what if she only said that because Uncle Randall was listening in?" I put in, stretching my legs out in front of me. My parents look at me, startled, as if they've forgotten I'm here. I'm surprised my mom's feminist training isn't rearing its head, that she isn't going on the warpath with *Ms.* magazines in hand to rescue Auntie Mina from oppression. I guess things are more complicated when it's happening in your own family.

"Oh, Sunny," my mom says, and sighs. "I hope you're wrong. I have faith in your Auntie Mina, that she's strong enough to tell us if and when she needs us. In the meantime, let's keep an extra close eye on her, okay? All of us."

I can't help wondering if that's true—or if she'll just suffer in silence. Like Shiri, who didn't even feel like she could talk to me, who took it all out on herself.

And then I wonder: What if I'd been able to listen in on Auntie Mina's house somehow? What if I'd been able to stop Uncle Randall *before* he hurt her?

My mouth goes dry. If Shiri had been able to under-hear, if she'd known her dad was like that…why didn't *she* make it stop? Then I realize: in her own awful way, she did.

fifteen

I pull the blankets up to my chin; then I break into a sweat, my skin crawling with heat, and kick the covers off again. Five minutes later, I'm cold. A lone annoying bird wakes up early and starts squawking in the tree outside.

It's four a.m.

I haven't been able to sleep, despite tea, despite Pixie snoozing at my feet, despite soothing music and candles and exhaustion. My thoughts keep bubbling up, making me toss and turn. When I do start to fall asleep, I doze fitfully, dreaming about being smothered in voluminous Wiccan robes, half-waking when I think I hear Shiri or Auntie Mina calling out for me, waking fully just long enough to realize it's only a dream.

At breakfast, I force down half a bowl of granola cereal. The rest of it turns to soggy mush as I sit there trying to avoid my parents' eyes. In our silence, we all know what isn't being said. On top of that, there's everything else that happened to me last night, before I got home. After Mom's one outburst about me not calling when I left the solstice party, she didn't ask about it again. And I can't help feeling sorry for myself, not that I want to talk about it.

It's like Shiri's absence tore a hole in our family; but that hole, instead of gradually going away, is like a black hole, expanding to take up more and more space.

I can't bear to sit here anymore, watching my mother sigh over her coffee while my dad stubbornly reads the same page of *Backstage* magazine over and over, so I dump the rest of my cereal in the garbage disposal.

"I'm going to make a phone call," I mumble, heading for the stairs.

Closing the door of my room, I pick up my phone from where it's lying on my desk. If I don't talk to someone about *something*... I feel a throbbing start in my temples, and I dial a number I haven't dialed in a long time.

It rings three times, then he answers.

Singing.

"Here comes the SUN, do-do-do-do, here comes the SUN, and I say, ooh yeah, it's all right, *ner ner ner ner ner nerrr*—"

"STOP. Now." I interrupt Spike's painful ruination of the Beatles song he always used to tease me with, only to hear his mom's faint Georgia twang in the background.

"Spencer, is that Miss Sunny you're torturing with your yowling? Sweet girl. Say hello to her for me. It's been ages." Hearing her voice makes me a little sad.

"So, the elusive Little Miss Sunshine herself," Spike says,

sounding muffled like he's chewing on something. "My mom says hi. As you probably heard."

"Yeah," I say, cautiously. "Look, do you have a few minutes? Are you eating or something?"

"Yeah, sure," he says. "I mean, sure, I have a few minutes. I just grabbed an extra piece of bacon. I'm done eating."

"You're never done eating," I scoff, before I can stop myself.

But Spike laughs, and I hope that means things are still okay between us, more or less. "Like you'd know," he says. "You've missed at least three barbecues. For all you know, my eating habits have undergone a complete transformation."

I grimace. "Sorry. I should have called sooner." I look out the window at the leaves fluttering against the grayish-blue sky.

"Yeah. Well, I could have called, too. You know I don't call people, though." His tone is light, but sort of brittle. "Plus I figured you were busy with your new friends," he adds pointedly.

"Oh, God, Spike, I—" My voice breaks, and I clear my throat. "Listen, everything is crazy right now. I don't know what to do. I had a huge fight with Mikaela after this party, and then I found out that Cody—she and Cody—I don't know. Why does everything have to be so complicated?"

He's silent for a minute and I squeeze my eyes shut, wondering if anything I just said made sense.

"I thought things would be simpler if I just started fresh," I add. "But they're not."

"Sunny … you know I'm not good with this kind of

thing." Spike's voice sounds pained. "I mean, why are you telling *me* all this?"

Almost in a whisper, I say, "Because maybe you were right. About them."

Silence.

"And I'm ... sorry I was such a bitch about it. That wasn't fair." Saying those words feels like I'm forcing out broken glass, but I can't help thinking about what Spike said, that he didn't trust Cody or his friends. I feel my chest constricting, like I'm about to cry.

"*Oh,*" he says. "Well, yeah, I heard some rumor about Cody getting arrested last year. But I don't even know if it's true. And I don't really know the rest of those people. I recognize one or two, I guess." He pauses. "You seem pretty buddy-buddy with that one girl, the short one with the braids. Is that who you're talking about?"

"Yeah. She told Cody something that should have been a secret. She shouldn't have said anything. *I* shouldn't have said anything. I'm so stupid."

"So what's this big secret?"

It sounds ridiculous, trying to tell him what happened without telling him about underhearing. It makes the whole thing seem insignificant. But I'm not ready to tell him everything yet, so I decide to lie.

Not a huge lie. Just a little one. A rearrangement of the truth.

"It's just ... there's been a lot going on in my family since Shiri died. Her mom—my Auntie Mina—has been having some marital problems. Her husband is kind of…" I swallow, and then I say the word I've been avoiding. "Abusive."

"Uh huh," Spike says, sounding uncomfortable.

I cross my fingers. "Anyway, I was telling Mikaela about some private stuff, and she told Cody, and…I found out last night at a party that she told him. Then we had a big argument about it and I'm pretty sure she never wants to talk to me again."

"Sunny."

"Yes."

"I'm going to have to be honest here."

"Okay." I sit forward, hunched, hugging my knees.

"Listen, and think about it. How many times did Cassie blab something you or Elisa or I told her to the rest of the group without even blinking?"

"Uh…" I don't want to think about Cassie. Is he *trying* to upset me?

"Remember the time she told everybody in our bio class about that pool party at James's house, when Mike sneaked in on Elisa in the bathroom while she was changing into her bathing suit and ran off with her bikini top? And then Cassie couldn't stop laughing about it?"

"Yeah," I say, sullenly.

"Do you really think Elisa *wanted* her to talk about that? And the time Cassie told Jenny Alvarez that my voice didn't finish changing until the end of freshman year?" Spike continues. "I was in love with Jenny Alvarez. That was a completely cold thing to do. But that's just Cassie. You can't tell her anything. She has boundary issues."

"Yeah, she doesn't *have* any boundaries," I say, and we both laugh a little, awkwardly. "But what does that have to do with this?"

"I'm just saying, Cassie told your 'secrets' to everyone on a regular basis, and you guys were still friends. I don't see why it's such a big drama just because what's-her-name's doing it."

"But—" I stop. This secret—it isn't like other secrets. But I can't tell him. Not yet. Now that we're finally talking again, like we used to, I don't want to make things weird.

"Fine," I force out. "I guess I'm being melodramatic. Thanks."

"Just call me Dr. Phil."

"Whatever." I sigh. "Dr. I-Have-No-Sympathy."

"Oh yeah—I'm still having my New Year's Eve party this year. My mom said to tell you. You should totally come. Oh, and *brriiing beeer,*" he adds in a stage whisper.

"Uh huh." We both know the likelihood of me showing up is pretty low, but I'm touched. "Well ... thanks," I tell him. "If I don't make it, tell everyone I said hi."

"Sure thang, sweet thang," he says, sounding like the old Spike again.

I hang up and put my head in my hands.

When I tried to explain my fight with Mikaela to him, it seemed so petty because I couldn't tell him the real reason for it. And telling him about Mikaela liking Cody would only have made it sound worse, like I was a jealous third wheel, like it was just a fight over a guy.

On top of that, he made me sound like a pushover because I always used to go along with whatever Cassie said.

And he's right. I did used to go along with it, used to laugh even if I didn't think it was funny. Am I being a hypocrite? Why do I expect so much out of Mikaela, when I always forgave Cassie? I'm not sure I understand it myself. I guess I'm not the same person anymore.

A while later—I'm not sure how long—I'm awakened from a doze by the doorbell. I look at the clock next to my bed: 4:15. The afternoon sun is already low, shining the last of the weak winter light through my window. I wonder who's here. I yawn and stretch my neck, stiff from falling asleep half-sitting up, and head downstairs.

I'm halfway down when I see my mom and dad open the door. Framed against the bare branches of the oak tree in our front yard is Auntie Mina, her face pinched but set with determination. Nobody says anything. Then the silence is broken with a loud thud, and I jump. It's a black suitcase, heavy and overbalanced, tipping over onto the front porch. Auntie Mina's suitcase.

From Shiri Langford's journal, May 20th

I had a fight with Brendan. We've never fought before. I forgot to call him to tell him tennis practice was going late and I wouldn't be able to meet him at the falafel place. I forgot. I honestly did. I was just playing so hard and knew I had the practice set in the bag and I forgot.

I tried to tell him. I got falafels and brought them by his apartment and he wouldn't even talk to me. He just sat there silently. I pleaded with him, begged him to talk to me. He finally said he waited an hour before he decided I'd blown him off. Was I with someone else?

I can't believe he would think that.

I fell apart. Then he apologized. His last girlfriend cheated on him. When I heard his thoughts the first time, all those months ago, he was feeling so betrayed and so vulnerable, and now I realize it was about her. I should have realized. I should have known. It's my fault.

sixteen

Mom and Dad lunge for Auntie Mina, all three of them talking at the same time. Mom hugs her, gently, and my dad holds her at arms' length, looking her up and down as if he's examining her for injuries. Maybe he is. I creep down the last few stairs and stare at her hard, as if I can figure out what happened just by reading it in the lines of her face, the wrinkles of her disheveled blouse.

Auntie Mina looks up at me briefly. Her gaze is steely, and I feel a surge of hope.

She says to my parents, "I don't want to impose, but..."

"Don't be silly," my mom says. "Here—come sit and have a cup of tea. Of course we'll help. Of course you can stay." She slides an arm around Auntie Mina's shoulders and steers her into the kitchen. My dad grabs the handle of the enormous suitcase.

"Sunny," he says, sighing. He lugs the suitcase inside and sets it in the front hallway. Frown lines crease the middle of his forehead as he glances at me distractedly. "Could you please check the guest room? And put out another towel."

Resentfully, I rush through prepping the guest room and go back downstairs to the kitchen. Dad glances at me as I pull up a chair. Auntie Mina is sitting next to him, her head resting on his shoulder, tears running down her face. My mom hands her a clean dishtowel and she wipes her face absently. I desperately want to ask what's going on, but my mom shoots me a quelling look. I bite the inside of my lip.

There's a long silence.

"We'll do everything we can," my dad finally says. "We can get you a new cell phone if you're worried about him harassing you."

"I don't think that's necessary," Auntie Mina says, straightening a little. "He just needs time to cool off. He didn't hurt me." My dad looks at her hard. An unspoken *this time* hangs in the air. "It was just an argument. But I've had enough."

"Mina, the guest room is yours for as long as you need it," my mom says. "We can talk more about the trial separation tomorrow. Just relax now."

"Thank you," she says, her voice thick with emotion. I'm not sure what to do, so I push the mug of tea closer to her. She grabs my hand, grips it almost desperately.

"Sunny, I should thank you, too. I know this must be disruptive for you. And so close to Christmas."

"I—no, it's okay." I'm taken aback, tongue-tied.

"You've always been such a treasure," she says, out of nowhere. "We'll get to spend some time together. I'm looking forward to that. I've missed you. You're growing up so fast." She sniffles a little. I want to pull away, but I don't. My body is tense, though. How long is she going to be here?

All I want to do is get past everything that's happened. Now I'm going to be reminded of it every day.

———————

That night, upstairs in my room, I close the door and take Shiri's journal out of my desk drawer. I run a hand over the battered faux-leather cover, but I don't open it. I could show it to Auntie Mina. Would Shiri have wanted that? I don't know. It wouldn't make things normal again. It wouldn't make Auntie Mina happy again, and it wouldn't bring Shiri back. And I feel just as powerless. I can't go back in time and do things differently. I can't go back and be a better cousin, a better friend. And so what if I'd sent her more emails, called her more often? Would it even have mattered?

I clench my jaw against unshed tears. I can't answer those questions. She stopped really confiding in me once she left for college; I think she started to change even before that. But I didn't notice. I don't think any of us did.

"Oh, I'm writing a paper about the existentialists for my philosophy class," Shiri said. It was a couple of weeks after she started college. She sounded excited about her classes, upbeat and energetic.

"Yeah?" I moved the phone to my other ear and absent-mindedly clicked the computer mouse, scrolling through the photos she'd emailed me from Blackwell Cliffs: her new dorm friends, scenes of the campus, an odd one of Shiri looking pen-

sively out a café window at the autumn leaves, her eyes shaded by a floppy knit hat. "What's that all about?"

"You'll read about it in English next year...Existentialists believed we live in an indifferent, uncaring universe. That life is basically meaningless and we're all essentially alone," she went on. I wasn't sure how something that sounded so depressing could get her so charged up. "So I'm going to try to refute that—that we're not essentially alone, that it IS possible to truly know other human beings. That the universe DOES care—and sometimes it's even out to get us."

I can't prove it, but I'm convinced now that she was talking about underhearing. By then, she'd been living with "that" for nine years.

If I'd been Shiri...if I had Uncle Randall for a father and I'd been underhearing his thoughts for years, totally unable to control it...maybe she had good reason to feel like the universe was out to get her.

————

On Christmas Day, my mom cooks up her usual huge brunch, complete with pancakes and a mystery-meat casserole. We light up the interfaith tree and open our small presents, and Mom laughs out loud at the bright-pink beaded curtain. In the evening, my dad sips at a beer and falls asleep in the armchair, while Auntie Mina and I cuddle up under a blanket and watch *A Christmas Story*, drinking hot chocolate and eating popcorn. Shiri loved that movie. It's almost like she's there with us, giggling next to us on the couch. It's almost like old times. Almost.

Auntie Mina's phone rings late that night, when we're cleaning up the popcorn mess and rinsing the hot chocolate mugs in the kitchen sink. It's Uncle Randall. She insists on talking to him and goes into Dad's study, closing the door on him when he tries to follow. She emerges a few minutes later, her face tear-streaked but set. Dad asks her what happened, but she refuses to talk about it. Exasperated, he goes into the kitchen and bangs dishes around, cleaning up the pots and pans from dinner.

The tension builds over the next few days.

Uncle Randall calls her phone, every day. One morning at breakfast, my dad sets his coffee mug down and asks bluntly, "Why do you keep talking to the man?" He fixes her in a steady gaze, a muscle working in his jaw.

Auntie Mina shifts a little, not quite meeting Dad's eyes. "He's just trying to help me get my resignation paperwork done. I have some unused sick days that they owe me. I should be able to use that money to help out here until I find a teaching job."

"You know that's not necessary," my dad says.

"But we're very glad you're following your bliss," my mom puts in. "And that you won't be working at the same place as Randall. That was never good for you two."

"Understatement of the year," I mumble into my plate. It wasn't just "not good," it was stifling. But Uncle Randall saw her quitting as evidence that she'd had this long-term grand plan to leave him. She can't seem to see how suspicious and vindictive he is.

She claims, even now, that he isn't still harassing her.

He hasn't called our home phone or dared to show up in person yet; at least, not that I know of. But he knows Auntie Mina's here. It's only a matter of time.

———————

The chocolate-chip cookies are fragrant, golden-brown, and perfect. At least they were when I threw them onto a paper plate and covered them with foil. I'm walking fast, but I know they're going to be stuck together by the time I get to the Dohertys' place.

I won't need to worry about it, though. I'm not staying for the party, no matter what Spike says. I refuse to hang around and make nice with Cassie. Or any of the others—it's not like they've tried to call me. Elisa just gives me this apologetic little look every time we see each other at school, and when I try to say hi, she finds an excuse to run off. Fine.

I walk faster.

Spike, at least, has been more or less his old self. So I'll make a brief pre-party appearance. I need a break from my house, anyway. Mom and Auntie Mina have been in the living room all day filling out job applications. My dad has been in his office with the door closed, preparing his classes for the spring semester. Mom keeps trying to get him to come out and "be sociable," but all he says is, "Ah, you guys don't need *me*."

I don't blame him for feeling useless. Mom's been a force of nature. She made Auntie Mina an appointment with the counselor; she's helping with the job applications, the trial separation. And Auntie Mina keeps looking at me with these sad eyes, as if there's anything I can do other than remind her of what she's missing.

It's nice to get some air, even if it's chilly winter air. It's almost dusk, and the streetlights are starting to come on. As I hurry past the empty neighborhood park and cross the street to Spike's house, my phone buzzes.

It's a text, from Mikaela. Mikaela, who I haven't seen in the week and a half since our big fight. She did send me a text on Christmas Eve: SORRY I WENT NUCLEAR. HAPPY CORPORATE GIFT-BUYING HOLIDAY. I wasn't sure how to react. She was so livid at the solstice party, I assumed she didn't want to talk to me anymore. I sent back a one-word reply—THX—but still, I haven't been quite ready to forgive and forget.

And now she wants to invite me to a New Year's Eve party at Cody's house as if everything's just fine. Maybe she's over it, but I'm not sure if I am.

For now, I push her to the back of my mind and knock on Spike's front door. Mrs. Doherty opens it and almost bowls me over with a big, floral-scented hug.

"Sunny, it's marvelous to see you. Do I smell cookies? You really didn't have to bring anything."

"I'm just sorry I can't stay," I say. I even mean it, a little. I wouldn't mind hanging out if it was just Spike and his parents.

"Did you walk? You sweet girl. Let me get you something to drink." Mrs. Doherty ushers me into their spacious living area and puts my cookies on the kitchen counter with the other food. The counter, which separates the kitchen from the living room, is covered with dishes of nuts, bowls of chips, vats of dip and salsa, trays of vegetables and cheeses. A huge cooler of sodas is open on the tiled floor next to the counter.

Spike walks in from the backyard, where I can see another cooler of sodas and a scattering of folding chairs set up next to the patio furniture.

"Dude, Mom. It's like a Costco exploded in here." He grins at his mother and then wiggles his eyebrows at me. "Hey. You brought *more* food?"

"Oh, you're going to complain about that? I can take these yummy, fresh, delicious chocolate-chip cookies back home with me if you don't want them." I press my lips together, trying not to smile.

"I never said *that*." He heads straight for the plate of cookies and grabs three. "Wanna check out the setup in the back?"

I accept a glass of Coke from Mrs. Doherty and follow Spike out the sliding glass door and into their spacious backyard.

"Welcome to my palace of decadence." He gestures extravagantly at the hanging strings of white lights illuminating the back patio, the little metal lanterns decorating the raised wooden deck where Mr. Doherty installed a hot tub last year.

I try to look suitably impressed. Inside, though, I'm feeling sad. Not quite nostalgic, but I've had some good times here.

I wonder if Spike told his mom why I haven't been around lately. Maybe she's talked to *my* mom. Probably not, though. They used to be on the PTA together when we were kids, but I'm positive they don't talk much anymore.

Sometimes it seems like the world is full of dead friendships.

I'm not going to let this bother me. I stuff my feelings down, deliberately relax my tense shoulders. Spike's quiet for once, fixing one of the strings of lights back into place. The backyard is empty except for us, and peaceful. A breeze whirs lightly past my ears, I shiver, and then—faintly—I hear voices:

> *—going to be SO fun, Spike's best party yet, can't wait*
> *to see everyone—*
> *—first party with Elisa and me as a couple—*
> *will she—will we—*
> *—hope this color doesn't make me look pale—*

Elisa. James. Cassie. I shake my head back and forth a little. My breath catches at their excitement, their happiness. The corners of my mouth turn up involuntarily. Then the elation dissipates like water running down a drain, leaving me feeling insignificant and small. My hands clench at my sides. Their happiness—it's got nothing to do with me.

Obviously they've moved on with their lives.

And now it's my turn.

Spike says something about James's brother's band playing during the party, and then he whispers something to me about the "special punch" that Cassie is bringing, but it doesn't matter. I hear the doorbell ring inside. It's time for me to go.

I hug Spike on my way out the side gate, surprising him.

"Sure you don't want to stay?" He cocks his head like a little puppy. "I have it on good authority that the punch contains only the finest generic vodka. And you don't have to talk to Cassie."

I shake my head. "I'm supposed to be home."

I don't belong here. I know that. Even though, when I look at Spike, I think about all the times I spent here before we met Cassie, and I feel like I'm already home.

———

It's the Monday after Winter Break. I drive to school feeling relieved to get out of the house, but I'm also apprehensive because today's the day I'm determined to talk everything out with Mikaela. We need to settle this. I know I want to. I know she wants to; she sent me enough emails over the break, though all I did in response was text her to say Happy New Year.

She has to know the things she said were unfair.

And I need to know that I can trust her.

My morning classes blur by. The lunch bell rings at the

end of fourth period and I'm startled enough to jump. I grab my backpack and grit my teeth.

After buying a diet soda, I walk as calmly as I can toward the back of campus, but my steps start to drag. Maybe she's going to want to keep fighting about this. It doesn't matter. I still have to talk to her. And at some point I need to figure out what to do about Cody. He needs to understand that this isn't just a joke, a trick. That this is serious, and my underhearing is real.

I hitch my backpack up and finger-comb my hair before rounding the corner of the art building. My stomach churns. I step around the back toward the awning.

Everyone's there. It looks like that first week I started sitting with them, before I broke into their tight-knit little group. Mikaela is standing at one end talking animatedly to Cody. She laughs and thumps him on the head. Cody flips her off. Becca is putting on burgundy lipstick. David is drawing in his sketchbook. Andy and a couple of his friends, dressed nearly identically in concert T-shirts and black jeans, are eating cafeteria pizza.

I stride forward before I lose my nerve. I head for an empty half-spot at the opposite end of the table from Cody and set down my brown paper lunch bag. Becca says hey, and David looks up briefly and smiles. Nothing seems out of the ordinary. Nobody seems to know what happened over the break.

Small favors.

I glance out of the corner of my eye at the other end of the bench. Mikaela looks at me and ... doesn't *smile*, exactly, but the corners of her mouth twitch into a sort of grimace. Cody just gives me a long, considering look. My hackles rise. I wonder if they've been talking about me. Again.

I'm not going to let it get to me. I pull out my sandwich and carrot sticks and start eating. After a few minutes, I catch myself smiling at something Becca says. Slowly the tension in my body eases. Mikaela walks to our side of the table to get something out of her messenger bag and says quietly, "Are we okay? You never answered my emails."

"That depends," I say. I swallow hard. "Got a few minutes to talk?"

She nods. When I get up a few minutes later and start walking, she grabs her bag and follows me around the corner. The ground is damp from an earlier drizzle, so instead of sitting, we stand awkwardly a few feet from each other.

"So, talk," she says. "I know you have something to say. You were glaring at me all through lunch."

"I wasn't glaring," I start, my voice croaking a little. I clear my throat. "Look. The last time we . . . after the party. I was really mad."

"Well, I was too," she says, staring over my shoulder at the jasmine. Then she sighs and looks directly at me. "I have to be honest. I was pissed. I felt like you didn't understand anything about me, even though you have this . . . you know. *Thing.* I felt like you should just be able to automatically, like, read my mind and figure it all out, know exactly what to say."

I open my mouth, then close it again.

"I know that's not true; you told me how it worked. But

that's the thing!" she bursts out, starting to pace back and forth. "You told me all this stuff about—you know. And it was hard to deal with. I freaked out. I couldn't handle it myself. So I told Cody. But I swear I didn't know he was going to tell anyone! I didn't know what to do during that stupid party. I was mad at him, and I was mad at you for running out and leaving me in there. But I'm sorry I yelled at you, okay?"

This is too hard. I don't know what to say. She's apologized, but she still sounds mad, and I'm still upset. And I don't know how to make it better between us.

"I shouldn't have said anything," I say miserably.

Mikaela lets out a frustrated noise. "No, that's not it. Don't think that. *I* shouldn't have said anything." She fidgets restlessly, shifting from foot to foot. "This sucks. It really does."

She looks at me. Even though she sounds angry, her eyes are pleading, as if she wants to say more but doesn't know what or how.

I sigh. "What if we just agree to be done fighting? Can we just … decide to be okay?" I'm still mad, but I don't know what else to do. We're at a stalemate, but we both regret what happened. We're both sorry.

"Yeah," she says. She looks relieved, and the tension in the air seems to dissipate a little. She moves as if to head back to the picnic table. But I still have something I need to say.

"Mikaela, wait." She stops and turns toward me again. "I didn't realize I felt that way about Cody. That's why I didn't say anything. I didn't realize you—that you—" I clear my throat. "If you guys are together—I didn't know."

She grimaces; waves a hand dismissively. "We're definitely not together."

"But—"

"No. Believe me. I've tried, but he's not interested. I think he likes that Rennie chick." A mixture of feelings roil around in my chest. Relief, hope, disappointment.

She pauses for a minute and her expression grows tense again. I can see she's trying to force out something difficult, something she's not sure she wants to say.

"You know, about Cody." She looks me in the eye. "He's not evil, even if he does think the sun shines out of his own ass. He really does want to help you with your ... power."

"Uh huh. I was thinking I'd give him a few more weeks of the silent treatment." We start walking back toward our lunch table.

"Seriously, you should talk to him. He might understand more than you think. He's got family issues too." She looks off into the distance again. "And he really is sorry. I know that for a fact because I ripped him a new one after the party."

I'm surprised. Lord knows he deserved it, but I still don't know what to think. Mikaela would probably prefer to keep Cody all to herself, if she had the option. If he didn't have a thing for someone else. Maybe she wouldn't even be telling me this if she thought there was the remotest possibility of something happening between the two of them.

She's looking at me expectantly. So I say, "Maybe I will

talk to him." I smile, a little weakly. In reply, she gives me a quick, fierce hug.

"You'll get through this," she says. I'm not sure about that, but I can't help being relieved anyway.

By the time we return to the lunch table, the group is already starting to scatter. Andy and C.J. are heading to the parking lot to try to sneak a cigarette before fifth period. I wander over, trying to look casual. I peer over David's shoulder at his latest sketch—a surprisingly realistic scene of the group eating lunch—and compliment him. He looks up, startled, and grins, ducking his head shyly. I move down to the table to Cody and try to figure out what to say.

"So, ring in the new year with a bang?" Cody asks, smiling sardonically.

"Well, there was some family melodrama," I say. "I don't know if I'd call that a bang, exactly. More like a whimper."

"T. S. Eliot," Cody says with a nod. "Nice."

"Yeah, we read that one in English class last semester."

"Mrs. DeMarco?" He grins at me. I don't smile back.

"Yup. Second period. You?"

"Fourth," he says. He cocks his head, his expression mildly curious. I look away from him for a moment, watching Becca as she touches up her black eyeliner.

"So did you hang out with those Wiccans again on New Year's?" I ask pointedly.

"Nah, Becca and Mikaela and I hung out at my house," he says. "I'm seeing Rennie and her group next week, though, if you want to come."

"Uh, no thanks." I look away, scowling. "That's exactly what I don't want to do."

"Hey, I already said I didn't know they were going to put you on the spot like that." He meets my eyes with an intense ice-blue stare. A challenging stare. "But I meant what I said that night."

"What, that you thought it was all a joke? A trick?" I cross my arms.

"No!" He lowers his voice so that only I can hear. "I mean, if you ever want to practice your ... ability, or just talk about it or something, tell me." He looks contrite now. "I promise. I won't tell anyone else about it. I won't say anything about your power unless you tell me it's okay."

I frown. "Okay. Thanks."

"So ... do you think you might *want* to try to practice sometime?" He doesn't quite look at me, just fiddles with the zipper on his jacket.

"I—don't know. Maybe." I feel confused, off-balance. The bell rings, and we gather up our bags and books. I start walking toward my fifth-period physics class. Cody falls into step beside me for a minute.

"Really, Sunny," he says, leaning close enough for me to feel his breath on my ear. "Just think about it." He smiles and starts walking off toward the history classrooms. I stare after him, watching him go.

He says he wants to help me practice. He wants to help me gain control over my underhearing. And I told Mikaela I'd try to give him a chance.

I'm afraid to say no, sort of. Problem is, I'm also afraid
to say yes.

———————

When I get home after school, I immediately go upstairs
to change into sweats and then flop down on my bed with
some physics homework. *Angular momentum and collisions:
Calculate the momentum of the cue ball as it hits the 8 Ball.*
That stupid 8 Ball again. At least this time it's a regular, non-
stolen 8 Ball.

I hear a knock at the door. Hear my mother say, in an
icy voice I've never heard before, "It's *him*. I don't believe it."

I rush back downstairs. Mom, Dad, and Auntie Mina
are gathered tensely near the closed front door like a huddle of penguins.

"What's he doing *here*?" My voice comes out plaintive.

"Not now," Dad says, making a shooing motion with
his hand. I ignore him.

"You sure you don't want me to send him away?" he
says to Auntie Mina.

"No," Auntie Mina says, her voice firm. "I'll do it."

"Well, we'll be right here behind you." My mom puts
an arm around Auntie Mina's shoulder. "We don't want him
threatening you."

Auntie Mina nods and opens the door.

"Hello, Randall," she says without a single tremor in her
voice, though her hands are clenched together, white-knuck-
led.

"Mina." Uncle Randall is dressed in a dark, perfectly pressed three-piece suit, and he's holding a single yellow rose—Auntie Mina's favorite color. He says a few perfunctory hellos to my parents and smiles ingratiatingly. "Madam, I'd like to request the pleasure of your company at the Armstrongs' dinner party. Your chariot awaits." He gestures at his Mercedes, parked on the street.

My mouth drops open. He's going to a *party*. Auntie Mina has been here, crying her eyes out, and he thinks she's going to want to go to a party with him? I start to say something, but my mom hushes me. I fidget, feeling like I want to burst.

"I don't think I'm up for a party," Auntie Mina says carefully. "Not on a Monday night. I appreciate the thought, but…"

Uncle Randall's still holding out the rose. He realizes she's not going to take it, and pulls his arm back. "What does it matter if it's Monday? You don't have work in the morning," he says pointedly.

"No, not yet," she says patiently. "I'm still waiting for a job offer."

There's a long, tense pause.

"Okay, look. Mina. Can we talk for a minute?" he says. "Please?" His cajoling tone makes me grimace.

"Okay," Auntie Mina says. "Go ahead."

He clears his throat meaningfully. Auntie Mina stays silent, and my parents and I stay where we are.

"All right," Uncle Randall says shortly. "I'll get to the

point. I want you to come to this party with me, but I also want to find out when you're coming home."

Auntie Mina swallows visibly. "I ... need some time before we can have this conversation."

"It's been almost two weeks. How much time do you need?" He's almost hissing now, as if he doesn't want anyone to overhear. "We planned to attend this party months ago. The Armstrongs are expecting to see you. What am I supposed to tell them?" My dad jerks a little, and my mom places a hand on his arm.

"I don't care what you tell them," Mina says, frowning. "Tell them the truth. And I'm still figuring things out. I'll call you in a few days, okay?"

There's an ominous silence. Uncle Randall glances at his watch. "A few days, then," he says. He holds out the yellow rose again until she finally gives in and takes it from him. Then he says, in a curt voice, "I'm not sure what you think this is going to accomplish, but I hope you get it out of your system."

He turns around abruptly and walks down our front steps to his car.

And then my dad does open his mouth, but before he can say anything, Auntie Mina reaches out and shuts the door. She sags, leaning against the door with her head in her hands.

"He treats you like a child!" My dad is incredulous; angry. "And he thinks you're planning to go back to him as if nothing happened?"

"Ali!" My mom reaches out, massages one of his shoulders. "Let's all go into the kitchen. I brought home some pie from work. Come on. We'll talk more in there."

They can talk. All the words I'd been planning to say have dribbled away. It's one thing to underhear Uncle Randall thinking awful things. It's another to actually hear him say them aloud, to have his words thunder and echo in the air between us.

I follow, mutely.

———————

A few nights later, between bites of rice, Auntie Mina says calmly, "I've scheduled a phone call with Randall for Sunday. We're going to talk things over."

"What do you mean, 'talk things over?'" I say, putting my fork down. "He's had his say."

"Sunny," my dad says sharply.

Mom looks at me, frowning a little. "Sometimes you have to give people a chance to talk, that's all." I look at Dad. He's not looking at anyone, just eating mechanically and staring at his plate.

I'm pretty sure he doesn't want to give Uncle Randall any more chances.

I look at Auntie Mina. A slight smile is fixed on her face, and I have no idea what she's thinking. Is she going to go *back* to him? She'd be nuts to do that. Especially with her new job starting in two weeks; her chance at a new life.

I wish I knew for sure. I could try to talk her out of it

somehow, try to prove to Auntie Mina that she wants nothing more to do with him. I could make her promise.

Things have changed so much. When I was little, they used to seem like a fairy-tale family to me. But fairy tales, like promises, are just words.

seventeen

That night, I pick up my cell phone and scroll down my list of contacts, my fingers twitching nervously. When I reach the C's, I linger for a second on Cassie's name. I never quite managed to delete her from my phone book. I don't know why. It's not like we've talked. But deleting her entry would feel like there's no going back, ever.

I sigh and scroll down to the number I was planning to dial. Cody.

Yesterday at school, we talked again about what happened over winter break, this time without Mikaela or the rest of the group potentially eavesdropping. He said that he'd been doing a little research and had some ideas about how I could try to get control over my underhearing. I think he might actually still feel bad about what happened. I know *I've* been wishing it never happened.

No matter what I do, though, I can't change it, any more than I can change what happened to Shiri. Still, I wake up every morning and go to bed every night trying to underhear something, anything, that could help Auntie Mina. Seeing her haggard face every day, her aimless puttering around the kitchen waiting for her new job to start, is almost too much for me to bear, so I keep trying.

But I can't do it alone.

The phone rings only once on the other end of the line before Cody picks up. "Hello." He sounds abrupt and distracted. I can hear voices in the background.

"It's Sunny," I say, my stomach doing flip-flops. I rush on before I lose my nerve. Just like a race—I just have to keep my eyes on the other end of the pool. "Look, I've been thinking about what you said. So ... tell me more about what you found out." My palm is sweating and I grip the phone more tightly in my hand.

I'm not sure how far I can trust him, but I don't want to be scared anymore. I want to be in control. I almost tell him that, but he jumps in, sounding a lot more enthusiastic now.

"Oh! Okay. Yeah. Wow," he says. "I wasn't sure you would want to, but—no, it's awesome."

"Well, good." I can imagine him pacing back and forth in his fidgety way, and I smile a little.

"You know, I had a feeling you were going to call. I'm really glad you did." His voice is low, as if he wants to talk to me and only me. A tiny shiver travels up my arms at the sound of his voice ... even though I know he's into witch chicks with flowing skirts and big candles.

"Me too," I say. "So what's this advice you were talking about?"

"Oh, man. I've been reading a *lot* of stuff, books from

Rennie and some articles on the Internet, and I think there's—" Cody stops mid-sentence. I hear a woman's voice muffled in the background, impatient and a little angry.

Cody says "O*kay!*" to whoever was talking and then makes a frustrated, wordless noise into the phone.

"Sorry about that. My mom. I have to wrap it up in ten minutes."

"I can call you back," I say.

"No, that's okay. I'm just on phone restriction until to-morrow night."

"Phone restriction?" I refrain from asking for details, but I'm curious. Maybe the Magic 8 Ball incident came back to haunt him. "Okay, we could talk about it at lunch tomor-row."

"I was kind of hoping we could get together outside of school. Like maybe at your place?" He sounds eager. I can't believe he just asked that. I jump up from my bed and walk over to the window, looking out at the drizzle that coats the lawn with a wet sparkle.

"Sure," I say, but in the back of my mind I think of Mikaela and wonder what she'd say. "I'll just have to tell my parents. When were you thinking?"

"Saturday? I'm going somewhere with Andy and David at four, but I can drive over before that. I'll be off restriction by then, so I should be able to borrow the car." He snorts, then adds in an undertone, "Like they really care anyway."

"Huh?"

"Oh, Mom and Pop are into the whole authority thing.

But it's all talk." He laughs, but it doesn't sound like he's really that amused.

"Okay." I'm not sure what to say. My parents sure aren't into the "authority thing," whatever he means by that.

"Anyway, I'll see you on Saturday."

I pause, then ask, "What do you want me to ... *do* on Saturday? Should I get candles, or something?"

"Leave it all to me," Cody says, this time with a real smile in his voice. "No spectators, though, don't worry. And you might want to do a little practicing in the meantime. I read that relaxation really helps."

"Like in what way?"

"Try lying flat on your back and tensing each muscle individually then relaxing it, until all your muscles are totally relaxed. Then, if you just concentrate on the sound of your breathing, for like five minutes or so with your eyes closed, you're supposed to reach a state of heightened awareness. Rennie says it works for her."

"Oh," I say. It sounds a lot like what I tried with Mikaela, but maybe it's something I need to practice alone for a while. It doesn't hurt to try. Even though I don't like the idea that he's still talking to Rennie about me.

I hear an exclamation in the background again, the same voice I heard earlier.

"I've gotta go," Cody says. "But let me know tomorrow if Saturday works."

"Sure. Talk to you then."

"Later."

I press the disconnect button a little reluctantly, though

I know he's already gone. I almost can't believe that phone call really happened. I have a crazy feeling in my stomach, and sort of a buzzing in my head . . . and it's not entirely bad.

Except that I know I should tell Mikaela. I don't want there to be secrets in our friendship. At the same time—I want to keep this to myself. So help me, despite knowing how she feels about him, and despite not quite trusting him, I want to keep this side of Cody to myself.

———

Thursday at lunch Cody walks up to me while Mikaela's in the bathroom and hands me a stack of Internet printouts.

"These should help you out. They're about reaching that state of heightened awareness I was telling you about." He gives me a sly smile.

"Thanks." I try for a cool smile back. "Saturday's fine with my parents. They've been wanting to meet you."

That's when Mikaela walks up.

"So your parents want to meet the man in black?" she asks, looking at me steadily.

I remind myself that I haven't done anything wrong. She didn't exactly stake a claim on Cody.

Of course, neither did I.

"Cody wanted to help me with the . . . you know. Practicing," I say, all too aware of David and Becca sitting just a few feet away. "He found some information on the Internet." I wave the papers Cody gave me.

"*Ohh.*" Mikaela relaxes visibly. "Good for you. Cody

is a fountain of obscure information." She bumps his arm with her shoulder.

I can't tell anything from her expression, but what does it matter? Mikaela was the one who kept encouraging me to talk to him, saying he'd understand.

"It can't hurt to try," I finally say.

"Damn straight," she answers.

I think of our awkward truce, the fight that preceded it, the realization that she likes Cody, too. I try again to read what's behind her enigmatic smile, but I can't.

———

That night, I look at the printouts Cody gave me. "Opening Your Chakras, Step-by-Step," says one. A laugh slips out, but I did promise to give this an honest effort. The other printout has a drawing of the body's meridian lines and talks about things like *chi* and the flow of energy along invisible pathways.

There's something about the drawing that strikes me: a simple black-and-white line diagram of a person's head, but the line representing the top of the head is dotted rather than solid and there are wavy arrows labeled "energy" radiating in and out of the top of the head. The expression on the person's face is serene, their eyes half-closed as if they're at peace with the universe.

I know it's just a drawing, but that's how I want to feel.

I close my door, sit on the floor next to the bed, and light my black-cherry candle. The printout says to try to focus on something simple and hold it in your mind, something like a candle flame flickering or the sound of the breath. I concentrate on feeling my lungs fill, then empty, over and over. I start to relax, my eyes closing. I can still see the image of the flickering candle flame against the backs of my eyelids, dancing. It absorbs my attention; the pale yellows and richer oranges, the tiny dark heart of the flame.

I try to release the tension in all of my muscles, still breathing evenly, focusing my attention on that one spot in my mind's eye with the slowly fading candle flame.

Then, on impulse, I try something completely new. It wasn't exactly mentioned in any of Cody's printouts, but it seems right. My eyes still closed, I picture the top of my head as…less than solid, open to the universe, to whatever feelings or images or sensations might flow in and out. When I inhale, I imagine energy is flowing in through the top of my head as well as into my nostrils and lungs; when I exhale, I picture those wavy lines in the diagram and feel almost as though I'm breathing through the crown of my head.

I get a strange, light tingling sensation in my scalp, traveling down to my eyes and ears. I almost imagine that the top of my head…isn't there, somehow. There's a slight humming in my ears, like electricity through wires.

And then the humming grows louder, and it becomes a voice, just out of the range of my hearing; but my room is quiet, and I know it's not the sound of somebody speaking out loud. It feels familiar, though, and there's a crackle, almost a smell, that's sharp but not unpleasant, like pine needles. It's a male voice, and I feel something like frustration? Exasperation? Is it my dad? Who else would be close enough for me to hear? Then it all fades. I open my eyes.

But I'm not unhappy. More like jubilant. Amazed.

Unlike Shiri, lost in the face of her unwanted ability, I feel powerful.

I can't help the huge grin that spreads across my face. This time, it almost worked.

From Shiri Langford's journal, June 15th

Our backpacking trip is already almost over. I can't believe it's been two weeks. Last night we sat at the edge of the lake, all seven of us just watching the night sky, talking, laughing. I'd been so scared that something would go wrong while I was there, that THAT would happen while I was in the tent with Brendan and I'd have to explain why I went so still, why I was shivering and exhausted afterward.

But every night was like a party. We'd drink, get high, and stay up until the sun came up again and it was time to go, or until we were so tired we just passed out. THAT didn't happen once. I didn't even need my medication.

Sometimes I would just walk out into the woods, so different from the hills and shrubs, beaches and deserts back home, and lose myself for a while in the complete silence. I wish my head were silent like that all the time.

eighteen

Cody saunters into my front hall, wearing his usual black coat and smiling slightly. He takes in the old photos of me on the walls, the shiny brass vase on the hall table, a few pairs of shoes lying haphazardly on the floor, in fidgety, quick glances. His eyes finally settle on me, and my stomach jumps.

"How goes it?"

"I'm good," I say cautiously. "Listen, I think we should do this...somewhere else." I glance furtively into the kitchen, where Auntie Mina is busy going over paperwork for her new job. Her stuff is everywhere, and the house has seemed too full the past few weeks, like I can't get any privacy.

"Okay," Cody says, agreeably. "Whatever works." After a rushed explanation to my parents, something completely made up about a writing assignment that has to be done outside, I hurry us back toward the front door.

"I was thinking we could go over to the park," I tell him, grabbing my backpack. He nods. I don't explain to him that

I'm not ready to underhear my family yet. But I do have a plan.

I lead the way out, hyper-conscious of Cody behind me and the unfamiliar tread of his boots on my front steps. We walk most of the four blocks to the park in edgy silence, dodging four of the eight Abronzino kids playing a game of tackle football in their front yard, and then getting chased half a block by somebody's loose Chihuahua.

I'm shocked Cody's being so docile. I'd expected at least one crack about my house being smack dab in the Land of the Clones.

"Here we are, home away from home," I say as we walk onto the damp grass of the small neighborhood park across the street from Spike's house. There are a couple of bundled-up toddlers with their parents in the playground area, and two girls are kicking a soccer ball around, but nobody's at the picnic table under the trees. We go over there and I deliberately sit facing away from the Doherty house. I look at Cody, feeling awkward, shy. He perches on the edge of the table, smiling at me.

I can't help smiling back. "I have to tell you something."

"Uh-huh." Cody drums his fingers against the table, sort of like he's anxious to get started. He eyes me, looking down from his perch and making the butterflies start all over again. I wonder if he notices I'm wearing the necklace he gave me, the little sun charm.

"I tried last night. Some of the stuff you printed out for me. It…" I swallow. "I think it almost worked."

"It did?" Cody sits up straighter.

"Yeah. Well—at least, I heard something. A voice. Maybe my dad. I couldn't make out the words. But I think…I think I'm almost there." I'm a little awestruck at the thought. I describe what happened, from the visualization exercise to the moment I heard the elusive, not-quite-there voice, the moment I felt the ghosts of emotions passing through me.

Cody gets up and starts to pace back and forth in front of the picnic table. "Okay," he says. "Okay." I can practically see the gears turning in his brain. "So, I think what we should do is repeat the conditions of however you did it last night. As closely as possible. If you want, I can try to prompt you, you know, verbally." He takes off his jacket and tosses it carelessly onto the table. "And I think we should try for somebody you know really well." He looks at me expectantly.

"I guess that's why I picked the park," I say slowly. "I thought we might see someone I know, someone from the neighborhood." I swallow, feeling disloyal as I say, "And Spike lives around here."

"Yeah? You used to hang out with him all the time, right?"

"Yeah." Then my heart sinks. Since it's Saturday, there's every possibility that not just Spike will be at his house but also the rest of the Zombie Squad, hanging out in the back-yard, jumping in and out of the hot tub. Including Cassie.

I have no desire to underhear Cassie ever again.

"What?" Cody says.

"He might have friends over," I say reluctantly. "I don't know if I can pick and choose who I hear."

He smiles. "That's okay. If it works, it works, right?"

I don't quite smile back. He's right, of course. I need to

just get over it. If I want to be able to control this—instead of it controlling me, instead of spinning out of control like Shiri did—I'm going to have to set aside my fears.

"Okay. I'll try," I say, settling my legs into as comfortable a position as I can manage on the hard bench. "Can you light this?" I reach for my backpack and pull out my black-cherry candle. Cody takes his Zippo out of his pocket and lights the candle with a soft *tink* of metal.

"Okay," I say. "I think I'm ready." I take a deep breath and close my eyes.

He's quiet for a minute. I crack my eyelids a tiny bit and peek through. He's staring at the candle, his expression unreadable. Finally, he sits on the bench opposite me and leans his arms on the table. I close my eyes all the way again.

"Are you sure?" he says.

I say yes. A trickle of sweat rolls down the back of my neck.

Cody starts by prompting me to relax certain muscles in turn, and then, after a few minutes of this, he tells me in a soft, hypnotic voice that I am now completely relaxed and aware. At first it's hard to concentrate, but gradually, his voice fades, and all I can hear are birds in the trees and the faint laughter of the girls playing soccer. The crown of my head is light, airy, and I have a sense of floating, like I'm not quite touching the bench even though I can feel the hard boards under my butt in a sort of distant way.

Think of Spike. I'm not sure whether the words were spoken out loud or in my head, but I comply, my thoughts drifting, bobbing erratically as if they're on an ocean or a breeze.

There's a memory of one of Spike's beach barbecues, the summer after freshman year, his dad manning the grill and handing out hot dogs as soon as they cooked. Biting in and tasting the smoky richness, the slight dryness of charcoal, the grit of sea salt.

It's vivid, but it's just a memory. So I keep trying. I think about his house, right there across the street; his mom's soft accent.

But the harder I try, paradoxically, the more the idea of Spike seems to slip out of my grasp, like trying to grab water. He's there, but I can't keep hold of him. I breathe slowly, hold my desperation and eagerness down somehow, and then someone does come clear in my mind: Cassie.

Bitterness surges inside me. I don't want to underhear her. Is she at Spike's house? My breath catches when I realize that I'm sort of hovering beside her, my thoughts floating in a formless space next to her head. Her voice sharpens, clarifies, a wisp or memory of the acrid smell of permanent hair dye ghosting through my nostrils.

> —*Why did I ever go to that stupid party with James?*
> *Elisa wasn't even there—she—and then—*
> —*the bedroom with Damion, he brought me*
> *in there, I was drunk, and I don't even remember*
> *what happened—and I heard that he told*
> *his friends we—did we? God what if—*

And then it's over. Except that I can feel tears sliding down my cheeks, stinging my wind-chapped skin. Horror and revulsion and regret slither through me. Hers? Or my own? I'm over her, so why am I crying?

I breathe raggedly, and I'm about to open my eyes when I hear Cody say softly, "Not yet. Try again." I don't really want to keep going, but I have trouble focusing enough to snap out of it and tell him so. It's easier to just let it go, to follow wherever my mind leads. My thoughts slide along again.

> *—party with James? Elisa wasn't even there—*
>   *—Elisa wasn't even—*

Echoes of Cassie's thoughts spin in fragments around me and then disappear, fading into that increasingly familiar feeling of openness in the crown of my head. Almost too soon, soon enough to surprise me, I hear another voice. Is Spike having a party? My brief flare of curiosity fades and I'm distracted by the sound of crackling, tearing paper in my head, a phantom smell of something slowly burning, smoldering down to ashes.

It's another familiar voice.

> *—I can't tell him what happened with Marc,*
>   *how he told me he'd always wanted—no—*
>   *why did Marc kiss*
>   *me?—why did I—*
> *—have to get rid of this letter—*
>   *—can't tell him, can't tell James, can't tell James*
>   *can't tell can't tell can't tell—*

I feel like I'm drowning. The words smother me and colors well behind my eyes, intricate patterns laced with swirling strands black as Elisa's dark hair. My heart races with panic. I try to breathe. I remind myself where I am: the park. Outside. Safe. I remind myself *who* I am. The swirling eases, and the smell of burned paper turns into a faint tendril of black-cherry fragrance. I can feel my hands again, and I flex them.

My eyes fly open, and I start to shiver. Cody jumps off the bench and asks, "Did it work?" And then, when I don't say anything, he adds, "Are you okay?"

I nod, but my teeth are chattering too hard to respond. He slides onto the bench next to me but I hardly react, even when he puts both arms around me and hugs me until I stop shaking. That's when I realize I'm still crying, that my cheeks are wet and my nails are digging into my palms. My breath hitches, knowing all of these things that I'm not supposed to know.

Cody just sits quietly, holding my hand in his, his thumb slowly stroking mine. He gazes at me steadily, his expression serious.

I can't keep my feelings inside. I can't be alone with this secret. I'll burst.

Slowly, I start to tell Cody what I heard. Who I heard. What I felt. The more I talk, the more my resentment and anger grow—anger that I can't seem to get away from Cassie; anger at Elisa for never having the guts to talk to me at school; frustration at Spike for being able to stay friends with them; fury at Shiri for not being able to cope, and at the universe for causing this gift, this curse. The emotions are raging out of me, and the words just keep spilling out.

Cody inches his body a little closer. He puts his arm around my shoulders again and pulls me into him. I can feel the warmth radiating from his arm like it's a burning branch, and right now it feels like the most solid thing in the world to me.

nineteen

When I get home from the park, I wrap my fleece moon-and-stars blanket tightly around me and huddle against the side of the bed. I'm sitting on the floor of my room, the door closed and locked, even though I know my mom hates it when I lock the door. But I don't want to talk to anyone right now. I don't want to *hear* anyone right now.

I've tried candles, incense, a hot bath, and right now I'm sipping some of Mom's mossy-tasting herbal tea, but I can't stop my thoughts from marching forward into places I don't want to go. Being able to underhear at will—it scares me. What if I can't fully control it? What if it's more like a dam bursting open and less like a door with a nice little door-knob that I can push closed whenever I feel like it?

What if I've done something I can't ever reverse?

I've always taken it for granted that I can be alone with my thoughts any time I want. In my room. In the pool. At the beach, on the sand, lapping waves the only sound. Maybe it won't be that way ever again.

Feeling completely alone, yet never again being completely alone. How could anybody stand it? For the first time, maybe, I understand Shiri's desperation. Not why she made the choice to die, but why she might have felt so trapped.

I put down the tea, clench my fingers around the blanket. It could be dangerous, deliberately trying to underhear people. What if I do something really weird and give myself brain damage? I don't even know if it's healthy that I can do this.

At least I have Cody and Mikaela. They didn't know how serious it was at first; they didn't know how to react. But we've gotten past that. Forgive and forget. I have to learn to forgive people, to trust them.

Even if knowing what they're really thinking makes it a whole lot harder sometimes.

———

Later, lying in bed, I take some deep breaths, trying to envision the top of my head as an impenetrable wall. For the first time since I started underhearing people, I'm scared to sleep. What might happen when I'm dreaming?

After a few hours of tossing and turning, I finally drop off. Thankfully, I don't dream.

The next morning, I don't wake up until almost nine o'clock. I feel a pang, missing the peace and silence of the school pool in the early morning, the feeling of working my muscles until they're tired. We don't have a pool at home, but I could go for a jog.

I yawn and haul myself up, opening the curtains a little

to let in the grayish light from the overcast morning. My eyes feel dry and itchy. I rub grit out of the corners and reach down to pull my extra blanket off the floor, and that's when yesterday comes flooding back.

—Elisa wasn't even—
—can't tell can't tell can't tell—

I knot my hands in my hair, yanking at it painfully. I can't think about this now. I get up and start stretching my legs. My parents' yoga group is due to arrive any minute, so it's the perfect time to make an exit. I pull on gray sweats, grab a hoodie, and go.

My feet pound the sidewalk and I'm quickly breathing hard. I'm out of shape, but I push myself a little more, trying to drive everything out of my head except the feeling of my legs pumping. My course takes me on a long loop through the neighborhood, out to the main road, and back around the other side, past the park.

I pass the Dohertys' house. Spike is outside, loading the family's huge red-and-white cooler into his mom's minivan.

"Hey," he shouts, and I slow down, jogging across his driveway. I stop in front of him, a little breathless.

"What's up?"

"Nothing's up. You know me. Never need an excuse to celebrate, baby." He grins.

Ah. Beach party time. "Cool," I say halfheartedly. I should really leave.

"Listen, you should come out," Spike says. "My dad's

cooking dogs and burgers. He already asked if you were coming. I told him you were."

"You what?" I put one hand on my hip and glare at him.

"I'm relying on my superhuman powers of persuasion." He's looking at me innocently, lazily, his eyes half closed.

"I'm not seeing any evidence of these powers," I say. "Plus—"

"Cassie's not going to be there, if that's what you're worried about," Spike says. "She's on some kind of spa day with her mom. Putting mud in her hair or something." He grins wickedly.

Do I even want to go? There's a risk—a risk I might underhear someone. But that's a risk no matter what I do. Whether I'm home, whether I'm at school. At least at the beach, I can wander away. Be alone for a while. And I don't have to stay long.

"Okay. I'll stop by for a while," I tell him. Just for old times' sake. I haven't done stuff with Spike outside of school since last summer, and I do feel a little guilty about it.

"Sweet," Spike says. "My dad said he'd bring that nasty mustard you like."

"There is nothing wrong with Dijon mustard."

"Nothing except that it's *naaaasssty.*"

I laugh and tell him that I'll see him later. I miss these stupid conversations with Spike, conversations about nothing at all but that leave me feeling better anyway. For a few minutes, I can forget about everything important.

And, for a while there at the beach, it *is* like old times— me and Spike and his dad, James and Elisa and another guy from swim team, Jared, all hanging out and eating hot dogs and chips around the barbecue. It's less awkward than I thought, but I still avoid being alone with James or Elisa. I don't make eye contact with either one, and I keep thinking about what Elisa said; what I heard. What I shouldn't know.

The weather is clear but chilly. January is still too cold to swim, in my opinion, but the water in front of me is crisply blue, little wavelets running almost up to the toes of my sneakers. Something about the sheer scale of the ocean, its power and overwhelming size, puts things into perspective somehow. I feel small, but so do my problems.

"Wanna look for tide pools under the pier?" Spike comes up behind me, making me jump.

"Sure," I say, grinning back at him. We walk north along the shore for a few minutes. In my head is an image of Spike and me in junior high, me with my dorky haircut, Spike still short and a little doughy, before we started to swim all the time. Back then, we used to clamber around the rocks under the pier looking for starfish and sea anemones, poking the anemones to make them retract their tentacles. Later, we'd come here with the whole swim crew, but it was always different when it was just the two of us. I never felt like I had to put on an act with Spike.

"Remember that time you picked up a sea slug and tried to freak me out with it? And it peed purple ink all over your hands?"

Spike laughs. "I forgot about that. That was classic."

"It was." I smile, looking down at our feet making wet footprints in the sand at the water's edge. Finally, we get to the fall of stones that surrounds the base of the pier. After climbing around the rocks for a while, we reach a relatively dry, flat rock and sit on it, looking out at the ocean from just under the overhang of the boardwalk above us. Little waves lap against the rocks below.

"So..." Spike says. "Having a good time?"

"Yeah, I am," I say honestly. "I wasn't sure if things would be cool, but I guess it's just Cassie who's still mad at me."

"You're still mad at her," Spike points out.

I look away from him, down at the lichen-encrusted rock.

"Forget about it," he says. "She's doing her thing, you're doing your thing. Don't worry about her."

"I know." I sigh. "It's just hard."

There's a brief silence, and then Spike sort of snorts. I look up at him, startled.

He tries to control himself, and then a smirk spreads across his face. "That's what *she* said."

I swat him on the arm. "You cannot be serious for even five minutes."

"Sure I can," he says. "Check this out." He leans toward me, closer and closer as if in slow motion. I giggle. Knowing Spike, any minute now he's going to stick his finger up my nose or try to lick my face.

But he doesn't, and the closer he gets—so close I almost go cross-eyed—I'm suddenly paralyzed. It seems unreal, like I'm having an out-of-body experience, like it's not really happening. I feel... dazed and close my eyes. I smell chocolate.

*—want this, what if she doesn't, but it's worth a try isn't
it, not like she hates you—*

I hear it like an urgent litany in my head, and our lips touch. For a moment, I'm frozen in place. I feel the warmth of his breath mingling with mine. I'm caught. My body leans toward his, my hand rises to touch the back of his neck. My arms are covered in goose bumps.

—yes—

But the desire surging through me isn't my own.

My eyes fly open and I scoot frantically back.

It's not just a joke. He meant it this time. And I'm not ready for it. I still have goose bumps but now I'm shivering, hugging my knees, looking everywhere but at him.

He sits back, looking startled and a little crestfallen. To cover my embarrassment, my guilt at recoiling so abruptly, I say, "I've fallen for that one before. No face-licking." I force a smile. But I feel terrible.

Credit where credit's due; he's quick to save face.

"Face-licking? Please. So juvenile. You'll just have to wonder whether it was going to be nose-picking…or ear-snorting…or what." He grins like nothing's wrong. But I know the answer is "or what," and I know what the "or what" was going to be.

"Well, I'm not sure I want to stick around here and risk invasion of my facial space," I say casually, picking my way down the rock pile toward the sand. "I think it's time for another hot dog."

I expect Spike to say "that's what *she* said" again, but he just raises his eyebrows at me as we walk back toward the group in silence.

My breath catches. I can sense Spike glancing at me as we crunch across the wet sand, but I don't turn his way. What's wrong with me? I've known Spike since we were twelve. I've never thought about kissing him, not once. It's not that he's not attractive. He's nice, and he cares about me. And, after everything that's happened, we're still friends. He wants to kiss me. Maybe I've never considered it, but I *like* him. I always have. Why did I flinch?

If I hadn't underheard him, would I have reacted differently? I felt something—it felt *good*—but what if they weren't *my* emotions?

I don't even know how I feel about him, especially not now. But it's not going to be easy to look at our friendship the same way anymore.

Are all of my friendships going to turn weird, one by one?

I cross my arms and hug myself tightly. That's not going to happen. I can make this work. All I have to do is learn to control my underhearing; control when it happens—and when it doesn't. And I'm almost there.

Everything's going to be fine.

When I walk through the door, my mom calls out, "Sunny, honey, can you come in here, please?" in an overly cheerful voice. I walk into the kitchen and glance at the clock. That's when I remember: Tonight is Auntie Mina's scheduled phone call with Uncle Randall. Not just tonight; right now.

I want nothing to do with any of this, so I turn right back around.

Mom's voice stops me. "Sunny. Now." I look at her and lean against the counter, my arms crossed.

"We're going to have a little talk, now," she says, sitting at the table. She reaches for a brightly colored ceramic mug, probably some ridiculous tea blend that she thinks is going to solve everyone's problems. She pushes another mug in my general direction. I don't take it. Instead, I just stand there in stony silence, waiting.

"You see, this is exactly what I'm worried about, Sunshine," she says, as if I've done something wrong just by standing here. "You haven't talked to us lately. You're either out somewhere or you're hiding in your room." She gesticulates jerkily with her left hand. "You just breeze out of the house to go to school, and on the weekends you're out with your friends."

"I thought you were happy I've been going out. You kept saying you didn't want me to 'mope around.'" Who in their right mind would want to stick around here? I stare up at the ceiling.

"Yes, but honey, you need to understand that there's no such thing as a part-time family member. I want you to think about that. This is a difficult time, and we need you to be supportive."

I draw in a sharp breath. "I *have* been supportive. And if I'm such a full-time family member, how come I don't have the same rights as everyone else? I don't have any privacy around the house. Nobody cares or even asks me how *I* feel. Everything we do revolves around Auntie Mina."

"This is no time to start picking up an attitude." Mom's face is grim and her lips are set in a thin line.

My voice comes out in a hoarse croak. "An *attitude*? Mom, you don't know what it's been like for me. If I don't get the chance to get out of here, I'll go crazy."

"Sunny—"

"And now she's talking to him like he didn't do anything wrong. How can she give him that satisfaction?" I'm stomping back and forth across the kitchen now, agitated.

Mom makes a wordless noise of frustration. She looks up at me, her eyes tired. "Sunny, it's Mina's decision to talk to him," she says. "And they are both capable of acting like adults. They need to discuss a lot more than just the way he's been treating her. It's more complicated than you think."

"*I know it's complicated.*" I slam my hand on the counter. "You don't think my life has been complicated ever since Shiri died? Ever since Auntie Mina came here?" She doesn't know the half of it. I straighten up. "I don't want any more complications. I'm going upstairs." Upstairs, where it's quiet. Where I won't have to deal with any of this.

Mom looks at me, emotions warring on her face. Frustration. Sympathy. Sadness. But she doesn't try to stop me this time.

I only make it as far as the hall when Auntie Mina walks into the kitchen, her face pale but calm. Seconds later, Dad comes in from the garage; he must have been waiting around to hear the study door open.

I hover in the hallway, indecisive. I can't help wanting to know what happened. I hear soft voices talking around the kitchen table as I dither, and then the voices get louder.

"You're not going to tell us what he said?" my dad says loudly.

"Mina, you don't have to talk about it right now if you don't want to." My mom's voice is softer, and I strain to hear more, huddling against the wall in the darkened hallway.

"It's okay, really," Auntie Mina says. I'd expected more anger, but her voice is mild. "Surprisingly," she says, "it was actually … fine."

I frown. How can any of us believe that?

"It was *fine?*" My dad sounds like he's never heard anything more ludicrous in his life.

"It was," Auntie Mina insists. "He was calm. He listened to everything I had to say. He didn't really say much. I think it's finally sinking in, that I'm not just going to do what he wants all the time." She trails off. When she speaks up again, her voice is soft. "I really think he heard me this time. And I really think I might be able to work things out with him."

My stomach churns.

Could we have been wrong about him?

Shiri didn't think so, and she was the one who really knew.

It just isn't possible. Auntie Mina can't be willing to listen to him, to consider going back to him. But somehow, it's happening.

From Shiri Langford's journal, July 31st

My father. My father. I can't believe that we share genetics, that my mother somehow found him and married him and somewhere along the line I came along, that an entire X chromosome came from him and permeates my body. It makes me want to tear at my skin, rip my DNA apart.

When I was a kid he could do no wrong. He was different then, when Randall Jr. still lived at home, when we were like a regular family and I was too little to do anything that would really piss him off. When I was his princess.

But then… it all changed. I don't know why.

Earlier today, THAT happened and it was like I was buried under a pile of bricks. I couldn't breathe. I was lucky to be in my room, sitting at my old childhood desk that seems so small to me now, when I broke into a cold sweat and it was like swirling darkness inside my head when I heard him.

I don't know how much more of this I can take.

twenty

I creep closer, peer through the doorway into the kitchen.

"Talking to him on the phone is one thing, but getting together with him, alone?" My mother's face is pale, and her voice trembles. "Do you think—"

"Really, it's okay," Auntie Mina protests.

"It's not an option, Mina." My dad's voice is low and grim.

"Oh, for heaven's sake, it's not as though I'm moving back in with him. All we did was agree to talk things out," she says. "Maybe I can convince him to start going to therapy."

"Do you really think that's going to help? Is it worth it, Mina?" Dad looks helplessly at his sister.

"We've been together for twenty-six years," she points out, her voice strained. "I can't pretend none of that ever happened."

You can't pretend he never hurt you, either. I feel like saying it. I almost do, but I clench my hands into fists and dig my nails into my palms to stay quiet. Auntie Mina looks over at me momentarily, a frown crossing her face.

"Sunny, I'm so sorry. You of all people shouldn't worry about me. Everything's going to be fine with Uncle Randall. He's still your uncle, and he loves you. We just have to talk it out."

There's that word again: *fine.* I clench my jaw and don't respond. How can someone so sensitive to everyone else's needs handle living with someone like that? Uncle Randall's always been like this, and there's no way he's going to change.

I think of that whirling, horrible darkness, that feeling of something rotting from the inside. That feeling I was afraid wasn't just in him, but also in me. But this time, instead of being scared, I'm gripped with the uncontrollable need to know, to be certain, what Uncle Randall wants. If I could find out, maybe I could convince her.

My parents are both crowding around the kitchen table, trying to talk sense into Auntie Mina. I refuse to stand here feeling helpless.

I sidestep out of the kitchen, quietly grab my keys, and sneak out the front door. They'll hear me starting the car and driving off, but hopefully they'll be occupied with Auntie Mina for the next few minutes. All I need is a few minutes.

I start to drive. Speeding a little, I make it across town in record time. The houses start to get bigger, the gardens fancy and landscaped, and I'm in the neighborhood where Shiri lives. Used to live. Where Uncle Randall is right now.

I drive past the house; then, nervously, I pull around the corner, about a block away. It's dark outside, and when

I turn off the headlights, the yellow glow of the streetlights is the only illumination.

Getting as comfortable as I can in the driver's seat, I close my eyes and regulate my breathing, just like I did yesterday with Cody. It takes me a while to calm down enough to start the visualizations. Gradually, though, I can feel my heart rate slow from its angry gallop.

I start to relax into that increasingly familiar feeling of unreality. It makes me think of stepping off a cliff and having to believe that I can walk on air.

My thoughts want to tumble in freefall, but I strain to keep my attention focused. In my mind's eye, I envision one particular place. I'm floating along the street toward that huge, echoing house, the house I used to think was a palace. I pass through the concrete columns on either side of the porch that Shiri and I used to draw on with colored chalk. In through the door. I can picture it clearly, and then I feel the thoughts I'm looking for. His thoughts.

—have to find someone to replace her at work—
how can I?—I don't need this, can't believe
she'd—she knows how it is—
—how could she do this to me—
—not my fault not me not me NOT ME—

There's a smell, too, a tang like something toxic melting, like plastic on fire or burning rubber or acrid metal. Not a physical smell; I guess it's like those people who say they can taste colors or see sounds—but it feels real nonetheless. I'm choking on it; on the feelings of anger and blame and loss like bile rising in my throat. I can't take it anymore. And then I'm hurtling through space, my head spinning as I sit with my face in my hands, leaning against the steering wheel.

Shreds of emotion drift through me like wafting smoke, making me tense up again, and then they're gone. My palms throb where I was digging my nails into them, and my eyes sting.

I don't know why I thought this could help. It's just a burden of useless knowledge, of feelings that threaten to overwhelm me. To bury me.

And, I realize with growing despair, it's not like anybody in my family would believe me anyway.

The next morning I wake up early, feeling like I've been sleeping under a ton of bricks. My limbs are sore and achy, and my head feels fuzzy. I gingerly climb out of bed, testing my legs, and decide to go for a run before showering for school.

The midwinter air is chilly and the sky is full of low gray clouds. As I slowly warm up, lengthening my stride, I wonder if it's not just lack of exercise that made me so tired this morning. I wonder if it was the underhearing.

The more I think about it, the more I'm sure of it. Especially now—now that I can actually *make* it happen—it seems to take something out of me.

It makes sense. When I swim extra hard, I get tired. When I study too late, I get headaches. And when I underhear too intensely, when I pour everything I have into trying to use this power...I suffer for it. It happened to Shiri, too; I saw it in one of her journal entries. But I don't think she made the connection.

I quicken my stride, breathing hard. The cool air blows past me, whipping stray strands of hair into my face. Not for the first time, not even for the fiftieth time, I wonder why this happened to me. Why it happened to Shiri. Auntie Mina's never shown any signs of being a mind reader. And my dad doesn't seem like he's got any special talents.

I think about Auntie Mina again. If she's even just a little more sensitive to people's feelings, maybe something happened with Shiri, some...*mutation* that made it more powerful somehow? And if that's true, how did it happen to me? I think about Shiri's note. *Maybe one day you'll figure it out. I never could.* How could she know about me? Was she just guessing? What if she gave it to me, like an infection?

I'm running flat-out through the neighborhood, and I force myself to slow down. I don't need to hurt myself by running too hard. But when I get to school, my mind is still spinning with theories. Maybe it's something that only affects the women in the family. Maybe it was something in the water when Shiri and I were growing up. Antonia would probably say it was a blessing from the Goddess. At this point, it's no weirder a theory than anything else.

I space out through most of the morning, thinking about it. Mrs. Lam pauses next to my chair during French class and pointedly says, "Bon*jour*, Mademoiselle Soleil," tapping a perfectly manicured fingernail on my desk. Still, I manage to concentrate long enough to get a B on the pop quiz. By the time I get to lunch, though, my brain is fried.

"You've got the burnout look going. Very hipster," Mikaela says when I drop my brown bag on the table and collapse onto the bench.

"You're just jealous." I elbow her lightly and start picking at my carrot sticks.

"Ha ha." She takes a bite of cafeteria pizza, then says casually, "So how was your practice session?"

"It went well," I say. I glance around. Cody's still not here yet, and Becca's trapped David and Andy with an excited monologue about the latest in her string of girlfriends. I lower my voice a little. "I think I'm starting to get the hang of it. Doing it on purpose, I mean."

Mikaela is quiet for a minute. "That's good," she finally says. "Right?"

I look up at her. "Yeah, I guess."

"You *guess*?"

"It's just that…" I lean toward her. "It's exhausting." And scary, and confusing. "I just have to get used to it, probably, but…" I'm not sure what else to tell her. I cut my eyes in the direction of the rest of the group.

"Gotcha," she says, following my gaze. "Later. But I expect a full report on the amazing and mind-bending talents of Cody the Wanna-Be Warlock." She says this last part in a fake-spooky voice, grabbing a stick from the ground and swirling it around like a magic wand.

"Wanna-Be Warlock?"

"Yeah, get this." Mikaela puts down her stick-wand and

turns to face me, straddling the picnic bench. "Saturday night after he left your house, he's driving around with that stupid coven chick from the Wiccan thing, and I guess he's trying to impress her with his dad's Lexus, and he rear-ends this guy who's stopped at a red light."

"No way!" I almost choke on a carrot. "So is he okay?"

"Oh, totally," Mikaela says. "The air bags went off and the witch-bitch got some kind of chemical burn from the powder in the air bags, but Cody's fine. Physically, anyway."

"Physically?" I'm confused. "So he's, like, suffering from PTSD?"

"Yeah, right. No, he's in major trouble at home. His dad was *pissed off*. I mean majorly. No car for the next three months, no going anywhere *at all* besides school for the next two weeks … poor baby." Mikaela has a tiny smirk. "And he has to actually get a job to pay for the repairs to the Lexus."

"Oooh, a *job*," I say. "But apparently he can still make calls to the outside world. He called you, right?"

"On a five-minute restriction, yeah."

"Jeez." I roll up my reusable lunch bag and stuff it into my backpack. "You know what, though? He gets away with everything."

"Yeah," Mikaela says, "but he's in for it now. His parents have been pretty easy on him, just cutting off his phone privileges and stuff like that, but now they're doing a 180." She tosses a few crumbs from her pizza crust out into the grass, where some birds are pecking around. She looks sad for a minute, but then her expression hardens. "He might be a jackass, but they're kind of being tyrants, you know?"

I don't really know, don't know at all, but I nod. Then Uncle Randall comes to mind, and I feel bad for Cody. If his dad is anything like that... if it were me, I'd feel like I was walking on a knife edge, just trying not to fall off.

twenty-one

Cody is absent on Tuesday but shows up on Wednesday, glowering so fiercely that lunch is nearly silent. The atmosphere is brittle, and even Becca doesn't say much. I'm edgy, afraid that my mind will drift and I'll underhear one of them, so I picture the top of my head as solid and impenetrable, the opposite of those dotted lines in the drawing Cody printed out. It seems to help, and I'm relieved that I don't have to hear Cody's fury or Becca's uncharacteristic listlessness.

It's enough just to see it, and know.

Thursday after school, Mikaela and I go to a used-CD store with Becca, who acts like such a spaz that it's impossible to worry about, or even concentrate on, anything else. She darts around the store, chattering about this girl she met who's a guitarist for some goth band, flirting with all of the store employees and leaving a black lipstick kiss mark on the credit card receipt she hands back to the cashier.

We all leave the store laughing, but when Becca drops me off at home, I notice Auntie Mina sitting on the front porch bench, alone. I wave, let myself in through the garage door, and put down my backpack. Mom and Dad aren't home yet and the house is quiet. I could have some time to myself.

My conscience nags at me. I open the front door and lean out.

"Hi, Sunny," Auntie Mina says, turning to face me with a wan smile.

"Is everything okay?"

She sets down a stack of papers on the bench next to her. "Yes...no. Well, I'm not sure. I'm trying to figure some things out. Come on—have a seat." She pats the bench.

Reluctantly, I sit next to her. I catch a glimpse of the papers on her other side: computer printouts. The top page says, "Trial Separation or Legal Separation?" in big black letters. I feel a wave of relief.

"Are you..." I gesture toward the stack of printouts, not sure what I really want to ask. Nothing's happened yet. Has it?

"Oh, sweetheart," Auntie Mina says, sighing. "I'll be honest with you. This is really tough. I didn't know it would be this hard."

I'm not sure if she's talking about the paperwork or the idea of leaving Uncle Randall, but I say, "He hurts you. You *have* to leave." My voice sounds small and I can't bring myself to look at her, so I stare out at the road. Mrs. Abronzino drives by in her silver station wagon and waves at us.

"The thing is, he really does care, in his own way. This is hard for him, too. Shiri is..." She pauses, then continues. "Shiri was his daughter. Our daughter. He's looking out for the family. That's how he sees it, anyway. It's all falling apart for him, and he's trying his best to keep it together."

"It doesn't matter," I insist. I struggle to articulate my thoughts. "The *why* doesn't matter. If the way he deals with it is to hurt you, then you can't stay with him."

Auntie Mina puts her arm around my shoulders. "It's okay," she says soothingly. "For now, I'm here. I don't know what's going to happen, not yet, but I'm here, okay?"

I can't help noticing: she hasn't said she'll never go back to him. Still, I lean into her and drop the subject.

We stay on the porch for a few more minutes, not talking. I close my eyes and drift a little. I don't even consciously realize that I'm reaching gently for Auntie Mina's thoughts until, softly, almost like a whisper, I hear her:

> —*reminds me so much of Shiri, miss her so much—*
> —*if I can just get Randall to listen, if I can*
> *convince—maybe he'll be different*
> *maybe all we need is a break—*
> —*love him, still love him, do I love him?*
> *I don't know—*
> *I don't want to be alone but I love him but*
> *I don't know, I don't know—*

Her agonized confusion, her loneliness, her desperation and love roil through me like a flood, and I feel tears spring to my eyes. Before they have a chance to spill over, I make some halfhearted excuse and run up to my room. I could feel how close to tears she was herself, how many emotions were surging just under the surface, yet she was so calm. She made it sound so simple.

Sometimes I feel like I don't really know anybody at all. None of us does.

But for some reason, now that I can find out more than anyone else can, I feel even more lost. And there's an undercurrent of worry that won't go away, because I'm not sure Auntie Mina is over Uncle Randall, no matter what she says.

———

On Friday, Cody corners me after school in the parking lot. When I go to my car, he's leaning against the driver's-side door, flipping his Zippo open and shut and smiling that little secret smile. It brings a smile to my own face in response.

Things have been different between us since the weekend. It feels like we have an unspoken understanding, something that goes deeper than ordinary friendship. He saw me at my worst, my most vulnerable, and he didn't freak out or get scared. He just held me closer, gave me the silence I needed.

It makes me feel a lot less alone.

When I walk up and jingle my keys in front of him pointedly, his smile broadens and he says, "Give me a ride to my house?"

The bottom drops out of my stomach for a second. Am I going to have to meet the Parents from Hell? Part of me doesn't care if they're there or not; part of me *wants* to go inside his house, see inside that part of his life.

"Earth to Sunshine," Cody says, and laughs at his own turn of phrase. "Ride?"

I swat his arm. "Sure, but it's a lot easier to drive people places when I can get *into* the car."

"What, you can't walk through walls?" he says jokingly. He gives my ponytail a tug and walks around to the passenger side. I unlock the doors and he slides in, not bothering with the seat belt. I refrain from making a snide remark about his fender-bender. In fact, as we drive away from school, I have trouble thinking of anything to say. Cody is thrumming with edgy energy, tapping his fingers on the dashboard, flipping radio stations back and forth, and smiling to himself.

"So," I say eventually, "What's the deal?"

"Turn here," he says, pointing at a stoplight that goes into a ritzy housing development I've never been in before. It isn't gated, but palm trees line the entry road and everything seems to be painted in trendy colors. There are a lot of fake columns and stonework facades and SUVs.

"Here," he says again, pointing to a cul-de-sac on the left with five or six big houses on it. "Hang on—you can park right there." He points at the curb next to a two-story house with giant glass picture windows and two cars, a Hummer and a Lexus, parked in front. The silver Lexus has been backed into the driveway, and I can see the crumpled part of the front bumper. I wince as I pull up to the curb and turn off the car.

"It's fine," Cody says shortly. "I'll be able to pay it off by the end of the school year if I can get a cashier job at Thumbscrew. "

"But if you can't drive there..." I trail off, not wanting to piss him off.

"Pop says I'll have to take the bus. Not that there's a bus stop anywhere near *this* neighborhood. Nobody wants the noise or the diesel fumes or 'those kinds of people' wandering around here." His voice is sarcastic. "Or I might be able to—I don't know." He fidgets with his Zippo again. He's all serious now, and he turns to look at me intently.

"So what is it?" I tilt my head and smile at him a little, trying to lighten the mood. It feels like we're trapped in a heavy silence.

"I—okay, listen," Cody says, sounding urgent now. "I have to ask you something. A favor."

I nod warily. He leans toward me, close enough in my little car that I can smell his shampoo. He closes his eyes for a second, then opens them, but his expression is hard to read. "That accident—that wasn't the only reason I got in trouble. I didn't tell Mikaela everything that happened."

"So, what else was there?" I ask. Even though I'm worried, I'm the one he's taking into his confidence this time, and it feels good.

He sighs. "Since I'm not allowed to drive for the foreseeable future, I invited some of those people you met at the solstice thing to have their meeting at my house on Sunday. It turned into kind of a party, I guess. My parents were supposed to be at a charity dinner, but Mom came home early and caught some of them smoking pot in the backyard and drinking Pop's scotch. And they broke one of his highball glasses. It wasn't on purpose, and I didn't mean for them to find out. But my parents were fucking pissed. I've never seen them so..." He swallows. "Anyway. I just thought maybe you could help me. You know. With your..." He taps the side of his head, and I have a growing feeling of unease.

"Cody, I—"

"I'm a little freaked," he says, putting his hand on my hand where it's resting on the gearshift. There's a crease of worry between his eyebrows. "More than a little. I just want to know if they're planning on—I don't know what they're thinking. But I need to know. I just want to be ready. There's going to be some kind of 'big discussion' and I have to be prepared." His voice is hard, but then it softens. He looks right at me, his eyes intense. "I wouldn't be asking you this if I didn't think it was really important."

"I know," I say, still shaken that Cody, of all people, would admit that he's actually *scared*. Of course, he really screwed up this time. But that doesn't mean Mikaela was wrong about his parents being tyrants.

"It wasn't your fault, though," I point out. "The party got out of control. Can't you explain that?"

"I tried," he says flatly. "They don't want to listen to me."

I squeeze his hand. "Okay," I say. "I'll try. But... I can't guarantee anything. They might be thinking about something totally unrelated."

"Not a chance," he says, looking away from me and staring out the front windshield. "I'm supposed to check in with my mom right after I get home from school today, so I'll just go in the front door, pick a little fight, and then let her rip about what a big screw-up I am. You'll definitely hear something."

His voice is desolate; bitter. I can't control my frown or the sick feeling that wells up in the pit of my stomach, but I try not to let Cody see just how painful it is to hear him say that. I don't want to be yet another source of stress in his life. Instead, I lean back a little in my seat, put my hands loosely in my lap, and close my eyes.

Unlike last week, Cody doesn't say anything to prompt me. He just breathes loudly and tensely in the seat next to me for a moment, then gets out of the car and slams the door. I go through the visualization process on my own, trying not to think about Cody trudging heavily up to the door of his house, trying not to fixate on the hopelessness in his voice.

After a few minutes of silence, I start to relax, and my mind drifts.

My awareness, my sense of myself, is in that nothing-space, and it's starting to seem more familiar, less ... terrifying. Though it's not really a *space*, but something intangible I can't quite describe. I sort of nudge myself toward Cody's house, picturing my mind drifting through the walls of the building not thirty feet away and looking—*feeling*, really—around for other thoughts.

And I find them.

> —*is NOT a choice, this is it, this is the last time, not kidding, not playing around anymore—sick of it—wild—undisciplined—needs structure—summer work camp or maybe military school if he doesn't—*

—has to learn, I don't know what more to do—
—have to send him—send him away—

My muscles tense with rage. Sweat breaks out on my forehead, starts dripping down my back and sides. My breath quickens and my heart races. It takes me a moment to calm down enough to remind myself that these aren't my emotions, this isn't my anger. I'm so shocked at the anguished, bitter flavor of the thoughts—his mother's thoughts—that I'm almost flung back into consciousness. But not before I sense something else.

Some*one* else. Someone I do know, because he's walking toward me now, walking back to the car. My thoughts are already spinning away, out of control, and all I can read is a sense of desperation, a moment of

—have to—have to do something—

… and then my eyes are open and I'm breathing hard, like I just finished an 800-meter swim race.

From Shiri Langford's journal, August 5th

This morning I was jogging around the neighborhood and listening to my iPod, one of the Beatles mixes I made for Sunny before I left for college, and the song "Yesterday" came on. When Paul sang out those first few lines, I couldn't help it, I just stopped right in the middle of the sidewalk and bent over and started sobbing, thinking about how my life didn't used to be like this, how it used to be different until one day, I don't know exactly when, it just started changing.

Like Paul said, all my troubles used to seem far away. But it's not like that now. I'm not sure it ever really was.

twenty-two

When I open my eyes again, I nearly jump out of my skin. Cody is staring at me through the car window. He opens the door and sits back down in the passenger seat, his whole posture radiating tension. But there's a lump in my throat and I can't talk just yet. I rummage in the glove box for a tissue, find a crumpled napkin, and wipe damp sweat off my forehead. Finally, he breaks the silence.

"So did it work? What did you hear?" His voice is low and rough.

"I—they—" I cough, my throat dry, and shake my head. "How did you manage to leave the house?"

"Bathroom window. Mom has no idea." He lets a tiny self-satisfied smile flit across his face, but it's gone in a moment and his face is nervous again.

How can I tell him? What's it going to change?

"Sunny? What's going to happen to me?" Cody asks, a little more desperately. I swallow a few times and try again, a creeping feeling of dread making my palms sweat. I wipe them on my jeans.

"Your mom," I finally force out. "She was pretty mad."

He's quiet, waiting for me to continue, but he tenses up even more the second I mention his mom.

I hesitate again. "She was saying something about how they're not kidding around anymore, they're sick of it, it's the last straw, blah blah blah. Typical parent stuff, I guess." I'm forcing my tone to be light. I can't bring myself to tell him that I could *feel* how angry she was, how afraid for him, how desperate. How she was ready to do anything to make him into the son she wanted him to be.

"And then what?" He catches and holds my gaze, and I look away. A tear slides down my cheek involuntarily. He reaches out, gently turns my chin so that I'm facing him again, then strokes my cheek with his thumb. "What?"

I close my eyes, lean into his hand. I don't want to tell him. It almost makes me feel sick. But I do anyway.

"It was something about . . . you needing discipline. Like sending you away to work camp or military school. She sounded really insistent." I can't look at him. I pull away from his hand, sit back in my seat, and stare out the window at the street ahead of me and the identical palm trees punctuating the sidewalk. "She sounded desperate."

He swears explosively and slams his palm against the dashboard. "I should have known this would happen. This is so typical of them." I can hear his teeth grinding together as he clenches his jaw, and I try not to cringe.

But I have to admit, his anger scares me a little.

"Look," I say, trying to sound calming, "it could just be a threat. So, you try not to get on their nerves for a while."

"You don't know what they're like," he says abruptly.

"They'd really send you away?" I can't imagine my parents ever wanting to get rid of me, even if they thought I needed to learn a lesson. But then, I haven't crashed the car. Or shoplifted. Or gotten arrested. Or thrown a party at my house without my parents around.

"This *cannot happen.*" Cody sounds less angry now. More like eerily calm. I look at him. His jaw is still clenched, but he seems to be more in control of himself. He looks at me and his eyes are hard. "I won't let them. This is *my* life."

"You're not eighteen yet," I point out. "They can still—"

"They won't do anything. I won't let them. If they try . . . I'll make them sorry." His eyes glitter with something I can't fathom.

"Make them sorry? What are you talking about?" Suddenly I'm terrified. He wouldn't hurt himself. Would he? I peer at him, but he just stares past me, over my shoulder, his face grim.

I clutch my hands together in my lap to keep them from shaking. How could he even imply it in front of me? It's too cruel. But that sounds like what he's saying. Or maybe he's talking about hurting his parents. Or damaging their house.

In a moment, though, my hands relax. Because I know: that's not Cody. None of it is, not really. He's always talking about his big plans for his life, about moving to L.A. to live in a house full of artists or a Wiccan coven and start an underground music 'zine.

He's not going to hurt anyone. I don't even think he'd run away to L.A. He just wants his parents to think he will.

He's planning to manipulate them. Scare them into doing what he wants.

No matter how tough his parents are, I'm not sure they deserve that.

I must look shocked. "It's okay," Cody says, his voice softening. "I know what I need to do now."

"You're not going to do anything dumb, are you?" I try to sound casual, but inside I'm reeling. Cody, his parents—both of them desperate, both of them stubborn. What's going to happen now?

"Like I said, I'll do what I have to do to get them to listen. Even if it means...scaring them a little." Cody sees me start and puts his hand on my hand again; warm, gentle. "Hey, it's okay. Don't freak. Listen, I really appreciated this. You were...incredible. I couldn't have done this without you. Obviously."

And then he leans toward me, quickly, too quickly for me to react, and kisses me hard on the mouth. I can't help moving toward him, almost reflexively. I feel the tip of his tongue glide lightly against the inside of my upper lip, and I shiver.

The first thing I think is, *Oh. Wow.*

The second thing I think, as his other hand comes up to stroke the back of my neck, is *This feels wrong*. Oh, it feels *good*, but it's wrong. The timing...my mind's not exactly working clearly. I'm still reeling from his mother's thoughts, from what Cody might do. I shouldn't be kissing anyone right now.

264

And I shouldn't be kissing Cody, of all people. No matter how much I might want to. God, what if Mikaela finds out? She doesn't even think this is a possibility. But I'm still kissing him, aren't I? No. I pull away, my face hot.

Before I can say anything, he leans back and says, "I mean it. I won't forget this."

"Okay." My mind spins, and I wonder if he's going to kiss me again. I want him to and I don't at the same time. But he's already opening the door and getting out of the car.

At school the following Monday, I manage to act like everything's normal. Cody acts like his old self. Mikaela doesn't seem to think anything's weird.

I'm not about to tell her that Cody kissed me, even though it's not like I did anything wrong, because *he* kissed *me*. And it hasn't happened again.

Still, I didn't stop him. I kissed him back. And I can't help thinking about it.

A lot.

From Shiri Langford's journal, August 29th

Such a relief to be back at school, away from THAT. Except of course THAT follows me wherever I go. It doesn't seem to matter what I do. So I stopped taking those stupid antidepressants. I'm not convinced they help me anyway.

(Later)

I did something terrible.

*I tried to tell Brendan about the things I hear. What
a mistake. What a disaster. I'm ~~such a pointless waste
of space~~ so stupid. The other times it's happened
while we were together, I passed it off as side effects
from my medication. Now he knows I'm not taking
my medication any more. He asked what was wrong.
I started to lie, and then I just couldn't stand keeping
it inside anymore and I told him.*

*He didn't say anything at all, just clenched his hands
around the edge of the table. He turned kind of red,
his eyes cold, and he got up and walked out of my
apartment.*

I don't know why he was so angry.

*I haven't been able to get hold of him for the past two
hours. I keep calling and calling.*

twenty-three

The early February air is crisp and dry. A breeze cuts under the open zipper of my jacket as I rush out of my last-period class and into the bathroom along with about eight million other girls.

I retie my ponytail, craning my neck to see around a girl who's hogging the mirror as she applies lipstick. Then I duck into a stall. The swirl of noise and voices echoes around the room for a minute, and then dwindles as the restroom empties out.

I flush the toilet, unlatch the door, and as I'm washing my hands at the sink I hear the clop-clop of high-heeled boots. And who walks in but Cassie, tottering a little on her fancy designer shoes, and Elisa.

Great.

I knew I should have avoided the bathrooms in the social science block.

I don't meet their eyes. I just nod noncommittally and try to dry my hands as quickly as possible.

The electric dryer seems to be operating excruciatingly slowly. I'm about to wipe my hands on my cargo pants and leave when I notice that Elisa is crying.

Against my better judgment, I go up to the two of them where they're standing over in the far corner. I mean, Elisa *was* my friend. And it's not like she did anything to me directly. She just kind of followed along. Like I used to. When I see her crying it's like we're all struggling through freshman year again, and I can't just leave.

"Lise, are you okay?" My voice is tentative. "What's wrong?" Cassie is murmuring comfortingly in Elisa's ear, but when she hears my voice, her head whips up and she glares at me.

"It's none of *your* business," Cassie says. "Like you care about us anymore anyway. Go back to your new friends."

"I'm fine," Elisa says, her voice hoarse. "It's—don't worry about it." She turns away from me, toward Cassie.

"Okay," I say, hurt. "I'm not going to pretend I have any idea what's going on, but here." I fish a tissue out of my purse and hold it out to her.

"Oh, *come on*," Cassie says. She rips the tissue out of my hand almost violently and throws it in the trash can. "You have to know. Everyone does. You're on there, too." She stares at me challengingly, but I have no idea what she's talking about.

"On what?" I sneak a sideways glance at the defaced bathroom wall, half-expecting to see our names and phone numbers listed along with "for a good time, call."

"On the *blog*, stupid."

"I'm not on any blog," I protest. "I haven't even been online in a week."

"I'm talking about that *Voice of the Underground* thing. It got emailed to everyone on the school list. You seriously don't know?" Cassie rolls her eyes and flips her hair over one shoulder. She's looking at me like I'm beyond idiotic.

"I seriously don't know," I tell her, bewildered. I shift my gaze to Elisa, but she's not looking at me. She's still dabbing at tears with her sleeve.

"Yeah, right," Cassie says. "Just check your email."

I stand there for a minute, wondering what the hell is going on, wondering if I should offer Elisa another tissue, but they ignore me. The atmosphere feels brittle, like a dead leaf. So I go. Obviously they don't want me around. I should never have stopped to talk to them in the first place. I shove aside my worry about Elisa and leave.

I have better things to do. I have better friends to see.

First, though, I call home, slowly walking across campus as I hit the speed-dial button and wait for our old answering machine to pick up.

"Auntie Mina? Are you home? This is Sunny." I wait a minute, and she answers.

"Yes, Sunny? How are you? How was school?" She sounds tired.

"Fine," I say. "I wanted to let you know, I was invited to my friend Cody's house after school. I should still be home before Mom and Dad. Will you be okay until I get there?" It's like I'm the adult and Auntie Mina is the child. But I'm worried. Uncle Randall hasn't come over since that last time, but he's been calling a lot ever since they started talking again. Sometimes two or three times a day. That's why we told her not to pick up until whoever it was talked into the machine. She doesn't have to talk to him all the time.

There's been a lot of hang-up messages. Click, and then a dial tone.

"Oh, sweetie, I'll be fine," she says, but her voice sounds artificially cheerful. "You deserve some time with your friends."

I feel a stab of guilt. "Well, call me if you need me."

"Pshht. Go enjoy yourself," she says, and hangs up. But I don't feel any better. Especially since there's absolutely nothing I can do.

Mikaela and Cody are already waiting for me by the gate to the back parking lot, and they fall into step on either side of me as I head for my car. As we walk, I can't help feeling extra-conscious of Cody on my right, of the warmth of his skin as his bare arm brushes mine for a second.

"So why *do* girls take so long in the bathroom?" Cody asks, with fake earnestness.

"It wasn't me," I start to explain; but Mikaela pats me on the head.

"It's okay; we won't tell anyone about your secret girly makeup obsession. Your hidden collection of Cover Girl stuff. The perfume bottles stashed in your locker. The eyebrow pencils in your pencil case."

I start laughing, letting myself be distracted. "Okay, seriously, who carries a pencil case? Name one person."

"Billy Dorf," she says solemnly. Her dark eyes twinkle.

"Fine. Okay. Name *two*."

"I'm sorry to have to tell you this," Cody says, "but... here." He reaches into his backpack and pulls out a battered black plastic pencil case with a Transformers logo on the front and an "Anarchy in the UK" sticker plastered on the back. We all crack up. During the car ride, Cody plugs his iPod into the adapter and cranks the volume and we speed along with the windows open, an old Rob Zombie album streaming out into the breeze. By the time we pull into Cody's neighborhood I'm a little happier.

I'm nervous, though, stepping into Cody's house.

"Are you sure your parents aren't going to be pissed? You're supposed to start work later tonight." I look down at the marble-tiled entryway as I walk in. It's spotless and mirror-shiny, as if it's been recently buffed. A planter box full of fake flowers lines one side of the foyer, which extends out into an open-plan living room and kitchen. Everything looks clean, modern, and strangely empty.

"They're not even going to know," he says. "They won't be home for a few hours. By the time they get back, I'll already be at the theater." He smiles enigmatically. "Want anything from the kitchen? I can fix a mean whiskey and Coke."

"Uh, that's okay," I say. "It's a little early."

"I'll take one," Mikaela says, grinning at me mischievously. "Sunny can be a party pooper, but *somebody's* gotta have some fun around here."

"Fine, whatever," I say, but I'm not really in the mood. I feel like his parents could show up any second. I take a doctored Coke, though, and help carry enough chips and snacks to feed a small army. It's supposed to be an "anti-retirement" party, just the three of us, before he leaves for his first evening on the job.

I've tried—and failed—repeatedly to imagine him in that stupid red vest they make all the movie concessions workers wear. I don't think I've seen him wear anything but black or gray.

So much for that Thumbscrew job he kept talking about.

We plop down in the sunken living room and spread everything out on the glass coffee table. The hardwood floor is almost completely covered in a fancy white shag rug. I make sure my drink is on a coaster and far away from the edge of the table before I grab a handful of cheese puffs and start crunching away.

Mikaela rips open a bag of pretzels. Cody turns on the entertainment center and switches to a music video channel. We sit there for a few minutes, yelling and laughing over the music and cramming our faces with junk food. It's nice, not having to think.

After a while, Cody clicks a button on the remote and mutes the sound. The silence is almost painful after the crunching and wailing of guitars.

He pulls a fancy laptop from the bottom shelf of the coffee table.

"I have to show you guys something," he says with barely suppressed glee.

"Is it that band you were telling me about? The one with

the girl drummer? You better not *like* her," Mikaela says teasingly. I flinch inwardly.

"Nope." Cody is fidgety, waiting for the computer to boot up. "You'll see."

"C'mon, tell us," she says, scooting a little closer to him on the couch. I'm sitting on his other side, and I lean toward him for a better view as he opens up the web browser.

This close to him, I can't help thinking about what happened the last time we sat so close to each other. It's been over two weeks, but I can't get it out of my head.

"You can call this the last gasp of freedom before my corporate enslavement," Cody says.

"When are you going to learn? We're all already slaves to The Man." Mikaela pokes him in the arm.

"I'm going to have to agree with Mikaela on this one," I say.

"Fine," Cody says, "but The Man had nothing to do with this." He quickly enters a URL into the browser, too fast for me to read it before the page pops up.

When I see what the graphic at the top of the page says, I feel like I'm going to spew cheese balls all over the table.

"*Voice of the Underground*," Cody says. "AKA me."

"Oh, hilarious." Mikaela reaches out to scroll down the page, stroking one black-painted fingernail along the touch screen.

"Hang on a sec—let me see that," I say, finally finding my voice. I'm thinking of Elisa crying in the bathroom earlier and what Cassie said, and I have a nasty feeling of dread. I lean closer and read the top blog post.

DESPERATE FUTURE HOUSEWIVES AT C.V.H.S.!
screams the headline. *Who's in bed with who? It's not who you think it is. Did C.P. get with D.W. at a secret party? Is E.N.'s boy toy going to be suicidally depressed when he finds out she's been snogging somebody else? Or is he going to kick some ass?*

GOTHS GONE WILD. C.J.D. last seen at Palmwood Park with his shirt off, blinding thousands of innocent bystanders. It goes on for a while, making fun of some kids I barely know who apparently did something to get on Cody's bad side, but I'm hung up on the first paragraph.

C.P. Cassie Parker. E.N. Elisa Nguyen.

This is horrible. It's really, really mean and petty.

And there's only one way Cody could have been able to write this stuff. He wouldn't even have *known* any of it if it hadn't been for me. Me and my stupid underhearing.

I'm a terrible person.

So much for trying to use underhearing to do good. Instead, I've just ruined people's lives.

Correction: *Cody* has ruined people's lives.

But I helped.

twenty-four

Cody is sitting there beaming like he's a little kid who just drew a picture for his mommy. My stomach churns, and it's not from the whiskey and Coke I barely touched.

"Cody..." I swallow, hard. "This is kind of mean."

"This is need-to-know information," Cody says, still grinning. "Anyway, I thought you hated them. Why do you care?"

"Elisa was *crying*," I tell him. I lean away from him, my back rigid. "That's why I took so long in the bathroom earlier."

"So? It's just payback for all those times they were bitchy to you."

"You know, you're allowed to be angry at them," Mikaela says. "You can't just hold it in forever. Let it out. *Let it go.*" She sweeps one arm out, a little drunkenly. I glare at both of them.

"I thought you'd be grateful." Cody isn't smiling anymore. He's starting to look annoyed.

"Grateful? You are really..." *Clueless? Missing the point?*

Nothing seems adequate to describe what I'm feeling right now. I remember what Cassie said and I start wondering if I'm on the blog somewhere, revealed as some kind of magical psychic know-it-all. My face gets hot and I dig my fingers into my palms.

And *he* has the nerve to look pissed.

I force myself to calm down enough to talk.

"I don't need revenge, okay? I just don't want to talk to them anymore." Actually, if I'm honest with myself, the only person I don't want to see anymore is Cassie. Nobody else did anything all that bad. That's what makes this so wrong. That, and the fact that Cody went behind my back again, used my underhearing for his own personal gain.

"Not only that, it was a private conversation. I told you what I'd heard *in confidence*. It wasn't supposed to be public knowledge." My voice trembles, but I'm too upset to care. "I don't care if they're not my friends. It's a matter of ethics."

Mikaela snorts. "Ethics? It's a blog. And what about free speech? Plus, it's just people's initials. It could be anyone."

"Come on, like people can't guess," I tell her. "And the URL was sent out to the whole school."

Cody looks surprised for a second, then starts laughing. "I didn't do that. But hey, I guess somebody thinks it's of interest to the general public."

Mikaela looks a little worried. "So the whole school knows now?" She smacks Cody on the top of the head.

"Ow! Fuck, what was that for?"

"*Dumb*ass," Mikaela says. "For putting me on there, that's what it's for. I don't need two thousand people calling me 'a valued member of the Psychic Friends Network.'" But she's smiling a little, too. It's hard to know whether she's really even mad.

"You didn't talk about *me*, did you?" I look at him coldly.

"I didn't mention you by name, if that's what you're worried about," he says. "Not even by initials. I said...let's see... 'Former JV swim hottie seen cavorting with men in black.' And I didn't say a thing about your power. I told you I wouldn't tell anyone. I think it's awesome, what you can do."

Cody gives me a crooked smile. For a second, I almost believe him.

Then I come crashing down to earth again. He's still trying to flatter me, still trying to convince me that he cares. Trying to downplay the fact that he's using me.

But he doesn't understand what it's like to be able to do this. He doesn't understand how much just the smallest amount of knowledge can hurt people.

"I mean it," Cody says, still looking right at me. "You're one of the most amazing people I've ever met."

I look down, running one hand over the velvety, cream-colored surface of the couch cushion. I want to believe him. But his words make me feel sick.

"Sunny, just take a compliment, why don't you?" Mikaela throws a pretzel at me.

"You know, you could really help people," Cody says.

I remember the first time I ever told Mikaela about my underhearing, how she said it could be a real gift.

"I know," I whisper. And I do. But.

"You could help me again." His voice is low and urgent,

his eyes intense. For a moment, it's like Mikaela's not even in the room, like it's just the two of us.

There's a twinge in my chest.

"It's my parents, of course," he says, answering a question I didn't ask. "After what you found out, I asked them what was up. They said if I don't do everything right this time..." He trails off, picks up the remote control and turns it over and over in his hands. His face is set and angry. Suddenly, he draws his arm back and flings the remote across the room. It ricochets off the immaculate beige wall, chipping the paint, and falls to the floor. My whole body tenses up.

Mikaela just leans her head back against the couch and stares at the ceiling. "I can't believe them," she says. "They cannot send you to boarding school. That's freakin' ridiculous. What is this, the nineteenth century?"

Cody slumps back on the couch. Despite everything, I feel sorry for him.

"I hate asking this," he says. "But you—I think you can do this."

"Do what?" I look up at him from under my hair, suddenly nervous.

He pauses, glances at Mikaela, then looks back at me. "I was thinking that if your—uh, power—if it goes in one direction, maybe it goes in the other direction, right?"

I frown. "Like ... what? Other people reading *my* thoughts?" I'm not sure what Cody is getting at. "They're already reading my thoughts. You just published them on a web page for all the world to see."

"Well," he says, "I guess I mean—what I—I need you,

Sunny." His voice is pleading now. "I need you to...do something to my parents. Make them stop. I don't want to get sent off. If I went to military school—fuck." He swears some more, takes a long swig of his drink. "I can't go to military school."

"You would so get your cute little ass kicked," Mikaela says, laughing.

"Whatever." Cody slams the laptop shut and puts it on the floor. He looks back up at me. "You have to help. I don't know what else to do. You could...push back. I don't know."

Push back? I feel like I'm made of lead, like I'm sinking into the couch, into the floor.

"It doesn't work like that," I say finally. "I want to help, but...it just won't work." I wouldn't *want* to do it, wouldn't want to force my thoughts on other people, even if I could.

"You haven't tried it, though," Mikaela says.

"I don't have to try it." My voice is taut and angry. They don't understand. Every time my underhearing happens, I feel like I'm on the edge of a precipice, like I'm on the edge of losing myself.

I already lost Shiri. I won't lose myself. I can't.

"Why are you being so resistant?" Mikaela sits forward, leans around Cody to stare at me. "Don't you at least want to find out if it's possible? To influence someone?"

"No, I don't," I say. "Because it isn't." I start to get up.

"You of all people should know that anything is possible at this point," Cody says, his eyes glinting. "I think you *can* do it. You learned to control it in the first place."

It takes every ounce of self-control I have not to scream.

I stand, stepping away from the pristine beige couch and the junk-food-covered coffee table.

"I can barely control it in one direction," I say through clenched teeth. "What makes you think it even works any other way?" I fumble in my jeans pocket for my car keys.

"Wait," Cody says. "You're not even going to try? You could show *me* how to do it, if that makes you feel better."

"It doesn't matter. It isn't right. You can't just make people do what you want." It's absurd that he's even considering it. And he's using me to do it. He's manipulating everyone.

"Oh, come on, Sunny," Mikaela says, slumping against Cody and smirking at me.

I turn my back and walk out.

———

I sit in the car for a few minutes with the engine off. My forehead rests against the top of the steering wheel and I breathe deeply, the bridge of my nose throbbing with an impending headache.

My mind keeps circling the same set of thoughts, over and over. Elisa crying. The web page full of stupid gossip I was responsible for. Cody needing help; help that it's not in my power to give. Anger at him, but also guilt at walking out when maybe I should have stayed and helped somehow. I should have at least stuck around long enough to commiserate, like Mikaela.

But even if I could have helped, it didn't feel right. I don't even *know* his parents. Unfair or not, whether they send him away to school is still their choice. It's Cody's responsibility to talk to them, not mine.

The headache pinches a little more. I take deep, slow breaths, picturing the flickering of the flame on my black-cherry candle, ocean waves creeping back and forth along the sand, the meditative feeling of swimming endless laps in the pool.

I'm only trying to relax enough to drive home. But without consciously meaning to do it, my mind is inexorably pulled back toward the house, back toward Cody. Suddenly I want to know, more than anything, what his issue really is. What can make a person so oblivious about everyone around him. Determined, I push harder.

I get vertigo, like I'm being tipped upside down. Then it gets weird.

At first, all I find is a maelstrom of swirling darkness. It surrounds me, buffeting me like a windstorm. Suddenly I'm in the center, floating, slowly tumbling in the eye of the storm, my ears ringing in the silence. That's where I start to get a sensation of hiddenness, of the real Cody veiled beneath the chaos, protected by an ice-brittle surface layer. But there are cracks and melted spots in that icy surface, and I slip through.

Paradoxically, I smell heat. I smell smoke, like a burning tire, and

—it's not fair, nobody ever cares what I want,
what about me—

—me, I deserve better than this and they'll realize
I'm smarter than them one day and they'll be
begging me to come back—
—I won't be the one begging, not like this—
—not fair—NOT FAIR

The burning feeling becomes so strong that I cough, jolting myself back to reality as I spaz into the steering wheel, bumping my collarbone.

I grip the wheel, steadying myself. And I understand everything with perfect clarity. Yes, Cody's been using me. I was stupid not to realize it sooner. But I still feel sorry for him. Sorry because he's just a selfish, immature little boy who thinks everything revolves around him. Sorry because there's obviously something really wrong in his family, in his life, if the way he views relationships is in terms of what's in it for him.

Sorry because I thought he cared about something, anything, besides himself.

Tears are streaming down my face, but at the same time a part of me feels lighter.

I turn the keys in the ignition and drive home.

From Shiri Langford's journal, September 3rd

Pain is not my friend.

The pain pills they gave me are nothing more than glorified aspirin. My ankle is still swollen like a purple balloon and I'm benched for the next month at least, maybe two. Maybe more. The ligament is torn, they said. Don't put weight on it, they said. Wear this air cast, they said. I'll need crutches until I can put weight on it.

I was having such a good practice, too, until I landed wrong on the court and went down, my right ankle bending the wrong way with a tearing, burning twist.

I don't know what I'm going to do now. I think the only reason I've kept my scholarship is because I've been playing so well and coach made an exception for me. My grades just aren't high enough, and thanks to last semester I'm on probation. I have this semester to get my GPA back up. That's all. My dad would kill me if he found out.

I've been giving Brendan some space. He still hasn't called me.

twenty-five

By the time I get home, I've stopped crying, but my face is damp and sore and my throat is raw. I really thought I knew Cody. How stupid I was. I only saw one side of him. I only *wanted* to see one side of him. I wanted him to be the Cody who encouraged me to accept my underhearing, the Cody who helped me get control over it, who held me when I was scared and shaking. I didn't want to see the rest of it.

I have no idea where I stand with Mikaela now, either. She's got to be thinking I'm cold and heartless for not trying to help him. Then again, maybe she's glad to have Cody all to herself. I dash away a few more angry tears. Either way, I don't belong in the picture. I don't even know if I want to be in the picture. For all I know, she was aware of the blog as soon as he wrote it and just didn't bother to tell me about it. The thought makes me furious all over again.

When I walk inside, the house is quiet. My parents aren't home yet. I go into the kitchen, splash my face in the sink, and pat it dry with a dish towel. There's a small mess of breakfast dishes in the sink and the compost bowl smells like banana peel, but I think of Cody's sterile house and I'm profoundly relieved to be home.

On my way upstairs, I almost crash into Auntie Mina.

She looks at me with a startled half-smile. Then she gets a good look at my face and the smile falls away.

Maybe I should have taken the time to put cucumber slices on my eyes, make it a little less obvious that I've been weepy. But Auntie Mina doesn't ask questions. She just gathers me close into a warm, tight hug and holds me there for a minute.

At first I resist. I'm tired of my problems and I'm sick of everybody else's issues, too. And I don't want to cry anymore.

But for a second, I do.

"Sit with me for a minute, okay?" Auntie Mina says gently. "I'll make you a cup of hot tea with honey, and then you can escape."

I swallow, my throat dry and swollen. Tea and honey might not be a bad idea. Just for a minute.

I sit at the kitchen table, leaning my chin in my left hand as Auntie Mina fills the electric teakettle with water. I know she wants to talk, or she would have just put a cup of water in the microwave.

Correction: she wants *me* to talk.

But there's too much to say.

We sit in silence for a while, me clenching my teeth, Auntie Mina grading a stack of quizzes from the computer science class she's now teaching at the college extension. Every so often she looks up at me with a sympathetic smile, pushing one graying lock of dark hair back behind her ear.

Eventually, sitting and waiting for the kettle to whistle, I do say something. It sounds like a question. But it really isn't, because I think I already know the answer.

"What do you do if you're disappointed by somebody you really thought you cared about? Like maybe they're not the person you thought they were. And the person they are...isn't someone you want to be around." It sounds stupid, childish, when I say it out loud. But it's true.

Auntie Mina is quiet for a minute, thinking, but looking at me seriously. Then I'm horrified, because I wonder if she thinks I'm talking about her and Uncle Randall.

"I mean—" I start to try to backpedal.

"It's okay," she says with a small smile. "I know. It's hard at your age, when everybody's figuring out who they are and who they really want to be. Trying one thing out or another. Even new friends." She looks at me intently. "It can happen at any age."

"It's not just them who's different, though," I say. I look down, stare at a faint stain on the surface of the table. "It's me."

She gets up, pours the hot water into two mugs, and brings them to the table with a basket of tea bags. For a moment she just sits there pensively, dunking a tea bag in and out of her mug.

"It's always like that, I suppose," she finally says, sighing. "Yes, sometimes the person you thought you knew turns out to be very different after all. But sometimes—sometimes you figure something out about your own needs, too, your own goals and dreams, and those might not be the same as everybody else's. They *shouldn't* be, because you're your own person."

She puts one hand over mine. I look down at her neatly trimmed fingernails, the wiry strength in her slender fingers that I never seemed to notice before.

My own person. I think about Cody, about how I'd always thought he was so individualistic and determined. I thought he really wanted more out of his life than he was getting, like maybe he'd graduate and go on to be some kind of artistic mastermind or form his own startup company or something else that misunderstood geniuses do.

Oh, he wants things to be different. He wants everything to revolve around *him*.

And then I think about Uncle Randall, and how Auntie Mina must have felt over the years, slowly finding out with every argument that he wasn't the fairy-tale prince she thought he was. I feel like crying again, but instead I just let out a long, shaky breath.

"You have to be strong," Auntie Mina says, her voice thick with emotion, squeezing my hand once more before releasing it. I'm not quite sure whether she's talking to me or to both of us.

Later that night, lying in bed, I'm thinking again about what she said. About being strong. I assumed Cody was strong. Then I realized how easily cracked that icy shell really was. That isn't real strength. Clinging to your own petty little wants at any cost, even when they're impossible or hurtful.

Letting go, maybe, is what takes real strength.

Sometimes, though, you can't just let go. Sometimes you have to learn to live with things.

I wonder if I can be strong enough to learn to live with my underhearing, to really figure out how to use it, and how not to. I don't know if I'm capable of it. But I have more control over it now than I ever did. Nobody else can do it for me. I have to try.

I pull my knees in to my chest and huddle under the sheets. It seems so difficult. There are so many things I *can't* do. I can't go back in time and make Shiri not want to die. I can't force Uncle Randall to be the person Auntie Mina wants him to be. I can't help Cody, not the way he wants me to, because I'm not that kind of person.

It's hard enough to live with my ability to underhear. If I did help Cody, I wouldn't be able to live with myself.

———

During my library period the next day, I check my school email. Click on the link that takes me to *Voice of the Underground*. I read it all again, this time in its entirety. I check for references to me, to my underhearing. I have to know for sure if Cody said anything about me. Not because I can do anything about it. I just need to know what kind of person he really is; no illusions. I scour it twice; three times.

All I find are vague references to the Psychic Friends Network. To "mysterious sources" and "secret information."

And that stupid JV swim hottie thing. My name isn't anywhere. Not even my initials.

I'm surprised, and a little relieved. But I don't really feel better. All it does is drive home the point that I never really mattered to him; didn't really exist as a person in his eyes. Just a tool to be used.

———————

At lunchtime, I go to my car to eat, sitting on the driver's side with my food on the seat next to me. I put my earbuds in and blast the Beatles' "Nowhere Man." For the first time in a long time, I think about Shiri and don't feel like I'm being stabbed in the gut. But I'm not happy.

The rest of the day passes uneventfully, and by some miracle, I pull a B+ on a history pop quiz despite being a chapter behind on reading. After school, I sit on my bed dangling a toy mouse in front of Pixie. Should I call Mikaela? I don't know what I would say, but I want to make sure we're okay at least. Maybe she's not even mad at me. I should have called earlier. Yesterday, maybe.

I'm just digging my cell phone out of my backpack when the home phone rings. Auntie Mina comes out of the guest room and shouts down the stairs, "I'll get it. Don't pick it up! I'm on my way down." Her muffled footsteps recede.

How could I have forgotten? It's Uncle Randall. Right on schedule, and brought to you by the home phone. The only difference this time is that they've had their first marriage counseling appointment, but Auntie Mina refused to tell us how it went. All she told us was that they're supposed to talk more about the trial separation.

The ringing stops abruptly as Auntie Mina picks up. My stomach flip-flops and I decide to head downstairs. When I get there, I notice that the study door is closed. I can't hear anything. Mom's not home from work but Dad is sitting stiffly at the kitchen table, so I sink into one of the empty chairs and nervously start fiddling with the salt shaker. My hands are trembling and I drop it, scattering grains of salt.

"Sorry."

My dad glances up from the Sudoku puzzle he's pretending to do. He's sitting there with his pencil poised, but he's not actually filling in numbers. The pencil is shaking ever so slightly. My heart twists.

I sweep the grains of spilled salt into my hand, get up, and dump them into the sink. On the way back to the table, I stop behind my dad's chair and give him a hug, squeezing his neck the way I used to when I was little. His hair smells like tea-tree shampoo. "Love you, Dad."

"I love you, too, Sun." He sounds quiet, forlorn. He reaches up and squeezes my arm. "I'm glad you're here."

I sit back down. A few more minutes pass. My dad finally fills in a couple of numbers on his Sudoku puzzle.

I lean back in my chair and sigh loudly. "This is ridiculous. I'm sick of just waiting around like *he's* the one in control. Can't we—"

"Shh," my dad says. "I want to be able to hear if she needs us."

Hear. If she needs us. Now there's an idea. There *is* something I can do.

Something only I can do.

After what happened with Cody, I'm not sure if I can. I don't know if can stay calm enough, if I can bear to reach out again. But it's Auntie Mina, it's my *family* this time, so I have to try.

I sit back against the wooden slats of the chair and close my eyes. My dad is right across the table from me, but he might as well be in a different city. He's lost in his own little world.

And I'm in mine. But I'm not lost.

In fact, it's getting easier. This time I almost settle into it, like leaning back into space and trusting somebody is going to be there to catch me.

But I have to be focused. If something goes wrong, I might not be able to try again. Not in time to help; not with how depleted it makes me. I concentrate on letting go, on letting my attention leave the room and find Auntie Mina. I can hear my dad tapping his pencil point on the newspaper. He lets out a sigh, but the sound is far away.

And then I'm sort of spinning through my mind, my head aching like I'm being flung through space on a roller coaster. I take a slow breath; then another.

Gradually the spinning stops and I feel normal again. I tentatively reach out.

I find Auntie Mina. And I find something else. Someone else.

Something about this feels different. It feels like my consciousness is ping-ponging between two places, like I'm hearing a different voice in each ear. I don't like it; it scares me. And what I realize about it scares me even more.

It's not just Auntie Mina, but Uncle Randall, too. Somehow I'm hearing them both, as if he's in the house with her. It makes me want to clap my hands over my ears. But I can't move. There is a smell, almost a taste, of iron, of horseradish, and I suppress the urge to cough. I fight to hold on, and I—

> *—this is NOT what we agreed to when we got married*
> > *—counselor said she said I'm—*
> *—know what the counselor said, and that counselor is*
> > *full of—*
> *—she was right, he doesn't listen to me he just—*

I find myself thinking urgently, almost praying, *Auntie Mina, just be strong, be strong like you told me*, and I know it isn't going to work but I can't help thinking it, every fiber in me is straining toward her, and—

> *—always trying to tell you something's wrong with you,*
> > *nothing's wrong with ME—*
> > > *—how can I go back if he doesn't listen*
> > > > *—you owe me—listen to me!*
> *—face-to-face, at least give me the courtesy of—*
> > *—owe me*
> > > *—don't you dare tell me what to—*
> *—talk face-to-face? why not now? yes, NOW—*

The metallic smell intensifies and this time I do cough and sit up, opening my eyes abruptly. My dad slides his water glass toward me with an expression of concern, but I ignore it. Waves of fury, of frustration and defensiveness and desperation, threaten to drown me. I feel them pour through me, meld with my own desperate need to do something, to change things somehow; to keep Uncle Randall, who has to be nearby, from bullying Auntie Mina or any of us. I stumble out of my seat and into a half-run. When I get to the living room, I part the sheer curtains on the front window and peek out. Nothing. I peer down one side of the street, then the other, as far as I can from where I'm standing.

There it is, parked halfway down the street. Uncle Randall's white Mercedes. And the driver's side door is opening. My heart thuds.

I turn back around, letting the curtain drop. I have to tell Auntie Mina. I've almost reached the far end of the hall when the study door opens and she comes out. I stop short and stare at her, my fists clenched at my sides.

"He's here," I tell her. "His car is parked down the street. He's coming."

I swallow, and fight back hot tears that I refuse, refuse to cry.

"I know," Auntie Mina says. She smiles gently, sadly.

I don't even question how she knows. I don't know whether he told her or whether she found out some other, more unusual way, if somehow she sensed it when I was hoping with everything in me that she could be strong. Does it even matter? All of a sudden my fingers and toes start to tingle and I feel like I'm going to pass out. Cold sweat breaks out on my forehead and I lean against the wall for support.

Auntie Mina puts one hand on my cheek, then draws me into a fierce hug. I can feel myself tremble slightly.

What now? I don't know what to do. I look up at her questioningly.

"We wait," she says.

twenty-six

Auntie Mina puts her arm around my waist and we walk into the kitchen together. My dad is already on his feet. In one glance he takes in my face, drained of color, and Auntie Mina's, smiling unconvincingly. Dad comes up to us and puts a hand on each of our shoulders.

"What's happened now?" he asks, sounding more resigned than I expected.

"Uncle Randall's here," I say weakly. "I saw his car parked down the street. He's coming." I feel dad's hand tighten.

"I didn't realize he was planning to come here," Auntie Mina says in a quiet voice. "He said—well, he thinks he deserves a face-to-face conversation before we decide to finalize the separation. He's said it before."

"What? That's ridiculous," my dad says.

"Maybe we should call the police," I start saying, but nobody's listening.

"You talk about respect, Ali," Auntie Mina says, her voice strained now. "You always tell me that Randall needs to show me respect. If I show him this one small courtesy, I expect him to respect my space in return."

"He's *never* shown you enough respect." My dad's face is tight with tension.

Auntie Mina looks up at him, stubborn. "I know you've never liked him. But this is right for *me*. I'm comfortable just letting him have his say, and then we take a little time away and think about it. If it gets uncomfortable..." She sounds like she's trying to convince herself.

Dad makes an exasperated noise and starts pacing around the kitchen.

"You don't have to do anything you're not comfortable with," I say forcefully. "If we have to, we can call the police." Auntie Mina glances at me. I look down at my hand; my phone is still in it from when I was going to call Mikaela. That seems like a year ago now.

My dad brings his fist down on the kitchen counter, rattling a few dishes in the dish drainer. We all jump.

"I'm sorry," he says, his voice rough. "But I don't think it's a good idea. If you insist on talking to the man, you should have a mediator. There's just been too much—too much for all of us. I'm going to tell him that. I'm going to tell him it's time to go home and cool off." He moves toward the doorway to the front hall.

"I wish you'd just let me talk to him," Auntie Mina says.

"You've *been* talking to him," my dad points out. "And all it's done is keep you from living your life. You have to move on. Life is better than this, Mina. He isn't good for you."

For the first time, I notice the laugh and frown lines

together on my dad's face, and I wonder if the frown lines were there before all of this happened.

It's changed all of us.

"Mina, listen," my dad says, his voice softening. "I hate to sound like a domineering jerk, but I can't let you talk to him when he's like this. It's an issue of your safety. We don't want anything to happen to you."

Auntie Mina looks deflated. My stomach churns with worry. I hope she really understands what a loser he is, and how dangerous he is. All she has to do is remember that bruise on her shoulder, the one on her wrist. I sure can't forget.

But I guess if you've loved someone that long, it's hard to just stop.

There's a sharp, angry knock on the front door. I go cold. My dad strides briskly into the front hall and goes outside, closing the door behind him. My heart in my throat, I start to follow.

"Sunny, no," Auntie Mina says.

I keep walking to the door. I'm worried about Dad, but even more than that, I'm tired of hearing thoughts, snippets. This time I want the whole conversation. I want to see how Uncle Randall is going to *act*. And I want to be sure Auntie Mina treats him how he deserves to be treated.

What people think is one thing. What they do is another.

My mind flashes onto Spike—uncertain, hopeful, but kissing me as if there was no doubt in his mind what he wanted, no fear of repercussions. And Cody—who always seemed so confident, looking at me with fear, seething with desperation inside. I shake my head and focus.

I open the front door.

I sense Auntie Mina standing behind me, and she grabs my arm, but I pull away. I glance at her; she's holding a golf umbrella. I look down at it stupidly.

"Just in case," she says, the tiniest wry smile twitching at her lips. "I don't think we'll need it, but you never know." I show her the phone in my hand, the numbers 9-1-1 already punched in. She squeezes my shoulder, gently this time, and I feel some of the tension, some of the fear for Auntie Mina, release its grip. I feel like we're a united front.

I hope we are.

I turn back toward the open doorway. Dad is talking to Uncle Randall in the driveway. The white Mercedes is parked, somewhat sloppily, at the curb.

" ... doesn't want to see you right now," my dad is saying. His back is toward me, so I can't see his expression; and he's blocking Uncle Randall, too; standing between him and the cement walk leading up to our front steps.

"Well, at least let her tell me that herself," Uncle Randall says, his tone polite but brittle. He tries to sidestep Dad, but Dad moves to block him. I take a big step back, my heart pounding, and crash into Auntie Mina.

"I don't think that's a good idea," Dad says coldly. "I think you'd better leave now. You shouldn't be confronting her when you're both angry."

"Come on. You and Debby are always the ones so into talking and letting it all hang out." He's standing really close to Dad now, jabbing a finger at his chest belligerently. "Now you've got us going to a counselor, letting a stranger in on all our private family business and telling us how our marriage is supposed to work. All that talk, and you don't want me talking to *her*?" His voice oozes contempt and a dull fury swells within me. It's a good thing I'm not holding the golf umbrella. I feel like smashing the windows of his precious car.

Dad's back stiffens. "This has nothing to do with me or Debby," he says, practically spitting the words out one by one. "It has to do with my sister, and the fact that you've been bullying her."

"Oh, *bullying*," Uncle Randall says. His face is red now. "If I were going to bully my own wife, would I have brought flowers?" He waves a wilted bouquet in the air. "Would I be standing here right now arguing with someone who has no right to interfere?"

"Listen carefully," my dad says, enunciating every syllable. "I'm asking you very politely now to please leave our property. Mina will talk to you whenever and however she's comfortable doing so. Just *not now*." His voice is quiet and dangerous. But Uncle Randall doesn't leave.

I glance behind me. Auntie Mina looks pale and tight-lipped. Where's my mom? She should be home by now.

"I just want to talk to her for a minute," Uncle Randall says, his voice changing to a wheedle. "Can't you just give me a minute?"

"Whatever it is, you can say it over the phone," my dad says, standing his ground. I reach out to grasp Auntie Mina's hand.

"I *need to see her*. We can't accomplish anything over the phone."

"You mean, you can't dole out bruises over the phone," my dad says flatly. I close my eyes for a moment and sigh quietly. Auntie Mina starts to tremble, just a little. I don't know what to do, so I hold her hand tighter.

Uncle Randall says something very softly, so softly I can't make it out, and then, to my horror, my dad brings his balled fists up from his sides.

"I'm giving you one more chance to leave," Dad says, "before I call the police."

Uncle Randall stands taller, trying to see past him. "I'm giving *you* one more chance to let me see my *wife*."

My mouth drops open in disbelief as he shoves Dad in the chest. Dad takes a step backward but he doesn't give up any more ground.

And then Auntie Mina somehow slips away from me, and she's standing in front of us, in full view of Uncle Randall, the golf umbrella clutched to her chest like she's hanging on for dear life.

"Here I am," she says—in a different tone of voice, one I haven't heard. She sounds stronger. She sounds angry. "You've seen me. Now you can go."

"This is ridiculous," Uncle Randall says, his face almost purple. "I'm not leaving."

I take a deep breath. I can't leave Dad alone out there for one more moment, but even more, it's Auntie Mina who still needs me. Who needs us. But I'm terrified, my mind and heart are both racing, and I don't even have a golf umbrella.

All I have in my hands is my phone. All I have is me.

I step up to join Auntie Mina, standing just behind her and Dad.

"Yes, you are leaving."

The voice that comes out is strong, and hardly even sounds like me, somehow. Somehow it doesn't betray that my insides could shatter like glass.

I sound confident; I sound like my mother.

Uncle Randall looks at me like he's never seen me before, but he's still standing there.

"*Get off my property,*" Dad hisses. He grabs the collar of Uncle Randall's shirt before he can even react; he gives it one hard shake before letting go.

I suck in a startled breath. Uncle Randall stumbles backward a step, his eyes first widening with shock and possibly a little fear, then narrowing again as he regains composure. Moving forward again, he opens his mouth to say something, visibly enraged.

The automatic garage door opens. It's Mom. Her car pulls into the driveway.

Uncle Randall stops short. He says coldly, "We'll settle this later, then," and stalks back to his fancy car and drives off. I know he'll hire the best lawyer money can buy, and he might win that battle, but we're not going to let him win the war. I'm sure of that now.

I let out my breath, shakily. The house, the neighborhood, feel quiet again. Safe.

Mom, Auntie Mina, and I rush to meet Dad as he comes up the front steps. He looks bent, tired; he looks ten years older. Inside, he walks into the living room and sinks down on the couch with an explosive sigh. His eyes are sad, not angry like I expected.

"So, you heard," he says lightly.

I sit down next to my dad and hug him, leaning my head on his shoulder like when I was a little kid. I feel drained. At the same time I can't help feeling foolishly proud of my dad. I know it's all old-fashioned, and my mom would probably call it pre-feminist idealism and say she and Auntie Mina should have been the ones to go out there in the first place, but I like it that Dad's willing to fight to defend his family. And we were right there, ready to back him up.

"Dad, you were like our guard dog," I say, knowing it's inadequate to what I'm really feeling. But I have to say something. "You were great."

"Grrrr," he says, a little weakly.

"If it's all the same to you," my mom puts in with a small smile, "I'd rather be married to a lover, not a fighter." All of us, including Auntie Mina, laugh a little louder than is strictly necessary.

"Now I think we need some chamomile tea," my mom continues, steering Auntie Mina ahead of her toward the kitchen and yanking my dad up from the couch. "We all need to unwind after that. And then, I think I'd like to talk about restraining orders."

My mom is kind of a fighter herself. She doesn't usually show it—her days of protesting ended, she claims, when she graduated from college—but if she thinks injustice is involved, she can't help herself. It's just the way she is. She starts bringing up advocacy and civil rights, equality and respect, and we all roll our eyes and say she must have lived in Santa Cruz too long, but she's right.

My parents might be bizarre, but at times like these, I really do love them.

After all, I'm a little bizarre too.

From Shiri Langford's journal, September 25th

It's all arranged. By next weekend, I won't have to worry about any of this. Or about THAT.

Sunny, if you're reading this, I wish I could explain everything, but I can't. Just know that it wasn't anyone's fault, it was me. I just couldn't do it anymore. Any of it.

I'm afraid of what you'll think of me. I'm afraid you'll think I'm a coward.

I am. I'm sorry.

twenty-seven

Later that evening, I pull out Shiri's journal. I haven't looked at it in a couple of weeks but I've been thinking about what she said, about Auntie Mina being more sensitive to other people's emotions. I've been wondering, again, where it fits in with my underhearing. With *our* underhearing—mine and Shiri's. I know I won't be able to figure out anything I haven't already, but I still feel like looking at it.

As I'm taking the journal out of the desk drawer where it's been lying incognito, it slips out of my hands and falls to the floor, splayed open face-down. I pick it up and smooth out a few creased pages, and that's when I notice a folded page, almost at the back of the book. The top half is torn off—it's just the bottom half of the page—and it's been folded so the outside edge doesn't show, which was why I didn't see it before. I might never have seen it if I hadn't dropped the book, unless I'd gone through every single page one by one. And I guess I didn't.

My fingers tremble a little as I unfold it, though I tell

myself there probably isn't anything there. But there is. The small half-page is full, cramped with writing.

Something looks familiar about it, and on instinct I flip to the front of the book where I'd stashed her note to me. I pull it out. It's on a half-sheet of paper. I flip back to the folded page and set the note above it, torn edges together.

It's a perfect fit.

Dear Sunny: I don't expect you to understand any of this yet, but we'll always have yesterday ... and today, and tomorrow. Maybe one day you'll figure it out. I never could.

I said in my last entry that I couldn't explain it even if I wanted to. By now—if I'm right about what's been happening to me—I think you'll know what I mean. I know that's a cop-out, but I'm too weak and scared to try anymore, and all I can think is that if I tell anyone else, I'll lose them, too. I don't want to lose you. I've already lost Brendan; I've lost Mom. When I tried to tell her about Dad, she didn't want to listen. And I couldn't prove anything. It's a curse, being able to do something nobody else can. If it ever happens to you, you have to promise me you'll be strong. Be stronger than I was.

I love you, Sunny. And tell Mom I love her, too.

———

I sit on my bed for a while after that, staring at nothing.

———

Then I pick up the journal again and go downstairs.

———

Auntie Mina is in the living room with her laptop, the TV on quietly in the background. I can hear Mom in the kitchen, and I don't know where Dad is. That's fine, because I have something I need to say to Auntie Mina in private.

She looks up when I walk in and immediately sets her laptop on the coffee table. Silently, I sit down next to her. I think about my words for a moment more, and although she eyes the book in my lap, she doesn't press me.

"The day Shiri died," I begin, then stop. I have to swallow past a lump in my throat. "Before I even found out what happened, I got this in the mail." I pick up the journal, the plain navy-blue book that literally fell at my feet so many months ago, and place it gently into her hands.

With trembling fingers, she opens the cover; flips through page after page, reading some, skimming others. I stay quiet. I don't point out anything, I don't ask questions. I don't even watch her reading—I pretend to look at the television screen, though if you asked me what I was watching, I would have no clue.

After several minutes, I hear her close the cover with a quiet rustle of paper.

Auntie Mina puts her hand on mine.

"Thank you, Sunny."

I wipe my wet cheeks. "It's yours. I think you should have it. I've already read it."

"Well," she says, and then pauses, seems to rethink whatever she was about to say.

What she says is, "Shiri...she was always different." Her voice is sad, but she doesn't seem devastated like I was afraid she might be. Like she would have been even a few months ago.

Shiri *was* different. That was what made her who she was, that was why she was special and why she was so much more than a cousin to me. Why I wanted to *be* so much like her.

Past tense: wanted.

I realize something more, and I say it to Auntie Mina.

"I'm different, too," I say, but what I mean is, I'm different from Shiri, not just from everyone else.

"Yes, you are," she says, and hugs me tightly. Somehow, without explaining it, I'm certain she understands.

––––––––––

The next day, when I see that neither Mikaela nor Cody is at the picnic table behind the art building, I sit down gingerly. I don't know what's going to happen. I'm a little afraid that Becca and David and Andy are all going to turn and glare at me, tell me to leave, but they don't.

David says hi, shyly, looking up briefly from his sketchbook. Andy nods and continues snarfing down a meatball sandwich, talking with his mouth full about a concert he wants to go to in Hollywood somewhere. Twelve o'clock and all's well.

Becca says, "Hey, is Mikaela okay?"

"I don't know," I say cautiously. "I haven't talked to her since two days ago. Is she sick?" I worry again that I should have called her after I left Cody's, but then, I didn't have a chance.

"I think she's hung over." Becca smirks. "She called me around eight last night and gave me a mini-lecture about how Siouxsie and the Banshees are historically underappreciated as the root of modern underground music."

"Oh." I hesitate, then tell a white lie. "All I know is, Monday after school I dropped her and Cody off at his place. Maybe they were partying last night, too."

"Without us? Bitches," Becca says cheerfully. "Cody never has parties at his place."

David nods in agreement. "Mostly we go out to Soto Park," he says quietly. "Not lately, though. Too muddy."

"And now they're missing the most *awesomest lunch in the world*." Becca pulls a crinkle-cut pickle slice and a piece of wilted, paper-thin lettuce out of her veggie burger and throws them at the nearest tree. "Well, maybe she got a little hot goth-boy action."

I stiffen, feeling a reflexive stab of jealousy. Then I push the feeling away. I have nothing to feel jealous about. I shouldn't want Cody. And I don't.

I *really* don't.

Then I wonder: what if Mikaela, drunk, decided to do

something stupid? Would she sleep with Cody, even knowing all the things he's done? Does she even care about the fact that he's an asshole? I'm furious with her, but I can't just let things lie, even if she was in on the whole blog debacle. When I get home, despite the lurch in my stomach, I pull out my cell phone and dial her number.

I'm not sure why I care so much, but like my mom says, sometimes you just have to give people a chance to talk.

It rings four times, but nobody picks up.

I try again an hour later, and I try her house, too, but there's still no answer. I leave a message on her cell telling her to call me, but she doesn't. It could be that she's not feeling well, but she doesn't even answer my text message.

I don't know if something else happened, something bad. I don't know if she's angry at me or not.

I don't even know if we're still friends.

twenty-eight

The next day I'm still on edge. All I can think about is whether Mikaela is going to be at school; whether Cody's going to be there; whether I can bear to face them without completely blowing up; whether they're both going to hate me now. During French class, Marc from the Zombie Squad gives me a sneer. It's probably because of that stupid blog, but I honestly don't care what he thinks anymore.

At lunch, I buy a slice of pizza from the cart. As I'm waiting in line, I glance at the table where I used to sit with Cassie and everyone. It seems like a long time ago now. They're all eating, laughing together. I see Elisa put her arm around James, see him kiss her on the cheek. I'm glad she's okay now; glad both of them are happy.

Mikaela, though—I'm not sure I'm ready to talk to her, even though I've been worried about her. Deep down, I'm terrified that our friendship is done. That maybe it was always all about Cody for her; not so much about me. I decide I need some alone time before I brave that conversation, so I go straight to my car instead of chancing the picnic table. I'm so lost in thought as I slink past the volleyball courts that I don't see Spike until he's jumped right in front of me.

"Dude! Space girl. I waved at you, like, twenty-eight times." His hair is standing up in little tufts and he wipes the sweat off his forehead with the bottom of his T-shirt. "You gotta lay off the crack pipe."

Despite what happened between us on the beach, when I see Spike the tension inside me relaxes a little. "You've been playing volleyball a lot lately," I say.

He grins goofily. "Sometimes I get tired of the Bitchy Bunch."

I snort a laugh. I can't help it. "I call them the Zombie Squad," I admit.

"Nice." Spike glances at my pizza slice. "Where you headed?"

"I was going out to my car to get something." I duck my head.

"I'll go with you," Spike says. He jogs over to where the guys are hanging out under the net, taking a break, and talks to them for a second. I consider just leaving. I'm not sure I want company. But by the time the thought runs through my head, he's back and we're walking toward my car.

It still gives me a little twinge to hang out with Spike. I'm still not sure how I feel about him. And I don't know if I want to change things between us.

I open the trunk of the station wagon and we hop up to sit partway in, our legs dangling down over the bumper.

Spike leans back on his elbows while I nibble at my rapidly congealing pizza.

"For the record," Spike says suddenly, "I know you didn't have anything to do with that blog. Cassie keeps saying you must have been spreading dirt around, but she's just looking for someone to blame."

"Yeah, that sounds like Cassie," I say, a little glumly.

"Anyway, we all know the very idea of you blogging is ridiculous."

"Oh *really*?" I raise my eyebrows at him.

"Dude," he says. "Come on. *You* writing a blog? You barely go online. You don't even answer email. Even when you're *not* mad at people." He flicks me on the arm. "Plus, I know you're not the vengeful type."

"I'm not mad at you. I just—things have been weird lately. At home."

"Why, did your parents kick it up a notch? What is it now? Hot yoga? Bollywood music videos in your living room?"

I almost laugh.

"No. Not that." I swallow hard. "I think my aunt is going to divorce my uncle."

"Your aunt Mina? Isn't that a good thing? It sounded like your uncle was kind of a... um, douchebag," he says apologetically.

"Well, yeah. For a while I was afraid she was going to go back to him. But now that it seems like she's ready to leave him for good, I'm just..." My eyes sting for a moment and I hold my breath until I'm calm again. "It's weird, that's all.

She's living with us right now. My uncle's not taking it well. Things are really tense."

Spike reaches a hand up as if he's going to touch my shoulder, then pulls back. I feel a little hurt, but it's my own fault. I try to smile reassuringly at him.

"It's okay," I tell him. "It's just been kind of crazy. I—"

"I thought I'd find you here in your hidey-hole."

I whip my head around. Mikaela is standing in front of me, smiling slightly, one hand on her hip and one booted foot tapping.

Several different emotions start warring inside me: outrage, relief, anxiety. I put down my pizza, trying to look casual.

"I didn't know you were here today," I say neutrally.

"Yeah, well, I'm here on the good graces of Madam Ibuprofen," she says. "And I'm not going anywhere near the lunch line."

"Yeah? Must have been a wild night. All forty-eight hours of it," I can't resist saying.

"Yeah, ha ha. Look, no offense," Mikaela says, turning toward Spike, "but we need a girly moment here."

"Don't listen to her. She orders everyone around all the time." I don't want Spike to leave. I'm not ready for this conversation.

"It's fine." Spike swings himself off the trunk, grinning at both of us. "I should get back to my game anyway. But I get it. I'm too much man for you all, I know. Say no more." He rubs a hand back and forth over his hair until it stands on end, then saunters back toward the volleyball courts. I watch him walk off, feeling helpless.

"For Christ's sake," Mikaela mutters, leaning on the back bumper of the Volvo and picking at a hole in her purple tights. "He's so ... *sweaty*."

I don't answer. I know she didn't come here to talk about Spike.

"Sunny—" Mikaela looks up at the sky, then down at her tights again. "Look. Sorry I didn't call you back. Everything went a little nuts."

"I'll say." I look at her as steadily as I can. "When you didn't answer your phone last night, I figured you were irrevocably pissed at me, but you know what? I was pissed, too. You and Cody ganged up on me *again*, Mikaela." My voice rises a little. "What was I supposed to think?"

I don't even bother to tell her how worried I was, how afraid I was that she might have done something stupid with Cody, because right now, it's all I can do to keep my anger from overwhelming me.

"I *didn't*—" Mikaela lets out a frustrated noise. "Okay. I'll tell you the whole story. But you have to know I had nothing to do with that stupid blog! Couldn't your underhearing tell you that much?" She looks at me briefly. There are tears brimming in the corners of her eyes, but they don't spill.

I don't say anything.

"Fine," she says. "I know, I know. You're Miss Perfect. You'd never use your underhearing for anything other than to help other people. Oh, except for *Cody*," she concludes bitterly.

"That's not fair," I say quietly. But it still stings.

The silence stretches out between us like a minefield. And she still hasn't told me what happened.

"Well," she says, finally breaking the silence, "That's how I felt. After you left his house, I was really pissed at you. It seemed like you just walked off, like you didn't even want to help. I mean, shit, it's *Cody*. But a couple of hours later, his parents get home, and I'm scrambling my ass out of there as fast as I can, and I hear his dad yelling something about how Cody was supposed to be at work an hour ago, and what the hell kind of crap did he think he was trying to pull, not showing up for the job he'd helped him get, and how did he expect to ever pay for the repairs on the car."

"So... okay, so then what?" I gaze at Mikaela levelly, knowing there has to be more.

"So then, nothing. So then I hightail it to the nearest bus stop hoping his parents didn't notice I was there and drinking their booze. That's when I was most pissed at you. You were *supposed* to be my ride, and then on top of that I left my phone on the bus."

"Well, I figured you didn't need a ride. I figured you wanted some alone time with Cody," I say sarcastically. "Since you guys are so tight these days. And I'm apparently totally useless, since I'm not going to use my underhearing at everyone's beck and call."

"Oh, come *on*," Mikaela says. Her voice is frustrated. "I don't think that at all."

"Okay, but you were going along with him and pressuring me to do something I *really can't* do. I wouldn't lie about that. And even if I could do it... I wouldn't. You know that."

"I know!" She sounds miserable, cowed.

"So, what? You were drunk? Lust-crazed? You can't resist his eyebrow ring?"

She lets out a loud, aggravated groan. "Okay, so maybe I made out with him a little. I shouldn't have. It was dumb."

I think about that for a long minute, but I'm surprised to find I don't care much one way or the other. "Whatever."

Her voice is bleak. "I just kept trying to convince myself that he—that we had a chance. That if we got together, then somehow everything would just fall into place. And... I guess I already knew that was wrong. But I felt so desperate. And on top of that I was scared you were still mad at me about the stupid solstice party. I started acting crazy. I kind of went on a bender."

She shifts a little, turning to face me more directly. Her brown eyes are intense and her hands are knotted tensely in her lap.

"Listen. I'm done with him, Sunny. He's not important. He wasn't worth it."

I inhale, slowly. Exhale, slowly. Hear:

—*and you are.*—

For a moment, all I can feel is her urgency, her loneliness and regret. I shake myself.

"Look," she says, sliding off the bumper and standing in front of me. "I suck at saying sorry."

Before I can respond, she throws a small object into the back of the car, next to where I'm sitting, and briskly walks off, platform boots beating a fast rhythm against the pavement of the parking lot.

I look down to my left, at whatever it was she threw at me. It's long and narrow and wrapped in newspaper—the news briefs section, with one readable headline: "Morbidly Obese Man Found Comatose in Bathtub." I rip the paper. Inside is a black fountain pen, the simple kind that stationery stores always have. But all over it are Mikaela's signature decorative swirls and thorny vines, in shiny silver paint. It's beautiful.

There's a note wrapped around it. The note reads, in Mikaela's precise looping handwriting, "To match the blank book I gave you. It occurs to me that there are less invasive ways to get people to read your thoughts than, well, you know. Here's to writing them down, the old-fashioned way."

———

At lunch the following day, I head over to the picnic bench behind the art building, where Mikaela is sitting with David, Becca, and Andy.

I stop about ten feet away, take a deep breath, and walk right up to Mikaela.

"You don't suck at apologizing," I tell her quietly. I sit

down on the side of the bench next to her and, very deliberately, loop my hair up into a bun and fasten it in place with the pen she gave me.

She gives me a tentative smile. I return it, just as tentatively. But I feel better, like there's been an invisible wall between us and now it's gone.

"So," I say conversationally, "you never told me what happened to Cody. I can't help noticing his conspicuous absence."

"Funny you should ask," she replies. "I was just telling these guys that Cody's probably not coming back. He emailed me this morning—his parents pulled him out of school and everything. I think they're looking for a private school. He's staying with his aunt and uncle right now in Malibu."

"Malibu? Poor him," Andy says. "What a horrible, horrible punishment."

"No, seriously, his aunt is some kind of cop and his uncle is a bodyguard for rich people. I bet they're paying his uncle to keep an eye on him." Mikaela reaches over and steals a chocolate-chip cookie out of Andy's lunch. He tries to smack her hand away and misses.

David smiles faintly. "Remember how he used to drive us around all the time? Before he crashed the car, I mean. Even all the way out to Melrose. Good times."

"Ah, he'll still be an asshole even at private school," Becca says, winking at me. "He'll just be a rich private school asshole."

"But he was *our* asshole," Mikaela says with a forlorn sigh. We all stare at her. The corner of my mouth twitches, and then I dissolve into helpless laughter. Even the super-serious Andy looks like he's trying to fight a case of the giggles.

"Okay," I say, finally getting myself under control. "Now, wait, he emailed you? What else did he say? So help me, I'm curious."

"Well, not much. He claims he's going to 'work his connection' with that Wiccan coven thing he's always going on about, but I think it's just that he has a crush on that chick with the cloak. The one from the solstice party. I'm pretty sure she isn't interested in a high school junior, unless she has a thing for little boys."

"Ew."

"No kidding. Hmm," Mikaela says musingly, "I wonder if they've ever had hot and horny witch sex in the woods?"

"Oh, gross, you *have* to shut up," Becca says, throwing a handful of corn chips at Mikaela.

"You're always throwing food! Children are starving," Mikaela retorts, grinning evilly. I wonder if she really is over Cody or if she's putting on an act. I wonder if she's going to keep in touch with him. Email him. Call him.

"Well, I've lost my appetite thanks to that mental image," Becca says.

"Yeah, I think we need to change the subject," I say.

"Oh, *fine*. Prudes, all of you." Mikaela gets up and wanders around the table, stopping to look over David's shoulder. "Hey, this is good. *Really* good."

Andy leans over. "Nice, dude." He looks up at me.

"What?" I frown.

Andy shrugs. "You should show her."

David turns the sketchbook around to face me. He looks away, smiling a little, but his ears are red.

Inside is a tiny portrait. Of *me*. I mean, it's clearly *supposed* to be me, but I'm not that...wistful-looking. Am I? It looks like David's been working on it for a while, and I feel like I should say something, but I don't know what.

"*Yes*, you look like that, Sunny honey," Mikaela says.

"Like what?" I ask, suspiciously.

"*Gorgeous*, silly." She circles the table and grabs my shoulders and gives them an annoying shake, then a quick hug. "You're, like, the Queen of Sunshine."

"What the hell does that mean?" Is she joking?

"It means I am wildly jealous that Da Vinci here drew a portrait of *you*. He never draws portraits of any of us. Just sketches us in awkward lunchtime situations." Mikaela lets go of my shoulders and prances around, flitting her hands like they're little fairy wings and singing, "La la la! Queen of Sunshine!" In her ripped purple tights, knee-high black boots, short skirt, and "Not all who wander are lost" T-shirt, she looks completely ridiculous.

"If you're trying to imitate me, you're failing miserably." It's so unlike me—really, Queen of Sunshine?—that I start laughing helplessly.

For some reason, I think about the old me then, with her bleached-blond hair, her "safe" group of swim team friends and nobody she really felt close to. I feel sad for her, really sad. Mikaela whirls dizzyingly around a tree, whooping, and I remember Shiri and me as little kids, running around the

backyard in pillowcase capes and shrieking with giggles—
Wonder Nerd and Super Dork.

We'll always have yesterday ... and today, and tomorrow.

Shiri left me more than that. Grief, confusion, anger.
Maybe even underhearing, though I may never know for
sure. And I've spent so much time remembering the yester-
days I can never get back. So much time wasted, when it's
today that's really important.

That's not me anymore, though. Yes, some things are
worth fighting to keep. But some things you have to let go.

I take the pen out of my hair, and Mikaela's blank book
out of my bag.

In the middle of the first page, like a title, I write: *TOMOR-
ROW*. And then I turn to the next page and start writing.

Author's Note

Like far too many others, my life has been affected by the suicide of someone close to me. I'm also no stranger to the battle with depression and despair. These issues are serious, and social stigma can make it even more difficult to talk about it when we are hurting. Don't hesitate to reach out for help if you need it, whether it's you or a loved one who is suffering. There are resources out there to help teens (and adults) cope with depression, suicide, and other crises. These are just a few:

National Suicide Prevention Lifeline
1-800-273-TALK (8255)
The National Suicide Prevention Lifeline provides free and confidential emotional support to people in suicidal crisis or emotional distress 24 hours a day, 7 days a week.
http://www.suicidepreventionlifeline.org/

National Alliance of the Mentally Ill
1 (800) 950-NAMI (6264)
Their toll-free, confidential hotline operates Mon-Fri, 10 am –6 pm EST, and provides information, referrals, and support to anyone with questions about mental illness. You can reach them via email at info@nami.org.

Safe Place
1-888-290-7233
Project Safe Place provides access to immediate help and resources for young people in crisis. Call the hotline to find out if the program operates in your state, or look online.
http://nationalsafeplace.org/

TXT 4 HELP
Project Safe Place operates their TXT 4 HELP service nationwide. If you're in trouble or need help, text SAFE and your current location (address/city/state) to 69866 and the operators will connect you to the closest location where you can get immediate help and safety.

Society for the Prevention of Teen Suicide
The mission of the SPTS is to reduce the number of youth suicides and attempted suicides by encouraging overall public awareness. Their website includes resources for teens, parents, and educators.
http://www.sptsusa.org/

The Trevor Project
866-4-U-TREVOR
The Trevor Project is a nationwide, around-the-clock crisis and suicide prevention helpline for lesbian, gay, bisexual, transgender, and questioning (LGBTQ) youth. The Trevor Helpline is available as a resource to parents, family members, and friends of young people as well.
http://www.TheTrevorProject.org

Acknowledgments

Writing is a solitary activity, but this novel wouldn't have come to be without help, encouragement, feedback, and friendship.

First things first, though.

In 1998, my stepcousin Janet took her own life. She was twenty-four years old. I was twenty-one. Many of my experiences of working through grief, sadness, confusion, and depression have found their way into this book.

I'm pretty sure this book never would have gotten finished at all if it hadn't been for my writing group: Yat-Yee Chong, Tanita Davis, Kelly Herold, Anne Levy, Jennifer March Soloway, and JoNelle Toriseva. You are all amazing friends, dedicated writers, and wonderful companions to have on this journey. Special thanks to Tanita, who has probably had to listen to more of my griping and exasperation than anyone else (and who has always been there for last-minute advice), and to Jennifer, who has given me many pep talks and has always believed in this story.

Other readers have weighed in along the way, too. Particular thanks to Mike Adams for some very revealing insights into Sunny's underhearing, and to Katie Sinclair for helping me with swim race details.

Thanks to my agent Jennifer Laughran for being there at the exact right time to help this one out into the world; to my editor at Flux, Brian Farrey-Latz, for being the perfect combination of friend, advocate, sounding board, and editor; and to everyone else at Flux for making this latest project a reality and for believing in my work. Lastly, thanks to the Green Gulch Farm Zen Center and Margaret Speaker Yuan and Colette Weil Parrinello of the SCBWI North/East Bay for providing the perfect environment for a writing (and editing) retreat.

Thanks to my husband, Rob, for everything: reading and giving feedback; listening to me gripe, panic, and/or think out loud; taking care of countless extra meals and chores; and giving me time and space and understanding and love.

And thanks to everyone who had faith in this project, even when I didn't. Sometimes it doesn't feel like you're going to make it, but you just have to keep telling yourself, don't give up.